# SECOND CHANCE SPIRIT

HAUNTED
EVER
AFTER

BOOK TWO

# CARRIE PULKINEN

Second Chance Spirit

COPYRIGHT © 2017 & 2021 by Carrie Pulkinen

Contact Information: www.CarriePulkinen.com

Cover Art by Rebecca Poole of Dreams2Media
Edited by Victoria Miller

ISBN: 978-1-7347624-6-4

Originally published as To Shop a Shadow

# CHAPTER ONE

Snow crunched under Trent Austin's black dress shoes, the cutting February wind stinging his eyes, as he made his way to the front steps of the 1889 Victorian home. Peeling paint, once bright green, littered the half-rotten porch in a dingy, lead-filled mess. He exhaled a curse and took a step back to examine his new burden.

The grimy-gray gingerbread trim framing the door and every window probably used to be white. Arches of the same curling pattern accented the top of the porch and the eave. The three-story structure could have been quaint and inviting in its prime. Now it sat vacant and crumbling near the back of the property, rows of hedges and willow trees obscuring it from the street. The isolation of the house and the darkening sky above made it appear more like a scene from a horror movie than the lush, Victorian mansion it once was.

Trent ascended the stairs, stepping lightly on the creaky wood panels to avoid putting a foot through the floor. He slid the key into the lock and twisted the knob.

The hinges creaked as the door swung open, the knob pulling from his hand as if someone on the other side yanked it from his grasp. *Definitely like a horror film.*

He peered inside. Hollow darkness greeted him. Haunting. A shiver ran down his spine, and it wasn't from the chilling winter air whispering through the trees.

The whole scene creeped him out.

His great-uncle, Jack Austin, had died in the living room two weeks earlier, and his will had granted the house to Trent. He'd only met the man a handful of times, and the hostility he'd felt from his uncle made those few encounters more than enough. The man was off. Perpetually mad at the world. Insanity didn't run in the family, but Uncle Jack could have been an exception.

And judging from the ghoulish condition of his house, disturbed seemed like an appropriate description of Jack. Trent had always thought his great-uncle menacing. The unnatural silence engulfing the home only intensified the feeling.

He hesitated at the threshold, almost afraid to cross it. What if Jack's spirit still lingered inside? What if the basement was full of bodies, and their spirits were crouching in the shadows, waiting to attack?

If someone had asked him if he believed in ghosts four months ago, he would have laughed. He'd never given the idea much thought until he encountered one himself. Now, not only did he believe in ghosts, but he also believed in the power they could exert over the living. The way spirits could control people. Destroy their lives. He'd seen it firsthand. And if his uncle had left him the house so he could haunt him...

*Get a grip, man. Don't be an ass.*

He stepped one foot into the foyer and held his

breath. He reluctantly pulled the other foot in and flipped on the light switch before he exhaled. The stale, musty scent of mold and dust made his stomach turn. The place would have to be aired out before anyone would consider buying it. The smell of death—or what he imagined death would smell like—still lingered in the air. He shuddered.

He hung his coat on the rack to his left. The dark, cherry wood stand reached nearly six feet high and had intricately carved, claw-like feet with talons that looked like they could slice open a whale. Not the most inviting piece to welcome guests into a home. Then again, Uncle Jack didn't seem like the type of man who'd had many visitors.

Immediately to the right lay the living room. Blood-red upholstered furniture stood on clawed feet that almost matched the sinister-looking coat rack. The whole room had an eerie feel to it. Of course, that was probably because all the drapes were drawn. Hanging from tarnished brass rods, the heavy, dust-filled, crimson curtains appeared to be velvet and had dirty, gold tassels that brushed the hardwood floor.

The dark, papered walls and cherry wood enhanced the gloomy aesthetic of the space, making it look more like a chamber from Dracula's crypt than an old man's living room.

"A little light ought to cheer this place up. Maybe."

Before he could take a step toward the window, an icy breath on the back of his neck stopped him cold. His stomach tightened as the first tendrils of dread crawled up his spine, and he closed his eyes and took a deep breath. *This house is old. It's just a draft.* He opened his eyes and moved forward. A frigid hand grasped his shoulder.

He froze, his breath stopping mid-inhale, his heart rate

speeding into a sprint. It was his imagination. It had to be. He'd let his mind run wild since his encounter with the ghost in his friend Logan's house three months ago, but he had to control it now. He would not lose his shit in this dilapidated mansion. "Leave me alone." His voice came out much steadier than anticipated, and he straightened his spine, relaxing his shoulders.

The hand lifted. The cold breath dissipated. Was it gone?

*Yeah, right.* He had to turn around. Had to face whatever it was that didn't want him opening the windows. He held his breath; every muscle in his body tensed as he slowly pivoted, ready to bolt at the first sign of a spirit. His eyes widened as he found himself face to face with the coat rack.

He shook his head. *Paranoid idiot.*

"Hey, buddy. I don't suppose that was you breathing down my neck?" He chuckled. "Nah. You're just a block of wood, aren't you?" He patted the bulbous top of the stand.

Ever since he'd helped Logan vanquish the ghost from his house, he'd had the disturbing feeling he was being watched. Like he'd opened himself up to spirits, and they were slowly creeping into his life, waiting for the right moment to scare him to death.

Not that he'd encountered one since then, but something deep in his gut warned him that his run-ins with spirits were far from over. Especially now that his best friend was engaged to a psychic medium.

Satisfied the icy breath was nothing more than a draft, he took half a step toward the window. Before he could plant his foot, the coat rack fell—no, flew—into his shoulder, missing the side of his head by mere inches. The stand skidded across the wood floor and landed five feet away.

Trent turned on his heel and sprinted out the door. There was no way in hell he was sticking around to see what had pushed that coat rack. Whatever it was, it didn't want him going near the window.

He jumped into his car and slammed the door. Once he pulled back onto the road, his erratic breathing finally slowed. There had to be a logical explanation. It wasn't a ghost. The house was old and drafty. The floor was uneven. The coat rack had fallen over...like the door had swung open on its own.

Could it have been the spirit of Uncle Jack? Was it a ghost at all? It didn't matter. He didn't plan to keep the house very long. In fact, the quicker he could get rid of the decrepit heap, the better. He'd put it on the market as soon as he found a real estate agent willing to take it. It wouldn't be an easy sell, so he'd have to hire someone good.

A slow smile curved his lips as a name danced through his mind. He knew just the agent for the job.

---

Tina Sanders sat across from her best friend in a little café in downtown Detroit. The bright lights, cheerful yellow décor, and bustle of the lunch crowd should have been a welcome distraction, but a phone call from Trent a few days ago still had her mind reeling. She toyed with her napkin as she tried to calm the flutter in her heart. She hadn't heard from him in nearly three months. Not since she blew him off after the ghost incident at Logan's house.

She hadn't actually dumped him because of the ghost, but being a grounding force that sent a spirit to the other realm had been a good excuse to get out of that relationship before it started. When she looked at Trent, all she saw was forever. And forever was something she refused to commit to.

She chewed her bottom lip and glanced at Allison. "There are tons of real estate agents in Ann Arbor."

"I'm sure there are, babe, but he called you. He's got his reasons, whatever they are." Allison patted Tina's hand. "Don't read too much into it."

"Says the queen of overanalyzing."

Allison laughed. "You got that right. Now show your queen some respect and pass the pepper."

Tina handed her the shaker. Thinking things through, weighing all the options, analyzing. Those were all good traits. There was nothing wrong with contemplating the man's motivations. "I'd just like to know what his reasons are."

Why did he call *her?* Was it because he was still interested? Could he be trying to reconnect? Or was it the simple fact that she was good at her job?

Allison took a bite of her salad and tapped the fork against her lips. "Maybe it's because you could sell water to a drowning person. Trent's a man of action. He gets things done quickly. If he needs a property sold, he knows you're the best person to do it. And if he happens to have an ulterior motive, all the better."

Tina sighed. "It doesn't matter. It's not like I'm going to call him back."

Allison dropped her fork, wiped her hands on her napkin, and dabbed the red cloth on the edges of her lips. She opened her mouth to speak, and then she closed it and shook her head.

"What?" Tina braced herself for the tough love that

was sure to spill from Allison's lips. "Go ahead and say it, Allie. You know you want to."

"I don't know." Allison shrugged. "You and Trent seemed to really hit it off before. He's a great guy, and—"

"I know. That's the problem."

Trent was an amazing guy. He was smart, funny, and incredibly sexy. His deep chocolate eyes smoldered with a heat so intense, Tina's heart melted every time his gaze caught hers. And his wavy, dark brown hair beckoned her to run her fingers through it. She couldn't think of a single reason not to like him. Except for that forever problem. When it came to her heart, she could think of a million and one reasons *not* to give it away.

"Oh, don't be such a weenie. Call the man." Allison took Tina's phone and dialed Trent's number.

Tina snatched it out of her hands. "I can't."

"You can."

"I won't."

Allison tilted her head to cast Tina a sympathetic gaze. "We both know you will, so quit being stubborn. All you have to do is press the little green button."

Tina narrowed her eyes. "You're a bitch. You know that, Allie?"

"That's why you love me."

Tina swallowed, took a deep breath, and pressed the button. She didn't exhale as she listened to it ring. One, two, three times. *Please go to voicemail.* It rang a fourth time.

"Hello?" Trent's voice flowed like warm rum and honey, and Tina's heart raced as she tried to form some semblance of a coherent sentence. She cut her gaze to Allison, who gestured for Tina to speak.

"Um, hi, Trent. It's Tina. Returning your call. You had

a house for me to look at?" She held her breath again, her insides twisting into a knot.

"Yeah. I inherited it from my great-uncle, though I have no idea why. Anyway, it's in ill repair, and I want to get rid of it. Maybe one of those house flippers or someone will want it. Can you help me out?"

Listening to the familiar cadence of his voice, the knot in Tina's chest relaxed. Something about the way he spoke always seemed to have a calming effect on her. She could breathe again. "Sure. I can take a look at it. When do you want to meet?"

"The sooner, the better. I don't have time to deal with a run-down shit hole. But I've got meetings all week. Are you available now?"

Her breath caught. He couldn't be serious. She wasn't ready to see him again. She needed time to prepare. To make sure her walls were securely in place so her heart didn't fall to pieces as soon as she laid eyes on him. "Uh, now? As in right now?" She looked at Allison and pleaded with her gaze. If anyone could get her out of this mess, Allison could. But all her friend did was grin.

"Yes," Trent said. "But if it's too short of notice, I understand."

"No, no." Tina let out a nervous giggle. "Now's as good a time as any."

"Great. Are you at home? I can pick you up."

"I think I better drive myself. You know, in case I need to look around the neighborhood. See what other houses are going for." And because she might need to make a quick get-away if things got too heavy.

"No problem. I'll see you in about an hour. You still have the message with the address?"

"Yeah. I'll see you soon."

"Okay." He paused, his deep inhale resonating in her ear, sounding far more intimate than it should have. "And, Tina? I'm so glad you called me back."

"Uh-huh." She pressed the end button and glared at her friend.

Allison returned her gaze with a smug smile. "I'm proud of you, girlfriend."

"He said he was glad I called back."

She rolled her eyes. "Well, of course he's glad. Get up, put some powder on that shiny nose, get your ass to the car, and call me as soon as you're done."

Jeez Louise, what was she thinking? It had been easy to forget about Mr. Perfect as long as she avoided him completely. Now, the mere thought of seeing him again had the worms in her can banging on the lid to open it. What was she getting herself into?

She rose from her seat and nodded to her friend. She was a grown woman who knew how to handle herself around a man. She could do this.

CHAPTER TWO

*I*t had taken Tina three days to call him back. Three days for him to dwell on the incident at the manor. Three days for Trent to convince himself that his imagination had taken over. The coat rack had fallen and the door had swung open because the floor was uneven. That's all there was to it. No entities—evil or otherwise—waited for him inside that house. Still, he hadn't brought himself to venture back inside it.

And now he was meeting Tina there. A fluttering sensation formed in his stomach as he pictured her sensuous smile. Was he insane? Three months ago, they seemed to have had something going for them. Mutual attraction, good times, friends in common. It was the perfect foundation for a relationship, but just as they were getting close, Tina had called it off without warning. She'd all but slammed the door in his face the last time he'd tried to talk to her.

And she wouldn't give him a reason. Not a real one. She'd blamed it on the ghost, saying it disturbed her so much she needed to get away from everyone involved.

Everyone except her best friend, Allison. And Allison's fiancé, Logan, who happened to be Trent's best friend.

Yeah, it was obvious the only person she wanted to get away from was Trent. So why did he call her when he needed a real estate agent?

Because she was the best.

That's what he told himself, anyway. He was over her. No, there was nothing to get over because they'd never really gotten started.

As he grabbed his keys and locked the front door to his two-bedroom bungalow on the outskirts of the city, he replayed in his mind the events of his first visit to the manor. The drafty old house. The unlevel foundation. No doubt his encounter with the "spirit" was his imagination. He'd explained away any sliver of dread that remained days ago.

So why were his palms slick with sweat and his mouth as dry as cotton?

Trent shoved his hands in his pockets as he made his way to the garage. He pressed the disarm button on his remote, and the familiar *chirp-chirp* of his silver Audi A4 eased his mind. The flashing lights led him to the beauty he'd affectionately named Bertha.

He smiled as he ran his hand along the sexy curve of the front wheel well. "How ya doing, baby? You ready for this?" He slipped into the driver's seat and turned the ignition, revving the engine. The sweet purr was music to his ears. "I don't know what I'm getting myself into, but you're going to take me there."

He tuned the radio to his favorite driving station—True Country 98.4—and started the forty-five-minute trek to the house of doom.

"It's just business." Tina flipped the stations on her car stereo, trying to find some decent music. To find anything to take her mind off seeing Trent's smoldering eyes again. The incessant chatter of radio talents and beer commercials grated on her nerves, so she jammed the preset buttons harder and harder, until one of them got stuck.

"Fantastic." She tried to pry the button loose with her fingernail but nearly chipped yesterday's manicure in the process.

"Great. Just superb. Forced to listen to the only country music station in Michigan." As Garth Brooks belted "Shameless," she sighed. "And it's not even the new stuff."

Tina despised country music. The only reason she'd programmed the damn station into her presets was Trent. He'd said his guilty pleasure was the pitiful, lonesome twang of the genre—in not so many words. She didn't enjoy the music, but seeing Trent's face light up when some sad, lonely cowboy crooned his favorite song had been well worth the audible torture. Sometimes he even sang along. He didn't hit every note, but his smooth voice always seemed to melt her heart like a stick of butter.

*Crap.* What was she doing? She'd never been attached to any man. Not that she hadn't had plenty of offers. She could bed almost any man she wanted with a simple smile, and she didn't need relationships. Her life was perfect the way it was—great friends, an awesome job, plenty of sex. She certainly didn't need love complicating things.

And she didn't need Trent. He surely would've thrown a wrench into her plans for world domination—or at least dominion over Michigan. She laughed. She'd been accused of having delusions of grandeur a time or two, but who could blame a girl for being confident? Sure, she probably wouldn't take over the world, but her aspirations were far from being reached. She didn't know what she wanted to be when she grew up, but she'd be something big. Like Wonder Woman. And she definitely didn't need a man getting in her way, telling her what to do.

She turned off Business 23 onto Depot Street. The frantic rush of the freeway subsided into a cozy quaintness as she rolled through the residential area. Victorian and Colonial homes with massive yards and hundred-year-old trees lined the street. She'd always considered herself a big-city girl, but something about the charm of this neighborhood drew her in.

The homes—some grand and some modest—resembled gingerbread houses, and she couldn't help but think of the classic fairytale *Hansel and Gretel.* Even Tina could've been fooled into entering a witch's home if it looked as charming as these.

She turned right and slowed to a crawl as she searched the homes for numbers. "One-thirty-six Acorn Street. Let's see…there's one-seventeen, so the house has to be on the right. One-twenty-two. One-twenty-four…" There wasn't much left on the street. Hopefully she hadn't written down the address wrong.

The road curved to the right and extended another fifty feet. The house numbers stopped at one-thirty. Letting out a frustrated grumble, Tina began a three-point-turn, but stopped when a small driveway came into view at the end of the road. She put the car in drive and slowly approached the clearing—if you could call it that. Two large willow trees stood on either side of the drive, their tendrils of branches blocking the house from view.

As she pulled through, the boughs scraped against her windows, creating a menacing sound like the claws of a monster scratching at the glass. She leaned forward, clutching the steering wheel, to get a better look. Though it was mid-morning, the property seemed dark. Ominous. Like eternal clouds had gathered above the manor, threatening to spill their tears at the slightest provocation.

"Jeez Louise."

No sun reflected off the silver Audi in the driveway, but Trent's car stood like a beacon of hope against the bleak, dismal property. Tina started to breathe a sigh of relief, until Trent got out of the car. Standing just over six feet tall, he looked like a god with his broad shoulders and chiseled features. He'd combed his hair into that messy-chic style that looked like he rolled out of bed that way but that probably took him half an hour to get every strand into perfect position.

She'd expected him to be in his lawyer suit, but the charcoal peacoat and dark jeans he wore suited him better. An onyx wool scarf peeked out of the neckline, and matching leather shoes completed the outfit. He looked drop-dead gorgeous. Just like she remembered him. She snapped her mouth shut to keep from drooling.

Of course, Trent would look good in a potato sack. Even better in nothing at all. *Don't go there, girl. It's just business.*

Seeing him again stirred up all the emotions she'd carefully tucked away—like she knew it would. The first worm started wriggling out of the can, but she shoved it back in. She had a job to do. That's why she'd come. It didn't matter who the client was.

*Yeah, right.*

Trent held his breath as Tina stepped out of her Mustang. One slender leg. Then the other. The three-inch heels on her brown boots didn't upset the sway of her hips as she glided through the snow. Her chocolate trench coat skimmed her knees, revealing the sexy curve of her calves, and her thick, black hair bounced with each step, glistening from an inner light that brightened when she smiled.

Sultry, mulberry lips curved across teeth as white as the snow, and her emerald eyes seemed to sparkle as she stepped closer. Good lord, he was in trouble.

"Hi, Trent. I almost didn't find the place. Your uncle sure liked his privacy, didn't he?" She tucked a piece of hair behind a delicate ear and placed her hand on his shoulder. "I'm sorry for your loss."

He instinctively took a step back. "Thanks." He cleared his voice. "I didn't know him that well."

"Oh, sorry." She dropped her gaze to the ground and then blinked up at him.

Damn, she was beautiful. More so than he remembered. Not that he thought of her often. After the way she'd bruised his pride, he'd be damned if he'd give her another chance. A man could only take so much rejection.

But seeing her here…after all these months…he couldn't help but feel the familiar spark igniting in his core. The frigid temperature of the air couldn't stop the sweat from beading on his forehead or the heat from flushing his cheeks. But he wouldn't let her get to him. He was her client and nothing more. That's probably how she saw it, anyway.

Awkward silence hung between them as he tried to

think of something to say. Trent was a straight shooter. Not big on small talk, he usually got right to the point. He hadn't planned on his smooth demeanor being derailed by the beauty before him, and he stumbled over his words.

"I, um…about the house." *Get it together, man.*

Tina straightened her spine, adjusted the purse strap on her shoulder, and flashed a nervous grin. "Right. The house. Let's go take a look."

He trodded two steps ahead on their way to the porch. He had to get control of himself. He'd sounded like a blubbering idiot instead of a professional. With his gaze fixed on the dreary sky, he plowed forward until he stepped on a patch of ice and his left foot slipped out from under him.

"Son of a bitch!" He stumbled, landing on his knee in the snow. "Goddammit!" The fall didn't hurt as bad as the stifled giggle coming from behind him. He must have looked like an ass.

"Are you okay?" Tina knelt by his side.

"Yeah. Fine." He rose to his feet and brushed the wet mess from his jeans.

She giggled again. "You're cute when you're flustered." As soon as the words left her lips, she covered her mouth with her pristinely manicured hand. "I mean…" She rubbed her arms as if to warm them. "How old is this house?"

"It was built in 1889." He furrowed his brow. *Cute? I nearly bust my ass on the ice and she says I'm cute?* Puppies were cute. Sweet little girls holding kittens were cute. Grown men were *not*.

Tina grinned and pressed her lips together. She reached up to muss his hair as she trotted up the front stairs. "C'mon, slow poke. What are you waiting for?"

He smoothed his hair back into place and tried to ignore the fluttering in his stomach. Tina acted playful like this with everyone. It was her nature, and he needed to remember that.

She turned around and smiled at him. "You coming?"

"Yeah." He shook his head and climbed the steps.

Was Tina flirting with him or simply giving him a hard time? It was hard to tell with her. Her poised, carefree attitude had been what attracted him to her in the first place—aside from her silky, onyx hair, porcelain-perfect skin, and voluptuous curves. She merely had to flash that infectious smile his way, and every thought drained from his head along with the blood rushing to his groin.

"The porch is a mess." Tina kicked the paint chips and pressed her toe against a rotten board. The snapping sound it made under her gentle pressure unnerved him. They could fall through with one wrong step.

"I'm sure the whole house is in bad shape. That's why I want to target house flippers. You know, someone who's looking for a fixer-upper." He fished in his pocket for the key.

Tina went into professional mode in an instant. Her posture straightened and her head rose slightly, like she was a woman who knew she was good at her job. "How many bedrooms?"

He held her gaze. "I'm not sure."

"Central heating?"

"I don't know."

She raised an eyebrow. "Have you even been inside?"

He toyed with the key in his hand. "I've been in the foyer. I saw the living room." His ears warmed with embarrassment. Thank goodness she wasn't there the first time he went inside. A confident woman like Tina would've laughed in his face when he ran out the door, and his chances of ever starting over with her would've crumbled to bits.

Not that he was thinking about starting anything with her. Not again. Where had that thought even come from?

Tina put a hand on her hip. "Well, I guess we'll find out together." She stepped aside and motioned for him to open the door.

When he put the key in the lock, the first drops of dread trickled through his system. As he turned it, cold hands of fear gripped his spine. What if he was wrong about the draft and the foundation? What if some sinister being really haunted the place? He could put her life in danger just by going inside.

*Get a grip.*

He swallowed down the lump in his throat and pushed the door open. It creaked on its hinges like the lid to Dracula's casket. Stale darkness crept from the entrance, and Trent's heart raced.

Tina peered inside and scrunched her nose. "It looks like a haunted house from a horror movie."

He let out a nervous laugh. "Sure does." Without crossing the threshold, he reached along the wall and flipped on the lights, jerking his hand back like he expected a monster to jump out and get them. Tina gave him a perplexed look, and he shook his head.

They stepped into the foyer, and Trent picked up the coat rack that had fallen over last time he was here. He turned it to the left. Then he scooted it to the right and pointed at it. "You. Stay put. I mean it."

Tina gave him a curious look. "I don't think you have to worry about it growing legs and walking away."

He patted his hand on the wood. "You never know with these things. What do you think about the house?"

Tina turned to examine the doorjamb. "The structure appears sound." She stomped on the floor. "Solid hardwood. This can easily be refinished. Is there wood throughout the whole house?" She stepped from the foyer, into the living room.

"Wait." Trent called.

"What is it?" She spun in a circle, examining the walls, the windows, the furniture.

"Nothing." He shook his head and shuffled to the living room. Of course it was nothing. Why the hell did he let this place get to him like this? He was making an ass of himself in front of the one woman whose opinion actually mattered to him. It shouldn't have mattered, but damn it, it did.

Tina ran a finger down the wood on the back of a chaise and blew the dust into the air. "The dreadful décor needs to go, but the inside is definitely in better shape than the outside. Clean it up, refinish the floors, repair the porch and give it a fresh coat of paint…it's definitely salable. And livable. It just needs a little light."

Trent cringed as she reached for the drapes. With the coat rack in his peripheral vision, he held his breath as she threw the curtains open. A cloud of dust puffed in the air, and Tina waved her arms frantically. "Ah!"

Was the ghost after her?

"Ahhh…ahhhh…"

What was happening? He could barely see through the haze of dust.

"AHHHH—CHOO!"

It was the loudest sneeze he had ever heard. So loud, she could've been a monster herself. Maybe it was the release of the irrational fear he'd let build up in his mind. Or maybe all the tension brewing between the two of them caused him to lose control, but he couldn't help himself. He doubled over with laughter. "I've never heard a sound like that come out of such a dainty thing as you."

Tina rubbed her nose and glared at him. "Oh, you think that's funny, huh? You breathe in six pounds of dust and we'll see what kind of sounds come out of you, mister."

"It's just…" He put his hands on his knees as he tried to regain his composure. He took a deep breath and stood upright. "I'm sorry. That was an impressive sneeze."

Tina's grimace lifted into a grin. "Hey, at least it only happened once this time. I usually sneeze four or five times in row." She crinkled her nose and rubbed the tip.

"I'm glad you didn't. You might have blown out the window. Anyway, bless you."

"Thank you. Let's see the rest of the house."

"Let's." Trent chuckled and followed Tina into the kitchen as the cold fingers of dread finally released their grip on his spine. No ghost or goblin tried to stop her from opening the drapes. Just like nothing had tried to stop him a few days ago. This house wasn't haunted. He'd merely let his imagination run rampant and psyched himself out. *There's nothing to worry about.*

---

Tina examined the kitchen. The appliances were ancient, as expected, but those could easily be replaced. The musty stench could be remedied with a can of Lysol and a day or two with the windows open. The rest of the downstairs seemed in decent condition, so she ascended the steps to the second floor. A deep forest green rug ran the entire length of the hallway, and dust plumed around her boots as she stepped.

"Jeez. Did your uncle know about vacuum cleaners?"

"He was an old fart. He probably hadn't been upstairs in years."

Her breath caught at the sound of Trent's voice behind her. He'd followed her up the stairs, so she shouldn't have been startled by his close proximity. But being near him after all these months set her nerves on edge. Her body hummed when she was close to him, and that could only mean trouble. "True. That's why a lot of older people sell their homes. They don't use the upstairs anymore."

She stepped into a bedroom decorated for a small child. The pink bunny wallpaper and rose-colored bedding suggested it was a girl's room, and Tina's chest tightened as an inkling of sadness crept into her heart. What a strange feeling to have in such a cheerful room.

Trent moved to stand beside her, and her chest tightened even more. "I didn't know he had kids," he said. "I didn't even know he was married."

"That's odd. A little creepy, actually." Surely Jack would've talked about his wife and children. Brought them to the family gatherings. She moved into the hallway, and the sadness lifted.

"Tell me about it." Trent followed her out of the room. "Who else do you think lived here?"

She shrugged. "He was *your* family. Maybe he adopted or was a foster parent or something."

"If he was, I feel sorry for the kids. Uncle Jack was…scary."

"How so?"

"He was really tall and rail thin. I always thought he'd

make a good undertaker. He had a long face and a pointed nose. And he hunched over, like a lot of old people do. He always seemed mad, but not really mad…more like… wicked. Like the world had done him wrong and he wanted everyone else to suffer for it."

She glanced into the other bedrooms, but their drab décor suggested no one had lived in them in a long time. "I guess he didn't have to dress up for Halloween then."

He curled his lip, shuddering as if the thought disgusted him. "He was frightening enough on his own. Ready for the third floor?"

She peered up the stairs. "As I'll ever be."

The top floor consisted of a short hallway with a single door. An oval mirror hung on the wall to the left, and a small table sat off to the right. She grabbed the doorknob, and the icy metal bit at her skin, sending a tingling shock up her arm.

"Ow!" She jerked her arm back and rubbed her palm. "Son of a bitch."

"What happened?" Trent reached for her, but he let his arm drop to his side.

"The doorknob shocked me." She rubbed her hand on her skirt.

"It was probably static. Look." Trent grabbed it and tried to turn it. The knob wouldn't budge. He jiggled it and leaned into the door. "Hmm…it's locked."

"Do you have a key?"

He reached in his pocket and pulled out the front door key. "This is the only one. I doubt it will fit." He tried the lock, but the key was too big.

Tina pressed her ear to the door. "I wonder what's in there." She reached for the handle again, and a white stream of electricity, like a tiny bolt of lightning, shot into her finger. "Goddammit." She shook her hand and placed the tip of her finger in her mouth. "Now it's personal. There's got to be a key around here somewhere."

She was willing to chalk the first shock up to static, but the second time seemed deliberate. Someone—or something—didn't want her opening that door, and she never backed down from a challenge.

She ran her hand along the top of the molding; some people hid keys right by the doors. No luck. She lifted the rug in the hallway. Nothing. Something may not have wanted her getting inside, but another something— equally as strong—silently called to her from the other side of the door. She *had* to get into the room.

"We can call a locksmith." Trent watched as she lifted knickknacks and vases.

"No, no. I've been in enough old houses. People always leave spare keys around." She looked behind the mirror and under the rug again. Her pulse pounded. Her hands went slick with sweat. Something drew her to that room, and she couldn't stop until she got inside.

"Want me to break it down?"

She cut her gaze to Trent for only a second. Then a pewter dragon statue sitting on a small table against the wall caught her eye. She'd seen pieces like this in plenty of old houses, and the seam along the neck hinted at its purpose. "No need."

She marched to the dragon and ran her hand along its back. As she suspected, one of the scales was a lever that released the head. She pulled it back and found the key inside. "Eureka." She pranced toward the door and slipped the key into the lock.

Trent blinked. "How did you know it was in there?"

"A gut feeling, I guess. There's *something* inside that

room." She took a deep breath and slowly turned the key. *And whatever that something is, it isn't going to be good.* So why on Earth did she need to see it so badly?

She pushed open the door and took a step back, expecting a lightning bolt to shoot through the threshold like it did through the knob.

Nothing happened.

"Huh." She peeked inside and looked to the right, then to the left. It was empty. A big, dark, empty room. "What the hell?" She crept inside and stood in the middle of a large, round rug that nearly covered the entire floor. Black shutters blocked the light from seeping in the windows, and she was blinded for a moment when Trent flipped on the light switch.

Aside from a vague feeling of familiarity, the room was void of any meaning—or any furniture. She couldn't find anything that would've caused the shock she'd received from the door knob. "Well, this sure isn't what I expected."

The light from the single, bare bulb didn't reach all the way to the corners of the room, leaving them cast in inky shadow. In her peripheral vision, the shadows seemed to roll, folding inward on themselves as if they were alive. But as soon as she focused on a corner, the movement stilled.

Something about this room wasn't right. It felt a good ten degrees colder than the rest of the house, but that could've been because it was closed up for so long. It seemed to grow colder the longer she stood there, and her breathing grew shallow as a feeling of dread gripped her chest. As badly as she'd needed to get into this room before, now she needed to get out. Out of this house.

"I need some fresh air." She brushed past Trent and

trotted down the stairs and out the front door. Careful not to put too much pressure on the rotting wood, she leaned on the front porch railing and tried to catch her breath. This house had to be the creepiest place she'd ever seen. And that room… Something about that room made her shiver.

***

Tina had bolted from the house like she'd seen a ghost. Maybe she had. Trent hadn't heard or felt anything unusual this time, but *something* had gotten to Tina. The way she'd been so intent on finding the key to the third-floor room. The way the color had drained from her face when she turned circles on the black rug. Her reactions to the home reignited his irrational fear that Uncle Jack still lingered inside.

He looked around the third-floor room. The faded black walls angled inward before they met the ceiling, forming a flat-topped A shape. The air was heavy, and it almost felt like the walls were closing in. Maybe the menacing atmosphere spooked her. He sighed. "What kind of trouble do you have in store for me, Uncle Jack?"

He made his way to the foyer and spotted Tina leaning over the front porch railing. "Hey, are you okay?" He eyed the coat rack as he stepped out the door, half-expecting it to fall on his head.

It didn't.

He rubbed the space between Tina's shoulder blades. "What happened? You jetted out of there so fast…it wasn't a… You didn't see a ghost, did you?"

Tina took a deep breath and stood straight, and Trent let his hand fall to his side. "No ghost. I guess I got creeped out. You might need to do a little cleaning. Try to brighten the place up before anyone looks at it."

"Yeah. I guess you're right."

Tina took two steps down the stairs and turned to look at him. "I'll get the paperwork drawn up tomorrow and give you a call then." She descended the rest of the steps.

Trent ran a hand through his hair. "Okay. Tina?"

She paused and turned to face him, a tiny smile curving her lips, though her eyes were still tight with worry. "Yes?"

"It was good to see you again."

Her smile reached her eyes. "Yeah…it was."

He watched her as she loped across the snowy ground, hopping over the ice slick he'd busted his ass on earlier. What was he going to do about that woman? If he'd known working with her would rekindle the small torch he secretly held for her, he never would've called her.

Or maybe that was *why* he called her. Deep down, he'd really wanted to see her again. Was he masochistic? Hell, he probably was. "What's done is done."

He turned to pull the front door closed. With one hand on the knob, he glanced inside one more time, and his eyes widened.

"I know that's not where I put you, you bastard." The coat rack had rotated ninety degrees and stood a good two feet from where he'd told it to stay. He exhaled a curse and marched inside to put the rack back in its proper place.

"You're trying to make me think I'm insane, but it won't work. This house is mine. Now, your ass better stay put, or I'm going to turn you into a pile of toothpicks."

He marched out the door, slamming it behind him.

## CHAPTER THREE

"So, how'd it go with Tina? Did you two get it on in the living room?" Logan playfully elbowed Trent in the shoulder.

"Hell no. We never got it on when she actually liked me." The vibrating bass of the rock band on the small stage should've made it impossible for Trent to hear himself think. Add to that the three lagers he'd already downed and his mind should've been a blank slate. But no matter how hard he tried to forget about Tina's supple breasts stretching her sweater tight across her chest, her full lips, and her piercing emerald eyes, he couldn't get his mind off the woman.

"Aw, I'm sorry, man."

Trent chuckled. "Don't be. I wouldn't give her the time of day, anyway." And why should he? She'd slammed the door on their blooming relationship with no semblance of a reason. She'd gone from smoking hot to frigid in a matter of days…no, hours. It wasn't a bait and switch. It was a bait and run like hell.

He'd never been shit on like that by a woman, and he

sure wasn't going to set himself up to get flushed again. Didn't need to. A good-looking, successful lawyer could have any woman he wanted. He made good money, worked out, and whenever he was in a relationship, he always treated his woman with respect. He was quite a catch, if he said so himself.

So why didn't Tina want him?

It didn't matter. It was guys' night, and he planned to get shit-faced and enjoy the hell out of it.

Logan took a sip of Coke. "How much are you asking for the place?"

Trent shrugged. "I don't know yet. Tina was going to research the area and get back with me today, but she never called."

"She will."

"I'm not worried about it. But when you tell someone you're going to call the next day, you should call him. Even if you don't have any information yet." She could've at least had the decency to tell him she didn't have time or she'd get back with him Monday. He slid his half-finished mug across the bar from his right hand to his left and back again.

"Sounds like you may still have a chip on your shoulder, man."

Trent shook his head. "Nah." He swiveled his bar stool around to face the band and pretended to jam to the music. A chip on his shoulder? The hell he did. It was common professional courtesy to call a client back when you told him you would. And all they had was a professional relationship.

He chugged the second half of his beer and ordered a shot of Patron.

Logan put his hand on top of the glass. "Dude, are you sure you want to do that?"

"Positive." And to prove it to his friend, he was going to take someone home tonight. A tanned blonde with short hair and dark brown eyes. As far from Tina as possible.

The bartender gave him a lime, but Trent left it on the napkin. Patrón didn't need a chaser. The smooth liquid slid down his throat and warmed him from the inside out. He spotted his potential conquest, motioned for Logan to see, and slipped off his stool.

---

"I love girls' night in as much as going out." Tina swiped the final stroke of cherry red polish across Allison's pinkie toe. "There's no pressure to look good. I don't have to hold in my stomach or constantly check my makeup in the mirror."

"Oh, please." Allison fanned her wet nails with a magazine. "Your stomach is flat without an ounce of effort on your part."

"Says Twiggy herself." Tina picked up her glass of chardonnay and handed the bottle of polish to her friend.

"Hey…I run my ass off nearly every day."

"Literally."

Allison opened her mouth in feigned shock. "That's not nice. It's actually gotten rounder since I started running."

"If you say so, sweets."

She glared and grabbed Tina's foot. "Just remember who's got the bright red paint."

Tina giggled and sipped her wine. "So, how are things with Logan? Have you set a date yet?"

"Not a specific one." Her eyes gleamed. "We're thinking of having a summer wedding. Maybe June, somewhere outdoors."

"That'll be nice. Just, please…*please* let me go with you when you pick out the bridesmaids' dresses. If I have to wear one more pink taffeta, 1980s prom-style gown I'm going to puke."

"Don't worry. I'm leaning toward fuchsia polyester, anyway."

Allison had been Tina's best friend for as long as she could remember. They'd been there for each other through disease, suicide, nervous breakdowns, and all the happy times in-between. She was the only person who knew Tina inside and out. Of course, the fact that Allison was psychic and empathic probably helped with that.

Not only could Allison feel other people's emotions, she could also communicate with spirits. Tina had gotten the chance to see what that entailed three months ago when she, Trent, and Logan assisted her in helping a spirit cross over to the other side.

That was the only time Tina had ever encountered a ghost. She didn't have a psychic bone in her body, and she was glad. She'd seen the things Allison had been through, and she wanted no part of it.

Allison finished painting Tina's right foot and moved on to the left. "How did it go with Trent? You never told me."

*Crap.* The dreaded moment she'd been hoping to elude had finally arrived. She'd tried her best to block him out of her thoughts all day. She hadn't forgotten to research the home values in the neighborhood where his uncle's house was. Or to call him. She'd flat out avoided it. He probably didn't notice, anyway.

"Oh, it was fine. The house is huge and in decent condition, so he'll probably get a lot for it."

Allison stopped painting mid-stroke. "Uh-huh. But how did it go with him? Was it awkward? Did he ask you out? If he did, and you didn't tell me, I'm going to stick this paintbrush up your nose." She waved the brush in front of Tina's face before applying the last coat on her toe.

Tina snorted. "He didn't ask me out, Allie. He didn't even act interested...well, maybe a little...but he kept it all business." She propped her feet on the coffee table and fanned them with a magazine.

Allison grabbed the nail polish bottle and carried it to the bathroom. A *thud* sounded from across the room, followed by the sound of shattering glass and Allison cursing.

Tina jumped to her feet and walked on her heels toward the bathroom. "Are you okay?"

"Don't come in here." Allison sucked a breath in through her teeth. "I broke the bottle."

"I can help you clean it up."

"I cut myself."

"Oh." Instantly light-headed, Tina placed her hand against the wall to steady herself. "I'll be in the living room then." She heel-walked back to the sofa and sat down.

Ten minutes later, Allison emerged from the bathroom with a bandage wrapped tightly around her index finger. "Luckily, the paint didn't splatter too far. I cleaned it up, and I'll buy you a new bottle next time I'm at the store."

"Don't worry about it. There's, uh...no blood in the sink or anything is there?"

Allison patted her hand. "I wouldn't do that to you, babe. I even buried the tissue I used to clean myself up in the bottom of the trash. I'll take it to the dumpster on my way home if you want."

"That's okay." Some strong, independent woman she was. How could she expect to be Wonder Woman when she grew up if she fainted at the sight of blood? She sighed and shook her head. "I'm sorry."

Allison shrugged. "It's no big deal. Anyway…You and Trent kept it all business?"

"I tried to at first, but I couldn't stop myself from flirting with him. He's just so damn cute."

She rolled her eyes. "Tina, you flirt with everyone."

"Only the people I want to flirt with. That's the difference. I didn't want to do it with him, but I couldn't help it. The only thing that stopped me from making a complete idiot of myself was the creepy house. If I hadn't been distracted by that attic or room, or whatever it was, I might've asked him out myself."

Allison leaned forward, furrowing her brow. "What happened in the attic?"

"Nothing. That's what was so creepy." Tina recounted her experience in the Victorian manor, and it seemed even more ridiculous as she spoke. "I had to get into that room, but once I was there…there was nothing."

Allison looked at Tina with a concerned gaze. "Are you okay? Do you think it could be something from a past life? Or a spirit?"

Tina laughed. "I doubt it. It was probably my self-conscience trying to distract me from Trent. I'm not over him, Allie. I thought I was, but I'm not."

Trent made eye contact with the blonde, and she smiled before playfully looking away. *Oh, yeah.* This was going to be easy. He'd prove to Logan that he was over Tina. Even better, he'd prove it to himself.

He swaggered toward the other side of the room with a Heineken in his hand, but he stopped short when a wave of fatigue crashed into him like he'd been hit in the face with a frying pan.

His head dropped. His jaw slacked. His knees buckled. Everything went black.

Sharp pain shot through the back of Trent's head as he tried to focus on the people around him. He blinked, then opened his eyes wide. Logan stood in front of him and offered him a hand up. Trent accepted and rose to his feet, casting his gaze to the floor to avoid the inquisitive stares of the onlookers. His ears grew warm as embarrassment flushed through his system. How many people had seen him fall?

"Are you sure he should be standing?" the blonde said. "I mean, he passed out. He should go to a hospital."

"Nah." Logan put his arm around Trent and walked him toward the bar. "It happens all the time."

With his ass firmly planted in his seat, Trent rested his elbows on the bar. "How long was I out?"

"A couple of minutes."

"Damn. Feels like it was all night. Aside from the headache, I feel great." He laughed, and the pain shot to his temple. "Ow."

Trent was seventeen when his narcolepsy first set in. It started mild, with only a few episodes of fatigue a week. But as he reached adulthood, the symptoms worsened. By the time he reached twenty-five, the frequent bouts of sleep attacks forced him to seek medical help.

Through trial and error, he'd finally found the drug cocktail that eliminated his symptoms. Well, almost eliminated them. He still fought the fatigue, but the sleep attacks rarely peeked their evil heads unless he was drinking or extremely emotional. Tonight, he was both.

Logan looked at him with sympathy in his eyes. "I told you not to have that shot, man. You know alcohol makes it worse."

Trent rubbed the sore spot on his head. "I know, I know. But I hadn't had an episode in years. I thought I'd be okay."

"That's what you get for thinking."

## CHAPTER FOUR

*W*arm water trickled down Tina's skin like rain. She took a deep breath, inhaling the freesia scent of her conditioner as she worked it through her thick hair and tried to clear her mind.

Ever since Allison had left, Tina had been a nervous wreck trying to figure out how to work with Trent and not fall for him again. She had to get the image of his chiseled features, dark chocolate eyes, and charming smile out of her mind. She'd focus on the house. That's why he'd called her, after all.

She'd have to do some research to find a good asking price. A contractor to do the repairs and haul out the old furniture should be easy to find. A cleaning company would need to do a deep clean before she could move the staging furniture in. It probably wouldn't hurt to ask Allison to clear the energy in the home as well. Hopefully she could get rid of the eeriness that made the place seem so suffocating.

With her to-do list firmly formed in her mind, Tina turned off the water and stepped out of the shower. She towel-dried her hair and glanced at the full-length mirror on the inside of the bathroom door. *Who in their right mind would put a mirror right there when you step out of the shower?*

She wiped the fog off the glass and looked at her body, running her hands along the curves of her waist and over the saddlebags she had for hips. No matter how hard she tried, her hips would never be as slender as she'd have liked. At least she had nice calves, though they were covered with boots most of the year.

She cupped her hands under her breasts and lifted them. Since she'd turned thirty, it seemed like gravity was getting the best of her. She sighed and ran her hand through her damp locks. "You gotta work what you got, girl."

She slipped into her favorite pink and green flannel pajamas and climbed into bed. Her pale blue walls and navy bed linens were meant to calm her…lull her to sleep. The colors usually did the trick; she was often asleep as soon as her head hit the pillow. But not tonight.

After tossing and turning for half an hour, she switched on the bedside lamp and picked up a book. Half science fiction, half thriller, the novel consisted of a new race of people—born as adults from creation tanks—that would soon rule the world. Their mission was to kill every living human. It was full of suspense, twists and turns—probably not the best reading material for someone trying to fall asleep. But she couldn't help it. She was addicted to mystery and suspense.

Despite the excitement in the novel world, her eyelids began to droop. With a yawn, she returned the book to the table and switched off the light before drifting to sleep.

Tina's feet pounded the pavement as she turned the corner into the alley. The darkness that trailed her knew her well —knew all her fears. It had tormented her before, but this time, it was out for blood. For revenge.

The sound of her frantic breath and the pulse throbbing in her ears deafened her to the rest of the world. She ran with all her might...her life depended on it. She wore pajamas, her bare feet numb on the icy streets. Piercing pain shot up her legs, and her side cramped as if she'd been stabbed. But still, she pushed forward. She couldn't afford to look behind her to see if the dark mass was getting closer. Her head felt as if it would split in two...her chest like it would explode.

She ducked behind a dumpster and slipped through a service door in the back of a warehouse, locking it behind her. Maybe it hadn't seen her. Maybe it would pass her by this time.

With her hands on her knees, she bent down to catch her breath. Her matted hair spilled forward, blocking most of the room from view. But she didn't miss the fog—no, the black shadow—that crept beneath the doorway. That oozed in through the sides of the threshold.

It had found her.

After all these years, it was back.

Tina sprinted across the room, but there was no way out. She slipped behind a shelving unit and pressed her back against the wall. She was out of sight, but her furious, shallow breaths gave her away. She closed her eyes and prepared herself for whatever was about to happen.

*"Help us."* The hopeless cry seemed to come from

nowhere and everywhere at the same time. Tina opened her eyes, but she saw nothing. *"Please."*

Despite the mass of smoky shadow on her trail, Tina dared a whisper. "Who? Who are you?"

A guttural roar echoed through the room, bouncing off the walls to create a cacophony of terror. Her body trembled. Tears rained down her cheeks, and she bit back a scream. The smoke hissed as it poured toward her.

*"Wake up. We need your help."* The voice grew louder, urgent. *"Open your eyes and it will be gone. It's not that strong yet."*

Tina spoke through clenched teeth, "My eyes are open."

*"Only in your dream."*

Was she asleep? The threat was too close, too real, to be a dream. But as the disembodied voice called to her, the warehouse room seemed to evaporate into a wispy film of dust.

She lay in her bed with the cotton sheets tangled across her body. The scent of her lavender candle danced in the air. Though her nightclothes were drenched in sweat, she was home. Safe. Her eyelids fluttered open, and she pushed herself into a sitting position...

And screamed.

The translucent woman standing before her wore a simple, white gown stained with splattered blood. Red slime oozed from the place her hand should have been attached to her arm. While her eyes appeared swollen and bruised, and bright red capillaries spidered beneath her jaundiced skin, her features seemed fluid, rolling and fading in and out, morphing the woman's face into an unrecognizable blur.

Tina pushed back on her bed. "Wha...what...who are you? What are you doing here?"

The spirit reached out her good hand. *"We need your help. He's got us. He's holding us here."*

"Who?"

*"You know who. Please..."* The spirit began to fade away.

"Wait! Who?"

*"Help us..."*

Tina blinked and rubbed her eyes. Had she really just seen that? *Heard* that? *No. No way.* She'd imagined it. She hadn't been getting enough sleep, and now she was hallucinating. The shadow monster in her dream? Yeah, she'd seen that before. Same creature. Different location every time, like it wanted her to know it could find her anywhere. The recurring nightmare had haunted her most of her life, though she hadn't had the dream in years. But the ghost woman in her bedroom? It was her imagination. That was the only logical explanation.

She couldn't talk to spirits...but Allison could. She picked up her phone and started to dial her friend's number, until she looked at the clock. *Damn it. It's four in the morning.*

What the hell was she supposed to do for the next three hours? She wasn't due at the office until eight, but she sure as hell wasn't going back to sleep. She shoved the tangled mess of covers off, threw on her robe, and shuffled to the kitchen for her morning routine. *Three freaking hours early.*

With the coffee brewing and bread in the toaster, she took a quick shower to rinse off the night's ordeal.

She turned on the television and sipped her coffee while she tried to figure out what exactly had happened.

Unable to make sense of any of it, she flipped the channels and settled on watching an early morning news show. The weather looked bleak. The meteorologist forecasted snow for the next five days. *Lovely.*

Her phone buzzed on the nightstand, and she padded across the room to answer it. The last thing she expected at five o'clock in the morning was a phone call. She sat on the edge of the bed and put the receiver to her ear. "Hello?"

"Are you okay?"

Her throat tightened at the sound of Trent's voice. She swallowed and answered, "I'm fine. Why do you ask?" That sounded cool, didn't it? Calm. Nonchalant. She hoped her voice didn't give away the excitement she felt. Why on Earth was he calling her this early?

Trent let out a heavy sigh. "Good. I just had this weird dream. You were in trouble, and…" He chuckled. "But it was nothing, wasn't it? Never mind."

He was dreaming about her? "What kind of trouble was I in?"

"It's stupid. I'm sorry if I woke you."

"I was already up. It's nice to hear that you're dreaming about me, though." She couldn't fight her playful tone as she flirted.

He let out a nervous laugh. "It wasn't that kind of dream."

"But at least I'm on your mind." Why was she doing this to herself? Was she looking for heartache? "I'm sorry. That's not very professional of me. I should—"

"It's okay. It's nice to see this side of you again. You seemed uptight when you left before, and then you didn't call."

"I don't have an uptight bone in my body. The house was creepy…and I was planning to call you today."

"Okay, I get it. Forget I said anything."

"Why was I in trouble in your dream?" What could have possibly warranted a phone call at five in the morning? After the dream she'd had herself, and the…whatever it was she thought she saw when she woke up…she could only imagine what kind of nightmare he might have had. Maybe the eeriness of the house had gotten to them both.

A smile tugged at the corners of her lips. Even if it was a nightmare…Trent was dreaming about her. "Did you rescue me?"

"It was stupid. Don't worry about it. Listen, I'm sorry I called so early. Just get in touch with me when you have the paperwork ready."

"But—"

"I've got to get ready for work. See you soon."

"Okay."

*Click.*

What the hell just happened? Did he blow her off? No one ever blew her off when she flirted. True, he had every reason to, but still. She couldn't remember the last time a man rejected her. Was she losing her appeal? She knew all the burgers and fried food would catch up with her eventually, but she was only thirty.

She walked into the bathroom and examined her face in the mirror. Faint traces of laugh lines were beginning to show around her eyes and mouth. And…was that a gray hair? *Oh, no!* She wrapped the strand around her finger and yanked it out, wincing at the sharp pain that followed. The brief stinging sensation was worth it, though. She was too young to go gray.

She'd just have to step up her game to avoid rejection. Maybe a girls' night out, rather than in, would do her some good. Some male attention would boost her self-esteem.

Wait…What was she thinking?

She didn't need anything from a man. She was a complete, successful, independent woman all on her own. She slept around because she enjoyed sex. Not because desperation to be loved and accepted drove her to do anything a man told her to. That was her mom's game, and—while she loved the woman dearly—she'd never forget the parade of men coming in and out of her life as if their house had a revolving front door. The way her mom completely changed for each new potential husband who stuck around for more than a few days. Her hair, her clothes, the way she acted.

Tina loved and accepted herself, and herself was all she needed. She'd never used sex to gain acceptance, and she could bed any man she wanted.

Except for Trent.

He was one man she'd dated but hadn't slept with. And why hadn't she slept with him? She'd certainly had plenty of opportunity—and desire. But oddly enough, Trent was the one man whose opinion of her actually mattered. She found herself caring about him as a person —not just his body—and that scared her to death.

What if she fell for him, and he left her? She didn't want to end up like her mom, drowning herself in alcohol and chocolate every time a man walked out the door. It was better to never get serious in the first place. Then she'd never have to worry about being rejected.

That's why she'd shut Trent out the first time. It was also why she couldn't get him off her mind. Damn it, she cared about that man. And he must've cared about her too

—at least a little bit—since he called her at five in the morning after having a bad dream. Add to that the fact that he was hard to get now—whether he was playing that way or not. Who didn't love a challenge?

But was the prize really what she wanted?

CHAPTER FIVE

*T*rent grumbled as he marched through the garage to his Audi. Logan had insisted he call his doctor before he left for work. Of course, the doc told him not to drive until they ran some tests. Don't drive? How the fuck else was he supposed to get to work?

He climbed into the car, slammed the door, and crammed the key into the ignition. And how the hell did the doctor expect him to get to the office for the fucking tests? Clutching the steering wheel, he took a deep breath. He wasn't mad at the doctor. He was mad at himself.

Where had that sleep attack come from? He'd had maybe ten or fifteen his entire life, and they were when he was much younger. Years ago. So why now? The only symptoms he'd dealt with in the past five years were fatigue, occasional hallucinations, and sleep paralysis. And it had been two years since he'd experienced any of those.

For his narcolepsy to resurface with the worst symptom possible was beyond strange. And then the dream he'd had about Tina...that shadow monster was one of the scariest things he'd ever seen. He'd never had a dream so vivid. So real.

Then again, it was probably because of everything that had happened. The rush of emotions seeing Tina stirred in his soul. The creepy house. His fear of it being haunted. Yeah, there were plenty of reasons for him to have a dream like that. And nightmares were another symptom of his disease. It was most likely nothing. It had to be.

He drove straight to the doctor's office and underwent a series of tests: EKGs, MRIs, stress tests. He gave nearly half a pint of blood for analysis. Two hours later, light-headed and exhausted, he checked out of the office and walked to his car. The preliminary results showed nothing had changed, but the doctor increased Trent's medication dosage, just to be safe. His entire morning was wasted. *What a hassle.*

As he drove into downtown toward the office, his mind drifted back to Tina. He'd made an ass of himself by calling her at five in the morning. She must've thought he was insane. Or obsessed. Hell, maybe he was both. He couldn't hide his feelings for her if he wanted to. And if she hadn't picked up on his emotions at the house, surely she'd noticed the swell in his pants when she'd gotten out of the car. It had taken all his strength not to adjust himself and make it even more obvious.

And the fragrance of her perfume when she'd gotten close was sweet and floral—like a colorful meadow on a crisp, spring day. It was enough to make his knees weak. But that was as close as he'd get to being with her.

The mystery of the moving coat rack and Tina's determination to get into that attic room intrigued him enough to return to the house. It called to him. He chuckled at himself. If the house called to him, that would mean he had psychic abilities, and he *knew* he didn't.

Allison had said that everyone had them and it's just a matter of developing them. Trent didn't want them developed. Not with all the hassle Logan had gone through. The guy might have gone nuts if it weren't for Allison. She'd taught Logan how to control his empathic abilities and get a handle on his own emotions.

If only Trent could rein his in. He'd love to squelch his desire to feel Tina's naked body pressed against his. To extinguish the flame in his soul that flared every time she was near. She'd intruded on his thoughts far too much, and if he wasn't careful, the fire might consume him.

He shook his head to remove her from his mind and turned up the radio. With George Strait blasting through the speakers, he made a quick U-turn and headed toward his inherited hell house.

---

Tina looked at her cell phone and debated calling Trent. She'd done her research and found the house was worth way more than she'd first thought. He'd be better off selling it to a normal buyer than going for a flipper. With a new front porch, a fresh coat of paint, and a *lot* of cleaning, Trent stood to make at least 1.2 million dollars on the place.

She leaned back in her desk chair and gazed out the third-floor window to the parking lot below, but her eyes didn't focus on the cars. All she could see was the image of the way Trent's jeans hugged his muscular thighs and the nice view of his backside she'd gotten when he slipped on the ice in front of the house. The adorable way he'd cussed at the slick spot on the ground had her lips curving into a grin. The man was scrumptious, that was for sure.

She glanced at the time on her phone. Eleven-thirty. If he were a normal client, she'd invite him to lunch to discuss her findings, but that felt too much like a date when it came to Trent. And after the way he'd blown her off this morning, she definitely didn't want him to think she was still interested.

She could always email the information to him. Avoid talking to the man all together. But she cringed at the formality of emails. Business was best done in person. Face to face. She didn't hide behind a screen with her other clients. Why should Trent be any different? He'd hired her to do a job. Nothing more. She needed to put her feelings for him aside, do what she was hired to do, and be done with him.

She dialed his number before she could change her mind, but she couldn't ignore the tightening in her chest as the phone rang one, two, three times.

"Hello?" Trent's sharp, irritated tone made her breath catch.

"Is this a bad time?"

He sighed heavily. "No. What did you find out?"

So much for making small talk. "I have quite a bit of information to share with you. I think you'll be happy to hear it. Can you meet me for lunch in an hour so we can discuss it?" She held her breath as she awaited his answer. He was taking way too long to respond. With all the road noise in the background, he was obviously driving. Maybe he hadn't heard her. "Trent?"

He let out a slow exhale. "I don't think that's a good idea. I'm already on my way to the house anyway. If it's too much to tell me over the phone, can you meet me there?"

A sour feeling formed in her stomach. Blown off by the same man twice in one day. She wasn't used to the sting of rejection, and she certainly didn't like the way it felt. "Yeah. Sure. I'll be there in forty-five minutes."

"Great."

*Click.*

She stared at her phone as the screen went blank. What the hell was wrong with him? Even if he wasn't interested in dating her, he could still show a little niceness and say good-bye before he ended the call. Then again, she hadn't exactly shown professionalism—or niceness—when she'd avoided calling him yesterday. She was acting like a nervous teenager, and that needed to stop right now.

From this moment forward, she would be nothing but professional. She'd get used to the way her pulse sprinted when he was near. Who knew? Maybe they could even be friends. After the way she'd dumped him three months ago, she didn't deserve anything more.

---

Trent rolled his car up the long driveway, cringing as the drooping willow branches slid across the surface of his silver Audi, their leafless tendrils squealing across his custom paint job. Crazy Uncle Jack better have had a couple grand stashed in a mattress somewhere in that house to pay for the scratches these overgrown trees were causing to his car. Bertha would need some TLC when he was rid of this place. Hopefully a good buffing would get the scratches out. He mentally moved calling the tree trimmers to the top of his to-do list.

Putting the car in park, he flipped on the windshield wipers to swipe away the fresh flurries of snow, but the futile action did no good. February snow in Michigan was as insistent as his resurfacing feelings for the dark-haired vixen he'd hired as his real estate agent.

Why, exactly, had he wanted to see her again? He'd hoped it would prove once and for all that he was over her. But her deep green eyes and silky black hair had the exact opposite effect. And man, did she have some nerve trying to flirt with him like she hadn't already ripped his heart out and stomped on it. Every time a string of playful banter left her lips, he got pulled in.

It was all part of her charm. But Tina flirted with everyone, and he'd be damned if he was going to flirt back anymore. If he could keep things between them professional, he might be able to make it out of this with his heart intact this time. There was no way in hell he'd let her reject him again.

He cut the engine and jogged up the front porch steps. As soon as his right foot hit the landing, the rotten wood snapped. His leg plunged through the boards, and he toppled over, catching himself with his hands before a massive splinter sliced through his leg.

"Goddammit. Stupid rotten wood." He yanked his leg free to the splitting sound of tearing fabric and sat in the door jamb, leaning his back against the door.

"Motherfucker." His pants were torn from mid-calf to his ankle, and blood oozed from a two-inch gash in his shin. "Can this day get any worse?"

He hauled his ass up and pushed open the door. Maybe fixing the front porch should get the number one spot on his to-do list.

Flipping on the light switch, he turned to the sinister

coat rack and waved his finger at it. "I'm not in the mood for your shenanigans. Stay put." He limped into the kitchen and shook his head. If that coat rack really could move on its own, it probably wouldn't listen anyway.

He snatched a paper towel off the roll and wet it in the sink. His cut stung as he pressed the make-shift bandage against his shin. Once he got the blood cleaned up, he breathed a sigh of relief. It was just a scrape. The bleeding had already slowed to a manageable level, so he left it alone.

But the rancid stench of rotting garbage wouldn't leave *him* alone. If no one had bothered to take the trash out when Jack died, he could only imagine what must be in the fridge.

A severed head. The fingers of Jack's latest victims.

He jerked the trash bag out of the bin and carried it to the fridge. Resting his hand on the door, he nearly choked on the deep breath of putrid funk he tried to inhale. He braced himself for whatever atrocities he might find and pulled open the door.

Moldy oranges. A pack of green mystery meat that looked like it might have once been ham. A half-empty carton of chunky two-percent milk. Nothing out of the ordinary to make his skin crawl. Maybe crazy Uncle Jack wasn't as crazy as he'd thought. Or maybe all the body parts were in a freezer in the basement.

He chunked the rotten food into the trash bag and carried it out to the porch before returning to the kitchen. Something still didn't smell right. He raked his gaze across the countertops until he found the culprit. A bowl of apples sat on the counter, its contents turning into a melted-looking black sludge.

Damn it, he'd already tied the bag shut. There had to

be more garbage bags around somewhere. He rummaged through the cabinets and drawers, but he found nothing of use. Where did Jack keep his trash bags? Maybe the pantry?

A quick peek inside revealed a few cereal boxes and some instant oatmeal. Surely he didn't keep them in the basement with the bodies.

Trent let out a nervous chuckle and eyed the cellar door. The one room he hadn't checked out yet, and that's probably where the trash bags were kept. He'd seen enough scary movies to know the basement was always where the monsters lurked. Maybe he should wait until Tina got there and they could go down together.

What was he saying? If it was really as dangerous down there as his imagination made it out to be, he wouldn't let Tina step foot inside the door. He'd have to check it out on his own. And it was better to do it before she got there so she wouldn't hear him if he screamed like a teenaged girl.

Of course the door creaked on its hinges as he pushed it open. Horror movie doors always creaked. And it was no surprise he had to stumble halfway down the staircase before he could reach the light switch. With his luck, the bulb would be burnt out too. Then the monsters would descend and suck the life out of him.

He gritted his teeth and flipped the switch. Bright, white light flooded the barren room, and he squinted as his eyes adjusted. "That wasn't so bad." He took a few deep breaths to slow his racing heart and descended the rest of the steps to the concrete floor.

A contemporary washing machine and dryer sat against one wall, and a recently updated furnace lined the adjacent wall. Hopefully the modern appliances down here would add a little value to the house of horrors. The ones in the kitchen appeared to be from the 1990s.

He walked deeper into the room and found a plush, red-velvet chair facing a wooden easel. A painting of a woman holding a little girl sat on the easel, and Trent settled into the chair to examine it. He'd never seen either of them before. The woman appeared young—maybe in her twenties—and the child couldn't have been more than three years old. The woman's face held a pained expression, and the little girl's wide eyes stared back at him hauntingly. But even more disturbing—an ominous black shadow occupied most of the background.

His mind flashed back to the shadow monster chasing Tina in his dream. He shivered. It had to be a coincidence. Uncle Jack was a creepy man. A creepy painting in a creepy man's basement wasn't too far-fetched. And his dream was simply a symptom of his narcolepsy.

Still, this whole ordeal was a little too weird. This painting too damn freaky. The sooner he could rid himself of this house the better. He needed to get his ass upstairs to wait for Tina, but he couldn't make himself move from the chair. His body felt heavy; his limbs ached like he hadn't slept in days. In his mind, he moved to get up but his body wouldn't respond. *Shit.*

He leaned his head back against the velvet cushion and closed his eyes. He'd rest here for five minutes. Just a tiny nap, and he'd have control of his body again. Then the new number one on his to-do list would be to pick up the stronger prescription from the pharmacy.

## CHAPTER SIX

Tina shook the snow flurries out of her hair as she ascended the front steps of the Victorian mansion. The sour reek of old garbage greeted her, and she crinkled her nose at the offending bag sitting outside the door. She could carry it down to the curb, but by the time she trekked down and back the lengthy driveway, her favorite boots would be soaked. Better to leave it where it lay for now.

She stepped around the foot-sized hole in the landing —Trent needed to fix this front porch pronto—and knocked on the door. Silence answered, so she pressed the doorbell. A deep ringing like church bells vibrated through the building, and she adjusted her scarf against the crisp breeze as she waited.

No answer.

Trent's car sat next to hers in the driveway, so he had to be here. She pressed the bell one more time and knocked harder. "Trent? Are you going to leave me out here in the cold all day?"

Nothing.

She pressed her ear against the wood, hoping to hear music or the sounds of Trent cleaning, but silence hung on the other side of the door. "Come on, Trent, this isn't funny."

Was he messing with her, or could something really be wrong? Knowing Trent, he didn't answer the door just to prove a point. He could probably tell by the way she acted that she wasn't over him, and this was his subtle way of rubbing it in.

Still, he couldn't leave her standing on the porch all afternoon. She twisted the knob and, thankfully, found it unlocked. Pushing open the door, she tentatively stepped inside and closed it behind her. "Trent?" At least it was warm inside the house.

Slipping out of her coat, she turned to the evil-looking rack by the door. "Mind holding my stuff for me?" She hung her coat and scarf on one of its coiling branches and followed the light toward the kitchen.

Holy moly, this house was unsettling. Dust motes hung in the air so thick she felt the need to swat them out of her way. Central heating chased away any chance for a draft, but goose bumps rose on her arms as she shivered. And she couldn't shake the feeling that someone—or something—was watching her.

She chuckled at herself. "I've obviously seen too many scary movies. Trent?"

Continuing on her path to the kitchen, she paused at the staircase. What was up with that third-floor room? She'd gotten the willies so bad the last time she was in it, she'd darted out before she'd had the chance to examine it. Maybe Trent was upstairs. It wouldn't hurt to check.

Climbing the steps, slowly placing one foot above the other, she clutched the rail as if it were her lifeline. Something up there called to her silently, drawing her in like a flame beckoning a moth to its warm light. Her heart pounded against her ribcage as she ascended the staircase, pulled by some mysterious force from above, ushered up from below. Her mouth went dry at the sight of the open door, the key still sitting in the lock where she'd left it yesterday.

She hesitated to reach for the key. Would the knob shock her again like it had done before? Only one way to find out.

Squeezing her eyes shut, she gripped the key and slid it from the lock. She opened one eye, then the other, half-expecting a bolt of electricity to shoot from the empty keyhole.

Nothing happened.

"I'm being ridiculous." She returned the key to the dragon statue on the table and stepped into the room. Oddly-angled, dark gray walls surrounded her. This must've been the tower-looking section of the house she'd seen from outside. The shutters over the window looked like they hadn't been opened in fifty years, and the circular, black rug covering the floor probably hadn't been vacuumed in just as long.

Tina stood in the center of the room and stared at the wall. The place felt so eerily familiar, her skin crawled. She hadn't known this house existed until yesterday, but something about this room had her glued to the spot.

She shivered and exhaled, her breath creating a fog in front of her. Did the central heat not reach the third floor? A bronze vent in the corner suggested it did, but the temperature in the room was even more frigid than last time.

The pressure of an icy hand pressed on her shoulder,

and her throat tightened. She jerked her head around, her feet still firmly planted to the floor. She was alone.

"What the hell?"

*"Help us."* The disembodied voice seemed to echo through her mind. *"Please."*

"Oh, no. I'm out of here." She stepped toward the exit, but the door slammed shut as if a gust of wind had blown through the room. "This isn't funny." She reached for the knob, but it wouldn't turn. Cold sweat beaded on her forehead as she jiggled the handle, willing the stupid door to open. It didn't budge. "Damn it."

*"He's coming."* That same damn voice rolled through her head, and every hair on her body stood on end.

"Who's coming?" She scanned the empty room and turned back to the door. "Trent?" She banged against the wood. "Trent, the door's locked. Can you come up and let me out?"

Silence.

Where the hell was he?

The icy hand gripped her arm as the chill of dread crept up her spine. *"He's here. Get out."*

"I'm trying." She definitely didn't want to stick around to find out who *he* was, but the damn door wouldn't budge. "Trent," she screamed. "Let me out!"

*"It's too late."*

Electricity pricked at her skin as a static charge filled the room. The air grew thick. Heavy. A suffocating presence descended on her, squeezing the air from her lungs.

A familiar sense of fear sent ice racing through her veins. She'd felt this presence before. "Trent!" Her voice squeaked as she screamed, her frantic pounding on the door shooting sharp pains through her clenched fist.

The light bulb overhead popped, sending sparks

raining down on the rug, casting the room in darkness. But not total darkness. Enough light crept in through the shutters for her to see the inky shadow pouring from the floorboards, billowing like smoke. Blacker than black.

Her final scream caught in her throat as the shadow began to take form. Pressing her back to the wall, she squeezed her eyes shut and held her breath.

---

Trent's eyelids fluttered open at the muffled sound of someone calling his name. He lifted his head from the cushion and rubbed at the crick in his neck. As his eyes adjusted to the light, the haunting gaze of the little girl in the portrait stared back at him.

"*Trent!*"

Was that Tina calling his name? "Damn it, how long was I out this time?"

"*Let me out!*"

"Tina?" He darted up the stairs, her screams growing louder as he approached the third floor. What on Earth was she doing in that room again? He yanked on the handle, but it wouldn't budge.

A blood-curdling scream sounded from inside the room.

He slammed his shoulder into the door, splintering the jamb with a loud *thwack*. A ray of light from the hallway cut through the center of the darkened room, chasing the shadows away like a receding fog. He rubbed his eyes and blinked. It had dissipated quickly, but from the corner of his eye, the billowing shadow looked like the one from his dream.

It couldn't have been. He wouldn't even entertain the idea that the monster from his nightmares could be real.

He put a hand on Tina's shoulder. "Are you okay?"

Tina peeled herself off the wall and shot through the doorway, dragging him by the arm behind her. Visibly trembling, she wrapped her arms around herself and cut her gaze between the room and him. "The light burned out, and the door locked. I thought I saw something."

"What did you see?"

She clamped her mouth shut and shook her head.

He pulled his phone from his pocket and turned on the flashlight feature before stepping back into the room. Shining the beam across the walls and floor, he found no trace of the smoky shadow or anything else that might have spooked her. He shoved the phone into his pocket and returned to the hallway. "The room is empty."

She stared at him with wide, frightened eyes. "It wasn't."

"Did you see a ghost?"

"No." She ran her hands through her hair and smoothed her sweater down her stomach. "It was just the shadows." She straightened her spine and flashed a half-smile, but with the way her bottom lip trembled, he couldn't help but take her in his arms.

"Hey. You're okay."

She slid her arms around his neck and rested her head on his shoulder. The sweet floral scent of her hair wafted through his senses, and he closed his eyes. God, she felt good in his arms.

"That room creeps me out every time I go in it." She lifted her head and held him with her deep green eyes. "Thanks for busting the door down to save me."

"My pleasure." Of course, if he hadn't fallen asleep in

the basement, she never would've been locked in the room to begin with. He needed to start that new prescription sooner rather than later.

"My hero." She dropped her gaze to his mouth.

He swallowed. He needed to let her go. To walk away from this situation before he did something he'd regret. But he couldn't seem to move his hands from around her waist. Her tongue slipped out to moisten her lips, and his knees nearly buckled.

He would not kiss her. He would pry his arms from her tender curves, turn around, and walk away. That would be the smart thing to do.

She drifted toward him. He needed to pull back, but he couldn't make himself move. Her breath warmed his skin. Her lips brushed his. Softly. Tentatively, as if she were asking his permission. He wanted to tell her no. To leave with his heart still intact. But when her velvet lips brushed his a second time, he couldn't hold back.

Sliding his hand up her back to cup her neck, he leaned into the kiss, drinking her in, reveling in the taste of sweet mint on her tongue. She was as soft and warm as he remembered, and everything about this moment felt so right.

She pulled away and pressed her fingers to her lips. "I'm so sorry."

He shoved his hands in his pockets. "Don't be. Just don't do it again." His heart couldn't handle another rejection from a woman like Tina. He turned and started down the stairs. *Space.* He needed to put some distance between them before he let himself fall for her again. "You've got some info for me on the value of the house, right?"

"Yes." She followed him down the steps. "But Trent, I

really am sorry about what happened. I don't know what came over me."

"Nothing happened. Let's talk about the details downstairs." Maybe if he kept telling himself nothing happened, he'd eventually believe it.

In the living room, he paused and gazed out the window. The snow flurries had stopped falling, but a soft layer of white blanketed the front yard and the hoods of their cars. A stark contrast to the blacks and deep reds Uncle Jack liked to decorate with. If Trent didn't know any better, he'd wonder if the man were a vampire.

Tina perched on the edge of a burgundy cigar chair, her spine straight and her chin inclined, a perturbed expression raising a delicate eyebrow. He pressed his lips together and tried not to chuckle. She was a woman who was used to getting her way, but she wasn't getting her way with him. Not this time. Not if he could help it.

He stepped toward her and ran his hand across the back of the chair. "This is where they found his body."

"Eww!" She shot from the chair as if it had bitten her and dusted off her backside. "You could have told me that before I sat down."

Trent laughed. "Are you kidding? You nearly hit the ceiling, you jumped so high. I wouldn't want to miss a show like that."

"I see how you're going to be, mister." A playful smile tugged at her lips. "I'll have you know I was the high school high-jump champion way back when."

"Really?"

"I made it all the way to state only to be beaten by Sarah Vickerman. That tramp had legs up to her neck. It was unnatural."

"Was that the first time you didn't get what you wanted?"

"It was the *only* time I didn't get what I wanted." She slung her bag over her shoulder and marched toward the kitchen.

He stood there and watched her hips sway as she walked away. What was it about a confident woman that was so damn sexy? She could've had him if she'd wanted him three months ago. Right in the palm of her pristinely manicured hand. But not anymore.

Tina stopped in the foyer and picked up her coat from the floor. "I swear I hung this on the rack when I got here."

Trent narrowed his eyes at the hunk of wood as she hooked the collar of her jacket over one of the arms. "That thing's got a mind of its own." He motioned toward the kitchen and followed her through the foyer.

She ran a finger across the Formica surface before setting her bag down. "I think this is the only room not covered in dust." She glanced at his leg and narrowed her gaze. "Your pants are ripped."

"I fell through the porch and cut up my leg. It's okay now."

She clutched the countertop. "Are you bleeding?"

"I think it stopped." He reached for his pant leg. "Want to have a look?"

"That's okay." She paled and turned away, pulling a brown folder from her bag and pressing it to her chest. "Do you think this place is haunted?"

He let his pant leg drop and stood up straight. "What happened up there?"

She set the folder on the table and picked at the corner of the file. "I'm not sure. I had a weird nightmare last night, so it's probably my imagination. But I thought I heard voices. And the shadows seemed to move after the lights went out." She chuckled. "I suppose that's a typical reaction to being in a creepy place. The heat kicking on probably caused a draft and slammed the door shut. Then I freaked out. I guess I'm a little gun-shy after…"

"I understand. I've had some strange experiences here too. I chalked it up to my imagination at first, but if you're seeing things, it wouldn't hurt to have it checked out."

She nodded and let out a long breath. "I'll talk to Allison this evening."

"No, I'll call Logan first. He'd kill me if she got hurt again."

"Logan's still working on his *spirit sensors*." She made air quotes with her fingers. "If you want it done quickly, Allison needs to do it."

"I want Logan to check it out first. Let him decide if it's safe for her."

She crossed her arms. "He's not the boss of her. She can check it out on her own."

"And you're not the boss of me. This is my house, and I'm calling Logan first." He straightened his spine and crossed his arms to mirror her posture. Damn, she was cute when she was flustered.

"If I'm the one who's going to be listing it…" She sank into a chair and folded her hands on the table. "You're right. I don't want to argue with you."

"Good. Now tell me what I can get for this hell hole and how fast you can find someone to take it off my hands."

He plopped into a chair and fought to keep his eyes open as she rattled off a string of numbers and statistics. He needed a nap. Twenty minutes to recharge after all the excitement upstairs, and he'd be fine. But he would not fall asleep in front of her. A confident, take-charge woman like Tina would turn her nose up at a man with a weakness like his. If he was going to convince her he was worth her time, she could never find out about his narcolepsy.

Then again, it wasn't like he could actually convince her of anything. She'd already shot him down once. He shouldn't give her the chance to do it again, no matter how badly he wanted her…

"Trent? Are you okay?"

He opened his eyes to Tina's concerned gaze. "I'm fine. You were saying?"

"You looked like you were falling asleep."

*Shit.* "I didn't sleep well last night." He rose to his feet and paced around the table to keep himself awake. "In a nutshell, I'll double my money if I clean the place up and put it on the market rather than going with a flipper."

"The only thing that seems to need repair is the front porch. I know a fantastic contractor who can take care of that for you. Otherwise, a good, deep cleaning and a fresh coat of paint is all it needs. That and clear out the Dracula furniture."

*Damn.* He'd had no intention of spending any more time on this place than he had to. But if he could double his money by giving the place a little TLC, it was a no-brainer. He could hire out most of the work, so it wouldn't take too much time away from his own job. And of course, if he made more money on the deal, Tina would too.

Then he could use the money to take a nice, long vacation, far away from the temptress who wouldn't stop smiling at him. Maybe he'd go to Mexico. "How long do you think it will take? I don't want to waste any time."

"A month, maybe."

Hell, he couldn't wait a month. That would give Tina way too much time to shred his heart again. He needed to get it over with so he could get on with his life. "That's too long. If I'm going to do this, I want it done quickly."

"I have a contractor who owes me a favor. I might be able to sweet talk him into sending a team out in the next few days. I can probably pull some strings to get the permits pushed through faster too."

He handed her a key. "All right. Call the contractor. I'll find a cleaning company."

"Great. I'm looking forward to working with you." She held out her hand to shake, and he took it.

Her smooth skin felt as soft as a rose petal. Delicate. Yet her handshake was firm. He held on a little too long, and as she pulled her hand from his grasp, she glanced at the floor before gazing into his eyes.

"I really am glad we're talking again."

Warmth filled his chest, and he cleared his voice. "Yeah. Me too."

## CHAPTER SEVEN

*T*ina's leg bounced under the table at Molly's Place. With a restaurant serving delicious food in the back and a bar with live music in the front, it was one of Tina's favorite places to hang out. Sports paraphernalia decorated the walls of the restaurant, and she'd managed to secure her favorite table beneath an old photo of the University of Michigan football team.

The entire establishment always swarmed with good-looking men, and a few had already tried to make eye contact in the ten minutes she'd been sitting there. But she couldn't get her mind off the taste of that sexy lawyer's lips.

And where the hell was Allison?

She pulled out her phone to text her best friend when Allison slid into the booth across from her and picked up a menu. "Sorry I'm late. My last session ran over. How are you?"

Tina clenched her fists in her lap and leaned forward. The anticipation of telling her about her screw up had been eating away at her since yesterday. "I kissed him."

Allison dropped her menu. "Trent?"

"Yes." She leaned back and covered her face with her hands. "Oh, God. What am I going to do?"

Allison grinned. "Did he kiss you back?"

"Yes, but…"

The waitress arrived to take their orders. Allison asked for a Greek salad, and Tina started to order a burger and fries but thought better of it. "You know what? I'll have the Greek salad too." She handed the server her menu.

Allison raised an eyebrow. "Since when do you eat rabbit food?"

"I'm not getting any younger."

"But you get hotter every day."

"Please." She rolled her eyes and waved off the compliment.

Allison leaned forward, drumming her fingers on the table. "Trent seems to think so. Tell me about the kiss."

"There's not much to tell." Tina let out a heavy sigh and clasped her hands in her lap. "I kissed him. He kissed me back. Then he told me not to do it again."

"He what?"

She slumped her shoulders. "Ugh. I don't know what happened, Allie. That house is so creepy. I got locked in an upstairs room, and I freaked out and screamed. Trent came running in like a superhero and busted down the door."

"How chivalrous of him."

"I'm telling you, if he'd had guns, they would have been blazing. You should've seen the look in his eyes. He was going to beat the shit out of whatever was hurting me."

"So you kissed him?"

An image of his soft, full lips flashed behind her eyes. The sexy way one corner of his mouth curved into his signature smile…

"Tina?"

She blinked and focused her gaze on her friend. "I went into the hall, and he checked out the room. Of course, there was nothing there. But I was flustered, and he hugged me, and his arms felt so good wrapped around me. I couldn't help myself."

Allison leaned toward her. "And then?"

"As soon as I realized what I was doing, I pulled away and apologized. And he told me not to be sorry, but not to do it again."

Her friend studied her. "You're sure he kissed you back?"

"Positive." She shivered as the memory of his velvet tongue brushing against hers danced in her mind. "Then we went downstairs and talked about the house like nothing happened and went our separate ways. What am I going to do?"

"What do you want to do?"

That was the million-dollar question, and she had no idea how to answer it. She wrapped her arms around herself. "Crawl in a hole and die."

"Seriously."

"Go back in time and never return his call."

Allison sighed. "Tina."

"I still like him. A lot. But I don't know what to do about it. Can you find out if he still likes me?"

Allison laughed and held up her hands. "Oh, no. We aren't in high school anymore."

"I know, but…" Her life would be a lot easier if he

didn't like her. Then she wouldn't have to worry about what to do. She'd bury her feelings for him deep inside her chest and get on with her life. Like a normal person would.

"Look, babe. He was pretty upset when you dumped him before. I wouldn't be surprised if he still has feelings for you. But, honestly, your excuse was lame. Trent's a proud guy. I doubt he's going to let you walk all over him again."

She straightened her spine. "I didn't walk all over him. I just walked out."

"And you hurt him. Close enough. So, what are you going to do? Do you want to date him?"

"Maybe. I don't know." She rubbed her forehead and squeezed her eyes shut. If she dated Trent, she'd be throwing her rulebook out the window, and rule number one had always been *don't get attached. Ugh!* She couldn't think about this now. Her indecision made her head pound. "Let's talk about something else. I think you need to check out the house before he sells it."

Allison lifted her eyebrows. "You think it's haunted? Is that why you freaked out?"

"Maybe. It happened in that same room. The one I had to get into the first time I was there." She told her about the shadow chasing her in her dream and the vision of the ghost at the foot of her bed. "It's weird because I've had nightmares about the shadow my whole life. I always chalked it up to stress or from watching scary movies, and it's always stayed in my dreams. This time, I swear I saw that same shadow in the third-floor room. It was coming for me. But when Trent busted in, there was nothing there. I don't know if I imagined it or if it was real or what. What do you think?"

Allison pursed her lips. "It could be a little of both. I don't have any experience with shadow monsters, but I'll be happy to stop by and see if there are any human spirits that need help crossing over."

"Thanks. I told Trent I was going to ask you to come out, and he insisted he talk to Logan about it first. I told him you'd be able to handle it, but he said it was *his* house, so it was his decision to make."

"He has a point."

"I know he's right, but there's something about that house. When he said that, my first instinct was to argue that it was my house too. I feel invested in it for some reason. Hell, if I could afford it, I'd buy it from him."

"Even with the nightmares and possible shadow monster?"

Tina chuckled. "The more I think about it, the more I feel like it had to be my imagination. Once we got downstairs, all the fear drained away, and the house just felt like a home again."

"A home that belongs in a horror movie from the way you've described it."

She shrugged. "It needs a little TLC."

"And you don't think the reason you feel attached to the house is because you're attached to the man that owns it?"

"I am not attached to him. I just like him a little."

"Uh-huh."

The waitress brought their orders, and Tina curled her lip at her salad. What was she thinking ordering a big bowl of grass? "I may need to stop by McDonald's on my way home."

Trent dropped the last slice of bacon into the frying pan, sending a dollop of grease splashing onto his arm. He winced at the sharp sting and wiped it with a towel. That's what he got for making bacon for dinner.

He'd spent all morning trying to find a maid service willing to clean the thick layer of grime off everything inside his uncle's house and half the afternoon waiting for them to return his calls. But as soon as they looked up the address, every one of them told him, "Thanks but no thanks," and hung up the phone.

Seemed his uncle had a nasty reputation, and no one in town wanted anything to do with his estate. That wouldn't stop Trent though. As long as Tina pulled through with the contractor to fix the porch, Trent could handle the cleaning himself.

Tina.

What was he going to do about that woman? The more time he spent in her presence, the more he craved holding her in his arms. Why the hell did she have to kiss him? And why did it have to feel so damn good when she did? Everything about her felt right, from her playful attitude to her confident nature to her soft, supple body pressed against him.

His arm jerked, and he splattered hot bacon grease across the stove. Damn it, he needed to stop thinking about her. His pulse was already racing. And now...

*Fuck. Not again.*

His shoulder twitched, and his arm froze up, knocking the frying pan off the burner. His knees buckled, and he barely caught himself with his other arm before he smacked his head on the tile.

From his position on the floor, he had a front row

view of the grease fire that started on his stove and quickly spread to the paper towel rack on the countertop.

And all he could do was watch it blaze.

He was fully alert. His eyes were even open, for fuck's sake, but he couldn't move. His entire body was paralyzed as the flames licked up toward the wooden cabinets and spread to every goddamn flammable object in sight.

He tried to calm his breathing as he lay on his back, watching the thick, black smoke roll across the ceiling. It looked a lot like the shadow that had chased Tina in his dream.

Tina.

If he burned up with his house, she'd spend the rest of her life thinking he didn't want her. Fuck, why'd he tell her not to kiss him again? He had to make it out of this. If he could just move his damn legs. Or even his arms so he could drag his sorry ass out of the house.

The heat from the flames warmed his skin, making sweat droplets roll down his forehead. He couldn't move his arm to wipe them away. He should've been panicking, but there wasn't a goddamn thing he could do until he got his body back, so what was the point?

The inferno grew hotter. The cabinets were fully ablaze, and the flames licked upward, charring the white ceiling. Why the hell couldn't he have blacked out this time? At least if he was fully asleep, he might not have to feel himself being burned alive. He inhaled deeply, trying to calm his mind. Intense emotions triggered these attacks, so hopefully a sense of calm could end it.

The tiny fire extinguisher in his pantry would be no match for this blaze. If he ever moved again, he'd have get his ass out of the house and call the fire department.

His finger twitched. He could move his hand. Slowly, steadily, movement returned to his arms. He pushed himself upright and shook his legs. Finally, he had his body back. He clambered to his feet and ran for the front door.

## CHAPTER EIGHT

Trent rolled his car to a stop in Logan's driveway and pulled his suitcase from the trunk. The firefighters had put out the blaze before it did any structural damage to his house, but the stench of burnt, wet wood was enough to send him packing. All the sheetrock would have to be replaced. The floor. The countertops. It would be a month before the repairs would be finished and the place would be livable again.

He climbed the marble front steps and rang the doorbell. Allison swung open the huge, oak door and tilted her head to the side. "I thought Logan was going to pick you up after his dinner meeting." She stepped aside so he could enter.

He paused under a crystal chandelier in the foyer. "He was, but I got tired of waiting. My place reeks of smoke."

"I can imagine. He told me you had a grease fire get out of control. He was afraid you'd be too rattled to drive."

"I'm fine." Hopefully that was all Logan told her. Trent could always count on his best friend to cover for his weaknesses. And vice versa. Of course, Allison knew everything about Logan and his OCD now, but she didn't need to know about Trent's problems.

He followed her into the living room and plopped onto the sofa. He reached for the remote and was about to turn on the television, but thought better of it. This was Allison's house too, and he needed to show some manners. "Mind if I turn on the TV? I need to veg for a while."

"Go for it." She smiled and padded across the thick carpet toward a large, wooden cabinet. She opened the door and scooped a stack of CD cases off the shelf, placing them into a cardboard box.

"Does Logan know you're messing with his favorite form of therapy?"

"He asked me to pack them up for him. We're working on some coping mechanisms that are more beneficial than reorganizing CDs."

"Is it helping?"

She put more discs in the box. "It's starting to. The medication has made a big difference too."

He toyed with the remote in his hand and watched her empty the cabinet. Logan's own empathic abilities were making his OCD rage out of control before he met Allison. "I'm glad he found you. You're good for him."

She closed the box. "He's good for me too. What did Tina say when you told her about the fire?"

His pulse quickened at the mention of her name, but calling her hadn't even crossed his mind. He'd needed a friend he could depend on, and with Tina…he wasn't sure how she felt. "Why would I tell her about it?"

Allison shrugged. "Because you two are talking again. She'd probably want to know."

Would she? "I don't know if I'd say we're *talking* again. Communicating with words, maybe."

She grinned. "Words. Lips. Tongues."

His stomach sank. How much did Allison already know? "Shit. She told you about that?"

"She tells me everything."

Of course she did. The women had been best friends since high school. Allison was engaged to *his* best friend. She was psychic. She probably knew way more about Trent and his non-relationship with Tina than he did himself. "What's her deal?"

"What do you mean?"

He ran a hand through his hair and blew out a breath. "Why'd she kiss me?"

"Why'd you kiss her back?"

"Why'd she take the job after she dumped me?"

"Why did you offer it to her?"

"Damn it, woman. I don't know." He crossed his arms and let his head fall back on the couch.

Allison laughed. "Like I told Tina, we're not in high school anymore and I'm not being the go-between. If you want to know how she feels about you, ask her."

He scrubbed a hand down his face and lifted his head from the cushion. Ask her. And then what? She already apologized for kissing him, so she obviously thought it was a mistake. And if she regretted doing it, then she must not have the same feelings for him as he did for her.

"Honestly, I have no idea why I called her. I felt compelled to. I knew it was a bad idea, even as I dialed her number, but it was almost like a voice inside my head told me to do it."

She scooped the box into her arms and rose to her feet. "Maybe it was your subconscious."

"I've got a masochistic subconscious then."

"Or maybe it's meant to be."

He laughed. "I doubt it. It's not like—"

The front door swung open, and Logan stormed in, slamming it behind him. "Damn it, man, I told you not to drive."

Allison raised her eyebrows and carried the box to the next room.

Logan dropped into the chair adjacent to the couch. "It's not safe."

He lifted a shoulder. "I made it here in one piece."

"You nearly burned your house down. You shouldn't be driving in your condition."

"Your condition?" Allison returned to the living room and perched on the arm of Logan's chair. "I thought you had a grease fire."

"I did." He flashed Logan a warning look. "And now I'm fine."

His friend let out an exasperated sigh. "You're not fine. That's what, the third time it's happened in as many days? Why don't you let Allison help you?"

"No." The last thing he needed was to have the women worrying about him.

"Help him with what?" She cut her gaze between Logan and Trent.

"Dude." He shook his head at Logan, pleading with his eyes.

"I'm going to tell her."

"Don't."

"Trent's got narcolepsy."

"Fuck." Betrayed by his best friend. He put his hand over his eyes and leaned back on the couch. "Thanks a lot, man."

The cushion next to him compressed, and he opened his eyes to find Allison sitting next to him.

She patted his knee and gave him a sympathetic look. "I would love to help you, Trent. I've never worked on anyone with your condition before, but Reiki healing is good for everything. Will you let me help you?"

"Might as well, since the cat's out of the bag anyway." He glared at Logan, who smiled back smugly.

"Can you help me understand what happens to you?" Allison said. "You fell asleep while you were cooking?"

"Not this time. It was cataplexy."

"What's that?"

He glanced at Logan. Damn it, he didn't want to get into this with her. With anyone. He had enough stress in his life without having to deal with people worrying about him all the time. Thinking he was weak. He had his condition under control before. He could do it again.

"It's temporary paralysis. I lose control of my muscles for a few minutes, but I'm fully awake. Just can't move. It's not that big of a deal. It always goes away on its own."

She grimaced. "Except that your house almost burned down."

"But it didn't."

Logan shifted in his seat. "That hasn't happened in years. Were you drinking again?"

"No."

He rubbed a hand across the scruff on his chin. "What do you think triggered it?"

Trent leaned his elbows on his knees and dropped his head in his hands. "I was thinking."

"Doesn't it have to be some intense emotions for thinking to trigger an attack like that?"

"Usually." He lifted his head and tried to give his friend another warning look. Not that the first few helped him.

"What were you thinking about, man?"

*Fuck.* It was bad enough Logan told Allison about his weakness. Now he had to admit what triggered it in front of her too. He picked at some imaginary lint on his pants. "I was thinking about...*her.*"

Logan grinned. "Her? You mean your smokin' hot real estate agent?"

Allison elbowed him.

"Hey, that's his name for her. Not mine."

She looked at Trent. "That's okay. She used to call you 'Logan's cute lawyer friend.'"

Cute. There was that word again. "I'm a man. I'm not cute."

"What would you rather her call you?"

"I don't know. Handsome. Sexy. Hot. Masculine. Anything but cute. Baby penguins are cute."

Allison laughed. "Logan's *masculine* lawyer friend doesn't have the same ring to it."

"I can see why she'd call you cute," Logan said. "You do have those big, brown, puppy-dog eyes."

Trent narrowed his gaze at his friend. "At least I don't have dimples."

Logan crossed his arms. "My woman loves my dimples, don't you, babe?"

"They're adorably cute." Allison pinched his cheek.

Trent groaned. As much as their affectionate display irked him, he was glad to see them so happy together.

"Anyway," she said. "You have intense emotions for Tina?"

"Apparently, I do. Please don't tell her about this. It's bad enough I have to deal with the damn disease. She's so strong and confident. I don't want her knowing about my weakness."

Allison sighed and shook her head. "You have an illness, not a weakness."

"The illness means I'm weak."

"Or it means you're strong. Battling day by day to lead a normal life." She cast a loving gaze at Logan and reached for his hand. "And look how successful you are in spite of it all."

Trent chuckled. "I'm a fucking superhero."

"Well, boys." Allison rose to her feet. "It's late, and I'm tired. Why don't we all go to sleep, and I'll give you a treatment first thing in the morning, Trent. I don't have to be downtown until the afternoon."

He looked at Logan. "I assume you made the deal tonight?"

His friend nodded. "You assume correctly."

"I'll draw up the contracts in the morning then. Maybe we can try the treatment in the evening? I need to get caught up at work. This damn house has been such a time suck."

Logan stood and wrapped his arms around his fiancée. "You don't have to do anything tomorrow. You're taking the week off."

"The hell I am. Someone has to keep your company running."

"I've got other lawyers on staff. We'll be fine without you for a while. Take a week off. Slow down and take care of yourself. Take care of the house. Maybe the stress of your new inheritance is what brought your symptoms to the surface. It all started around the same time your uncle died, didn't it?"

"I guess it did, but I don't need to slow down. You know I don't like leaving things undone."

"Everyone needs to slow down once in a while, man. Even you."

Maybe Logan was right. He could get the house off his hands quicker if he took a few days off work. Hopefully the new medication could get his condition under control within the week so he didn't wind up falling asleep at the office. "Thanks, man. And I'll look into an extended-stay hotel tomorrow so I'll be out of your hair soon."

Allison shook her head. "Nonsense, Trent. This house is huge. You'll stay here until your place is repaired."

"I don't want to intrude."

"You're not intruding. It'll be easier for me to schedule your treatments if you're living here anyway. Please stay. We insist."

He looked at Logan. "You cool with that, man?"

"How many times have I crashed at your place?"

"True."

"Pick a bedroom."

"Thanks." Trent grabbed his bag and followed his friends up the stairs. He picked a guest room with a slate-gray duvet and beige walls with an en suite bathroom. He considered showering before climbing into bed, but with all the excitement of the day, he'd probably pass out in the tub. Instead, he stripped down to his boxer-briefs and crawled under the covers.

A break would help him get his life back under control. If he spent a day resting, catching up on some much-needed sleep, maybe he'd be able to stay conscious for an entire day.

Tina tossed and turned most of the night, barely slipping under the surface of sleep, only to be pulled back up to consciousness. When she finally settled into a solid slumber, she found the shadow monster waiting for her in the third-floor room. She hesitated in the hallway. Was this even the same house? Ornate, nineteenth century furnishings replaced the dusty, morbid-looking belongings of Trent's Uncle Jack. A plush, green runner lined the floor, and the scent of freshly-baked bread wafted up from below.

She stepped toward the room, but Trent darted through the door. He grabbed her around the waist and pulled her toward the stairs. "He's coming. Run!"

"Who's coming?"

"You know who." He dragged her down the steps and into the living room. "He has them all."

"Who?"

Trent took both her hands and stared hard into her eyes. "You started this, my love. You can stop it."

She took a step back and nearly tripped over an antique chair. "Your love? What the…?"

"He's coming." Trent shot out the front door as the inky shadow rolled down the steps.

Tina froze, her heart beating a frantic rhythm, her feet glued to the floor. The shadow seemed to bubble and fold, turning from thick fog to molten liquid as it slid across the floor and poured out the door after Trent.

Then he screamed.

She shot up in bed, the sheets in a tangled mess around her legs. The dryness in her mouth felt like she'd swallowed a desert, and she fought to catch her breath. *What the hell kind of dream was that?* She wiped the matted hair off her sweaty forehead and kicked the covers off the end of the bed. Bleary-eyed, she blinked at her alarm clock until it came into focus. The little red numbers on the face read five a.m.

At least no dismembered ghosts waited at her bedside when she woke, but going back to sleep was out of the question.

She swung her legs over the side of the bed and stretched. There was no way she'd really seen a ghost in her room. It sounded ridiculous. Even to her. She didn't have a psychic bone in her body. All this crazy crap was in her head. The dreams. The paranoid feeling she got every time she went into that third-floor room. She was stressed, and now her dreams were turning into nightmares about Trent and the stupid house. That's all there was to it, and the sooner she could get the damn thing on the market, the sooner she could go back to life as she knew it.

Though she wasn't sure life as she knew it was what she wanted to go back to.

## CHAPTER NINE

*T*ina leaned against the hood of her Mustang and sipped a latte from a paper cup.

The contractor put the finishing touches on Trent's new front porch and approached her with a clipboard. "We can get started on the exterior paint tomorrow morning if you'll sign off on the color."

She chewed her bottom lip and stared at the order form. She shouldn't have been making this decision without Trent, but he hadn't returned any of her calls today. And if they didn't start the work tomorrow, the contractor would move on to a different job and not be available again for another two weeks. Plus, Trent seemed to be in such a rush to get it done.

She took the pen he offered and signed the paper. "Let's go with the same blue as the original." It was a deep, gorgeous color, and with the white gingerbread trim to accent it, the house would be the most beautiful one on the street. Besides, getting it back to its original state seemed like the right thing to do. Trent would trust her decision. It wasn't like he was going to live in the house. He just wanted it sold.

The contractor took the clipboard and nodded. "We'll be back at six a.m. tomorrow."

"Thank you."

As the workers packed up their gear, Tina went around to the back door and entered through the kitchen. She'd called the movers to come out tomorrow to put all the Dracula furniture in storage. A deep cleaning, a quick coat of paint on the interior walls, and some staging furniture, and this place would be good to go.

She crinkled her nose at the thin layer of grime on the kitchen cabinets. It would be good to go as long as Trent had hired a cleaning service before he went into hiding.

She'd left him three messages before Allison finally called her and told her he was sick. Why the hell couldn't he tell her that himself?

"I don't know. Logan asked me to call you," Allison had said when she'd asked.

He'd better have really been sick and not just hiding from her after the kiss. Why on Earth had she done that? She wouldn't make that mistake again. His arms felt too damn good wrapped around her.

She shook her head to chase away the thoughts and padded into the living room. Everything here could probably go to the dumpster, but she'd have it all moved to storage for Trent to go through later if he wanted. He seemed to take a liking to that strange-looking coat rack, so she definitely didn't want to throw that out. She stepped toward it and ran her hand down the stem. The dark wood felt cool and smooth against her skin. Though heavy, old-fashioned designs weren't usually her style, this piece was starting to grow on her.

Truth be told, in the short amount of time she'd spent with Trent recently, he was starting to grow on her too. Fear of commitment had kept her from missing him over the three months since she dumped him. Now that they were talking again, though, she hated to admit it, but she was bummed she didn't get to see him today. And she was more than a little disappointed he didn't call her himself to tell her he wasn't coming.

She rubbed her forehead and let out a sigh. What was she doing? Feelings like this were exactly why she broke it off with him in the first place. Men were glorious creatures who definitely had their uses, but they were meant to be enjoyed, not to get all sappy about when they weren't around. She'd seen her mom cry into a bottle over a man way too many times, and she was not going there. Not with Trent. Not with anyone. She was who she was. Being in a relationship meant she had to change herself for the other person, and that wasn't a sacrifice she was willing to make. She'd rather spend the rest of her life alone than have to change.

Besides, she wouldn't always be alone. One day, she'd adopt a little girl and raise her to be just as fierce and independent as she was. She didn't need a man to be a mom, and she certainly didn't need Trent.

But she still missed him.

"Ugh." She turned toward the stairs. It was that damn dream that was doing it to her. Why did Trent have to call her *his love?* And what was up with the shadow monster going after him now? It had to be a warning from her self-conscious to stay away. If she pursued him, one of them would get hurt. That's what the shadow was about. The darkness that would consume her soul if she lost herself to a man.

*Stop being so dramatic.*

Maybe if she stayed away from the third floor, she'd have better dreams tonight. Or maybe she should go up there and prove to herself it was all her imagination. She put her foot on the first step but hesitated. If she got locked inside again, Trent wasn't here to rescue her. She chewed her bottom lip and gazed up the stairway. No need to tempt fate today. Better to stay on the first floor since she was alone.

She paced through the living room and pushed open the double doors leading into the study. The air seemed to grow colder as soon as she stepped into the room, and the hairs on her arms stood on end.

*This place definitely hasn't lost its creepiness factor.*

As she reached for the thick drapes covering the window, cool pressure pushed into her shoulder, as if a person were trying to stop her from letting the sunlight in. Her mouth went dry, and she slowly turned around.

Of course, no one was there. *I liked it better when I was ignorant about ghosts.*

"If there really is a spirit here, please leave me alone." She rubbed the goose bumps on her arms and yanked the heavy curtains open.

She turned to survey the room. Rows of dusty books lined one wall, and a massive, metal office desk sat in the center. A stack of unpaid bills rested on the corner of the desk. Trent would definitely want to go through all the stuff in here before he trashed anything.

She sat in the squeaky, vinyl chair at the desk and ran her finger across the surface. At least it wasn't covered in an inch of dust. An intricate pewter photo frame lay face-down on the edge of the desk. From the way Trent described him, Uncle Jack had been a hermit. And a mean one at that. Were there actually people he cared about enough to keep a photograph?

She picked up the frame and gazed at the image. A woman in her early twenties with dark hair and light eyes held a little girl who looked about three years old. They sat in a rocking chair in front of a wall with bunny wallpaper.

Bunny wallpaper? The second-floor bedroom.

She set the picture on the desk and headed upstairs to the room she'd seen on her first visit to the mansion. A child-sized bed sat in the far corner, and a white dresser lined one wall. The same rocking chair from the photo sat near the window. A thick layer of dust covered the bedspread and the surface of the furniture as if no one had been inside the room in years. She padded toward the rocking chair and ran her hand across the arm. No dust covered the chair. And the seat cushion appeared well-worn and torn around the edges.

Could Uncle Jack have had a family? What could have happened to them to cause him to preserve the bedroom this way?

A wave of sadness washed over Tina as she lowered herself into the rocking chair. Pressure mounted in the backs of her eyes at the thought of that poor little girl dying at such an early age. Why else would the room still be decorated for a small child, if she hadn't died young? What could have taken her? An accident? Disease? A sob bubbled up from her chest, and she leaned her head back and closed her eyes.

She could imagine the feeling of holding her dying child in her arms, rocking her in this very chair. The emotions swirling through her body felt too strong to be her imagination, though. They felt as if they were her own. A sharp ache followed by familiar numbness spread from her chest to her limbs. She had felt this way before. But when? Aside from Allison's parents, she'd never lost anyone she loved.

She rose to her feet and cleared the thickness from her throat. What was it about this house that had her emotions on a roller coaster? Perhaps she'd done enough for today. Some fresh air would do her some good. She took one last look at the chair and headed downstairs to lock up. She had to be back here at six a.m. to meet the painters anyway. She deserved a break. And hopefully Trent would actually show up tomorrow.

---

Trent lay on top of the slate gray duvet in Logan's guest bedroom and closed his eyes as Allison worked her Reiki magic on him. It was awkward at first to have his best friend's fiancée hovering her hands above his body, breathing deeply, a soft humming sound emanating from her throat. Hell, it was downright strange.

But after a few minutes, he started to relax. His whole body felt lighter. Healthier. Though it might not help his narcolepsy, whatever she was doing, it was helping something.

"I think that's good for today." She sat on the edge of the bed, and Trent opened his eyes.

"What's the verdict, doc? Am I going to survive?"

She patted his hand. "You'll live. How do you feel?"

"Better, actually." He pushed up onto his elbows. "Spending the day in bed had my back aching, but it's not so bad now."

"I'm glad I was able to help *something*."

"You mean I'm not cured?"

She sighed. "I can't *cure* anything. I only help your body with the healing process."

"Better than nothing." He didn't know much about Reiki, but he hadn't expected an instant recovery. If she could fix a chronic illness that fast, she'd be a celebrity.

"The problem is I can't pinpoint exactly what's blocked. Every time I think I've found the source of the problem, it moves. I've never encountered anything like this before."

"I've always been unique."

She chuckled. "There's definitely something strange going on inside your head."

"Tell me about it." He was a glutton for punishment, but he had to ask. "Was Tina mad when you told her I wasn't going to the house today?"

She shook her head. "She didn't sound mad. More disappointed than anything."

He shouldn't read into it. She was probably disappointed because she had to do all the work herself today, but the corners of his mouth still pulled up into a smile. "What do you think I should do about her?"

Allison rose to her feet. "I can't tell you that."

"I don't want to get hurt again."

"And I can't guarantee she won't hurt you." She sighed and sat on the bed again. "She does have feelings for you. But she's scared to death of those feelings."

He pushed back to lean against the headboard. "What did I do to make her scared?"

"Nothing. I don't think Tina knows what a healthy relationship looks like. Growing up, her parents weren't the best role models."

"What happened?"

"That's her story to tell." She stood and padded to the

door. Resting her hand on the frame, she turned to Trent. "Do you care about her?"

"Too much, it seems."

"You two have a strong connection. You always have. I think you'd be good together, if she can get past her commitment issues."

Logan appeared behind Allison and wrapped his arms around her waist, nuzzling into her neck. "Ready for bed, babe?"

She turned and snaked her hands behind his shoulders, pressing her lips to his. "You know it."

Thoughts of Tina's lips pressed against his own flashed in Trent's mind, and a pang of jealousy shot through his chest. Why had he told her not to kiss him again when kissing her was exactly what he wanted to do?

"Good night, Trent." Allison's voice brought him back to the present.

"Night, man," Logan said as he led his fiancée down the hall.

Trent lay on the pillow and stared at the ceiling. Tina did have feelings for him; he hadn't imagined it. Now the question was, what was he going to do about it?

Not a goddamn thing.

If he pursued her, he'd only be setting himself up for heartache. She had commitment issues, and he wasn't looking for a fling. So there could never be anything between them. Tomorrow, he'd lay down the rules. No more flirting. Definitely no more kissing. They'd keep their relationship in the friend zone, and no one would get hurt.

CHAPTER TEN

Trent rubbed his eyes as Allison turned her Prius onto Acorn Street and approached the Victorian mansion. He'd slept a solid twelve hours last night, but his body felt like he'd been up for days. By the time he'd woken and Allison had performed her Reiki treatment, it was ten o'clock. The entire morning wasted.

Logan and Allison had both insisted it was too dangerous for him to get behind the wheel until his sleep attacks were under control. They had a point, but damn, he hated to have to rely on other people. Now he'd wasted Allison's morning too.

"Thanks again for driving me out here. I'm sorry to take so much time out of your day."

She flashed him a warm smile. "It's no problem at all. There's a metaphysical store in Ann Arbor I've been meaning to visit, so now I've got the perfect excuse. Give me a call when you're done, and Logan or I will come and get you." She turned into the driveway.

"You can drop me off here. The trees are…" He gazed out the windshield at the willow branches. Rather than scraping the car like the uninviting fingers of death they were two days ago, they had been trimmed into a crescent-shaped tunnel, a good six feet of air between the lowest tendrils and the top of the car. "Never mind. I guess Tina got the contractors she was talking about."

"That's a pretty blue. What made you decide to change the color of the house?"

"I didn't." He'd been so busy looking at the trees, he hadn't noticed what Tina had already done to the house. The porch had been completely redone, and one quarter of the front façade was already painted a cheerful blue. "What the hell has that woman done?" Sure, the house was a burden, but it was *his* burden. She couldn't waltz in like she owned the place and start making changes.

Allison grinned. "Uh oh."

"Thanks for the ride." He slammed the car door and marched toward the house. She had some nerve doing all this work without consulting him first.

Tina stepped onto the porch and waved to Allison before focusing on him. "I was wondering if you were ever coming back. Feeling better?"

He nodded, and her smile disarmed him. Those soft pink lips curving into a perfect bow wiped every thought from his mind, and he stopped in the yard to admire the vision of beauty standing in the doorway. She wore tight jeans that hugged her curves and a pair of sexy black leather boots. Her deep purple sweater clung to her perfectly proportioned breasts, and his fingers twitched with the urge to cup them in his hands.

Damn it, he'd been mad at her a moment ago. Now, he couldn't for the life of him remember why.

She leaned against the door jamb. "Why did Allison drive you?"

*Shit.* He hadn't thought about needing an excuse for not driving himself. He couldn't tell her the real reason. "My car's in the shop."

She stepped forward, resting her hands on her hips, and beams of sunlight filtering through the willow branches reflected off her dark hair, making it glisten. Something about Tina standing on that porch, smiling at him as if she were welcoming him home, seemed so right. "Are you going to stand out in the cold all day, or are you coming inside?"

But this wasn't her home, and she had no right to start the renovations without him. He stomped up the steps and regarded the sturdy porch beneath his feet. The thick, painted wood didn't give or squeak with his heavy steps, and the nails were flush with the surface. Overall, an excellent job. He pressed his lips together and narrowed his gaze at her.

"It looks great, doesn't it?" she said. "My guys trimmed the trees, too, so no one scrapes their cars when they come to look at the house."

He wanted to be irritated. He *tried* to be mad, but trimming the trees and fixing the porch were both on the top of his to-do list. And if he'd been here yesterday, he'd have signed off on having them done exactly like Tina had arranged. What could he say?

But the paint. Changing the color of the house without his consent was stepping over the line. "They're painting it blue."

Her smiled beamed. "I know. Come look." She took his hand and pulled him through the door, holding on to him until they reached the kitchen. "I got in touch with the historical society. Since this place is so old, there are some rules about what you can do to it." She handed him a sheet of paper.

"What's this?"

"It's a list of every paint color ever used on this house. It's been green, purple, and four shades of blue." She pointed to the top entry. "It seemed right to put it back to its original color. Bring back the glory of the 1800s. It's a beautiful shade, don't you think?"

He rubbed a hand across his forehead. "It is a nice color, but—"

"And I've rented a storage unit for you. Later today, my guys are going to move out all this creepy furniture, so we can stage it with a more modern look. It's going to be beautiful." Her eyes shone as she spoke, her excitement evident in her voice.

Still, her audacity grated on his nerves. "What else have you done?"

"That's it so far. Oh, I found something interesting in the study I want to show you. Come on." She reached for his hand again, but he jerked it away.

"What are you doing, Tina?"

"What do you mean? I'm helping you get your house ready to sell."

He laid the paper on the table. "It's *my* house."

She tilted her head, giving him a quizzical look. "I know."

"Then why are you acting like you've got a claim to it? What makes you think you can make all these decisions without my consent?"

"I…"

"I was sick one day. I come back, and you've planned the entire renovation without me."

She fisted her hands on her hips. "Did I do something

wrong? I can go stop the painters. It's not too late to change the color. You want it the same green as before? I'll go tell them."

He pulled out a kitchen chair and lowered himself onto the vinyl seat. "No. The paint color is perfect. It's what I would have chosen."

She crossed her arms. "Is something wrong with the porch? Or did they not trim the trees the way you want?"

"Those are fine too."

"So, what's the problem?"

Everything she did was perfect. *That* was the problem. Sure, the fact that she went ahead with all this without consulting him irked him, but he hadn't exactly made himself available for consultation either. If he'd have answered his phone when she called, rather than having Allison call her for him, she probably would've asked for his input. And even without his input, she'd done everything exactly the way he would've done it. Almost as if she'd read his mind.

"There's no problem. But don't plan anything else without consulting me first."

She sat in the chair next to him. "You seemed to be in such a hurry to get this place on the market, I didn't want to waste a day doing nothing."

He stood and walked behind her, resting his hands on her shoulders. "And everything you did was right. Just check with me first next time." He squeezed her tight muscles, kneading her back with his thumbs. Her tension relaxed under his touch, and he fought the urge to slide his arms around her and kiss her cheek. "You wanted to show me something in the study?"

"Hmm?" She leaned her head against his stomach and

gazed up at him, her bright green eyes pulling him in like a magnet.

Good lord, this woman was perfect.

She blinked as if coming back to herself. "Oh, yeah. Come on." She jumped to her feet and padded through the foyer, stopping to pick up her coat from the floor. "This coat rack is beautiful, but it's not very functional, is it? Everything seems to fall off it." She threw her coat over a hook.

Trent slipped out of his own coat and hung it on the rack. "Stay put."

Tina giggled. "It kinda grows on you, doesn't it? It creeped me out at first, but it seems to have a personality of its own."

"No kidding." He followed her into the study, where she picked up a pewter picture frame and held it out to him.

"I found this on your uncle's desk. I think it's his wife and daughter."

He took the frame and stared at the happy image of the woman and the child. Goose bumps rose on his skin as a chill crept down his spine at the familiarity of the faces. "He's got a painting of them in the basement. Though they don't look nearly this happy. I had no idea he was married."

Tina stood behind him, resting her hands on his shoulders as she peered at the photograph in his hands. "They died in the 1940s. Her name was Lucy, and the little girl was Emily."

Tina's close proximity had his chest tightening. He stepped away and returned the frame to the desk. "How do you know all this? Did you go through his files?"

"I checked at the county clerk's office. Marriage and death certificates are public record."

He raised his eyebrows. Everything about this woman impressed him. When something needed to be done, she did it. When she wanted information, she got it. Tina was more than confident. She was capable. Intelligent. And so goddamn sexy.

"I didn't snoop through his stuff. I was going to move it all into storage, so you could go through it later when you have more time."

"It wouldn't have mattered if you did." He stepped toward her and ran the back of his fingers down her cheek. Her breath hitched with his touch, and he moved closer, erasing the distance between them.

He shouldn't have been doing this, but damn it, he wanted to. He wanted her. He might've been setting himself up for heartbreak, but at this moment, he didn't care. He needed to taste her. To feel her soft lips pressed to his, her body melting into him as he held her.

He slid his hand to the nape of her neck and lowered his gaze to her mouth. Her lips parted ever-so-slightly, and her tongue slipped out to moisten them. That was all the invitation he needed. He leaned in, brushing his lips to hers, giving her ample opportunity to walk away from what was sure to be his biggest mistake of the day.

She stepped closer, deepening the kiss, sliding her arms around his waist, and fire shot through his veins. He cupped her face in his hands, a soft moan escaping his throat as his tongue brushed hers. Everything about this woman felt so right. Her taste, her scent, the way she fit in his arms. When she slid her hands down to his ass and pulled his hips to hers, his knees nearly buckled. He could have taken her right here in the study if the entire room wasn't coated in a layer of dust.

As the kissed slowed, she pulled away and gazed into his eyes. "You said I wasn't supposed to kiss you again."

He pressed his lips to her forehead, her cheek, her mouth. "You're not. I'm kissing you."

"And that's okay?"

"Is it?"

She bit her bottom lip, furrowing her brow as if unsure of her answer. He traced his thumb across her mouth, tugging her lip from the grasp of her teeth.

She leaned into him. "I guess it's okay this time."

He kissed her again, allowing himself to get lost in her essence, just for a moment, as she held him tight. This was further than he'd gotten with her when they'd attempted to date three months ago. The way she pressed her hips into his arousal made him harder by the second. The passion, the intensity at which she kissed him…Had she finally gotten over her fear of commitment? Could they attempt a relationship again?

A knock on the study door brought him back to the present. "Ms. Sanders? The truck is here to move the furniture."

She smiled at the contractor, never removing her hands from Trent's ass. "Thanks, John. This is the homeowner, Trent Austin." She released her hold and gripped his bicep instead. "He'll be the one making all the decisions from here on out."

"Any special instructions, Mr. Austin?"

Trent ran a hand through his hair and adjusted his pants. "Just get it all out."

"And the stuff on the shelves?"

"Box it up and put it in storage with the furniture. I

want everything gone." He might go through his uncle's belongings later. Or he might not. He felt no attachment to anything inside the house. Except for one thing. "Leave the coat rack, though."

"Yes, sir."

"And the rocking chair in the baby's room." Tina gave him an apologetic look. "If that's all right with you. It looks like it might be original to the house, and with a new cushion, it will make a great staging piece."

He wrapped his arm around her shoulders and looked at the contractor. "Leave the coat rack and the rocking chair. Everything else can go."

The man nodded and left the room.

Trent rested his head on top of Tina's, inhaling her sweet floral scent. "I've missed you."

She slid from his grasp and smoothed her sweater. "Me too, but...we should probably get some work done. Can I see that painting you found in the basement? I might make a good staging piece too."

"I don't think it will, but I'll show it to you."

---

Tina followed Trent into the basement, silently berating herself the entire way down. That kiss had felt so good. So...right. She'd lost herself to the moment, melding to his body, fitting in his arms as if she were made to be there.

Then he said he'd missed her.

As soon as he'd uttered the words, her fight or flight instinct kicked into full flight mode. Truth was, she'd missed him too...and Tina didn't miss men. Her feelings for Trent ran way deeper than anything she'd felt before, and the only thing she could think to do was run.

He deserved better. He deserved someone who would stick around, and Tina wasn't the sticking around type. If they continued on the path they were heading down, she'd only break his heart. It's what she always did. She didn't know how to have a relationship. She'd never wanted one before.

Did she want one now?

He flipped on a light switch and motioned toward a canvas and easel standing in the center of the room. "It's here, but I don't think it'll give the warm and inviting feeling you're hoping for."

She stepped around the painting and inhaled a sharp breath. The haunting faces of the people in this picture were a far cry from the cheerful smiles in the photograph. And what was up with the background? The smoky-black mist hovering behind the girls made her shiver. *Creepy.*

Trent stood behind the canvas and shoved his hands in his pockets. "You mentioned death certificates. Do you know what happened to them? I'm not going to find their bodies buried in the backyard, am I?"

"That, I don't know. You did say your uncle was crazy." She smiled at him, and he chuckled. Her chest tightened at the musical sound of his laugh. "The little girl died from an aneurism. Her mom died a month later from heart failure."

"That would be enough to drive anyone mad."

"Yeah, I guess it would."

He held her gaze for a moment. "Let's go have a look at that rocking chair. I didn't notice it before."

She took one last look at the sad portrait and followed Trent toward the stairs. As she reached the fourth step, a *thud* sounded from behind her. She turned around to find the painting lying on the floor beside the chair. "That was weird."

"The central heat kicked on. It was probably a draft." Trent continued up the stairs.

"Yeah. A draft." Though she didn't feel the slightest breeze. There weren't even any air vents down here. She shivered and continued up the stairs.

Trent stepped around the movers as they carried the red velvet sofa out the front door, and he headed up to the second floor. For assuming it was a draft, he sure seemed to want to get the hell away from that basement.

"Hey, Trent." She caught up to him on the stairs. "Did you talk to Logan yet about checking for spirits?"

He stopped on the landing. "It's an old house. It makes noises. It's creepy. The more I think about the things that have happened, the more it feels like they were in our imaginations. Doesn't it?"

"I guess so. It still wouldn't hurt to have it checked out. Even if there aren't any ghosts, Allison can clear the residual energy from the walls. Take away the creepy factor." She stepped onto the landing next to him, so close her shoulder brushed his. Warmth spread through her body at the brief contact, and she pressed her back to wall as he took a step toward her.

"I'll talk to him. And in the meantime, I promise to keep you safe. Okay?" He trailed his fingers up her arm, raising a row of goose bumps with his touch.

God, she wanted to kiss him again. Her mouth watered at the thought of his soft, full lips pressed to hers. To feel his hands on her body. His tongue gliding across her skin. She wanted this man, but she cared about him. And that was exactly why she couldn't have him.

His gaze slid down her mouth, and she swallowed hard. "Trent?"

"Hmm?" He leaned in, and she scooted away.

"I don't think we should do this."

He let out a heavy sigh. "Why not?"

"Because I don't want to hurt you."

"What makes you think you're going to hurt me?"

*Because I hurt you before. Because it's what I do.* She let out her own sigh, pleading with him silently. *Please don't make me explain.*

"All right, I can take a hint. Let's have a look at that chair." He brushed past her on his way to the child's bedroom.

"It's not that I'm not attracted to you, Trent. I just think we should try staying friends for now."

He stopped in the doorway and flashed a fake smile. "You're absolutely right. I hired you to do a job, and we need to maintain a professional relationship. I won't make a move on you again, if you promise not to make one on me." He turned and stepped inside the room, leaving her alone in the hallway.

"Okay." She followed him through the door.

"This chair is beautiful. Look at the craftsmanship." He ran his hand across the intricately-carved wood and sat in the seat. "Definitely needs a new cushion though."

It appeared their discussion about their relationship— or lack thereof—was over. Well, if he wanted it to be all business, she could certainly oblige. It was better than the awkwardness she thought she'd have to endure. "I think we should keep this a baby's room for the staging."

"I agree. This is definitely the baby's room. It has that feeling to it." He ran his hands over the arms of the chair and leaned his head back.

Why did he look so comfortable in that chair? In this house? Her mind flashed back to her experience in the room the day before. To the overwhelming sadness that had suddenly engulfed her. Why was this scene so familiar? She shook her head and stepped into the hallway before the emotions could overcome her again. "And these other rooms can also be set up as children's rooms. I think a neutral beige for the walls would be nice."

She padded into the next room and turned on the light. "A bed in that corner. A dresser against the far wall. What do you think?" She turned for Trent's opinion, but he hadn't followed her. He wasn't in the hallway either.

"Trent?" She shuffled back to the baby's room and found him sitting in the rocking chair, head leaned back, eyes closed. Was he sleeping?

"Trent?" She stepped closer and rested a hand on his chest. It rose and fell steadily with his breaths, but he didn't move when she gently shook his shoulder.

"Wake up, Trent." She shook him harder.

"What?" He opened his eyes and stared wildly around the room. "I wasn't asleep."

"Yes, you were. Are you still sick? Do you need to go home?"

"No, no." He rose to his feet and straightened his clothes. "I'm fine."

"Are you sure? What was wrong with you yesterday?"

He flipped a hand in the air. "I think I ate something that didn't agree with me. I'm okay."

"I can take you home if you need to rest."

He touched her shoulder. "I'm fine."

"Okay."

"I need to get started cleaning this place, anyway. I

couldn't find a maid service within fifty miles that was willing to do it."

"Really?"

"Seems crazy Uncle Jack had a nasty reputation. As soon as they looked up the address, they couldn't get off the phone with me fast enough." He left the room and started down the stairs.

"Wow." She followed after him. "Well, I'll help you. If we work together, it shouldn't take too long once all the furniture is out."

"You don't have to do that."

But she did. She owed it to him for being such a flake. "I want to help."

He continued down the stairs, refusing to look at her. "Why?"

"We're friends, aren't we? I hope we are."

Stopping by the coat rack, he rested a hand on the top and held her gaze, his eyes searching hers for…something. "Yeah. We're friends."

"So, friends help each other. Let's get started."

CHAPTER ELEVEN

Trent spent the rest of the afternoon with Tina, scrubbing floors and cleaning out the kitchen cabinets. He tried his best to ignore the emotions raging inside him, but damn it if that woman wasn't bending over to scrub something every time he turned around. He peeled his gaze away from her heart-shaped backside for the umpteenth time and cursed himself for giving in to his whims.

She'd rejected him again, like he knew she would. But when he wanted something, he had to go after it. It was his nature, and he'd wanted Tina from the moment he saw her. He'd moved too quickly last time—like he always did —and scared her away. He was about to scare her away again if he wasn't careful.

The dust rag slipped from his hands, and he bent down to pick it up, only to drop it again. He was so goddamn tired; he couldn't even focus his thoughts on berating himself, much less on cleaning this shit hole. He would not fall asleep in front of her again.

He tossed the rag on the counter and pulled out his

phone. "I've had enough of this for today. I'm calling Logan to pick me up."

Tina brushed her hair away from her face, leaving a smudge of oven grease on her forehead. "I can take you home."

"It's all right. Logan owes me one."

She dropped her rag on the counter and stepped toward him. "Don't make him drive all the way out here. Stop being a stubborn man and ride with me."

He arched an eyebrow. "I'm not stubborn."

"All men are stubborn."

"I'm not all men."

She grinned. "We'll see. Let me grab my purse."

"Hold on." He caught her by the hand and yanked a paper towel from the roll on the counter. "You've got a little smudge there." She seemed to hold her breath as he wiped the soot from her skin, her gaze never leaving his face until he released her.

Exactly the reaction he was looking for. She wanted him. So why was she fighting it? He tossed the towel in the trash and turned around to find her still staring at him. She licked her lips, and he stepped past her as quickly as he could. He'd given in to the temptation too many times today. It wouldn't happen again.

"Let's get out of here. All this cleaning is giving me a headache." And if he didn't get some rest soon, he might collapse right in front of her.

He grabbed their coats from the rack. He was certain it had moved a good two feet from where it was before, but the movers could've bumped it while they were taking out the furniture. Or hell, he could've imagined it. Between the fatigue and the racing thoughts tumbling through his head, he wouldn't have been surprised if he started hallucinating too.

Neither of them said much on the ride back to Detroit, but it was just as well. He was having a hard enough time keeping his eyes open. Small talk would've only made it worse. Tina put on her blinker to take the exit toward his house, and he cleared his voice. "I'm, uh… staying with Logan for a while."

She cast him a sideways glance and changed lanes. "Why?"

"Kitchen fire. It's being repaired."

She turned off the freeway and crossed the bridge to Grayhaven Island. "You burned your house down?"

"I didn't burn it down. The fire stayed in the kitchen."

"What happened?"

He leaned his head back against the seat and closed his eyes for a long blink. "A grease fire that spread too fast for me to put it out."

She grasped his arm and glanced at him before focusing on the road. "Trent, you could have been killed."

He rolled his eyes. He'd been scolded for this enough already. "I'm still alive."

"You should have told me." She returned her hand to the steering wheel and gripped it as if she were trying to choke it.

"Why should I have told you?" So she could worry about him too? Or worse, think him incompetent? "It's taken care of."

"Well, because we're friends. I could have helped you."

He shrugged and stared out the window. "I called Logan. He helped me. Why would I need to call you too?"

She rolled the car to a stop in Logan's driveway. "I would have liked to have known. I care about you."

"Do you?" He slid out of the car and slammed the door. She couldn't have it both ways. She couldn't expect him to act like they were more than acquaintances if she didn't reciprocate. Her back and forth attitude grated on his nerves. He was tired of playing games. Hell, he was just so goddamn tired.

"Of course I do." She slammed her own door and caught up to him. "And why is your car here? You said it was in the shop."

*Shit.* "The mechanics finished it early and dropped it off." He picked up his pace. "I don't need you to walk me to the door."

"I'm not. I want to see Allison. She lives here too."

He groaned inwardly at the thought of how *that* conversation would go. "Fine." He turned his key in the lock and pushed open the door. Logan and Allison rose to their feet as he stormed inside.

Tina stopped in the threshold. "What's your problem?"

"No problem." He marched into the living room and mouthed the words, "Don't say anything," to Allison. She'd said Tina told her everything. Hopefully, she wouldn't reciprocate in this case.

She nodded and looked at Tina. "Hey girl, how'd it go?"

"Fine, apparently." She crossed her arms and glanced at Trent before turning to Allison. "Have you had dinner yet?"

"I'm getting ready to make something. Do you want to stay?"

"I want to go out. I need some girl time."

Trent shook his head and plopped onto the couch. Thank goodness she didn't want to stay here. He couldn't handle spending another minute with the impossible woman. Hell, it was all he could do to keep his eyes open.

Allison turned to Logan. "Do you mind if I go out with Tina tonight?"

Logan grinned and cut his gaze from Tina to Trent. "Nah. I'll order a pizza. Looks like I might need some *guy* time." He swept her into his arms, lifting her feet from the ground as he kissed her.

Tina caught Trent's gaze for a moment before rolling her eyes. "Come on, Allie. You'll have plenty of time for hanky panky later." She picked up Allison's purse and handed it to her.

Logan released his hold on Allison and kissed her cheek. "Stay safe, my love."

"Always."

A look of surprise flashed in Tina's eyes, like she remembered something. She gave Trent a quizzical look before quickly shaking her head as if dismissing the thought.

Whatever she was thinking, it couldn't have been more pressing than the sleep threatening to overtake him any second now. If she didn't get her fine, curvy ass out that door, he would fall asleep in front of her, and he couldn't let that happen again. He took a deep breath and leaned forward, resting his elbows on his knees.

"Bye, Trent," Allison said. "We'll, um…talk later."

"Yeah."

Tina followed her friend out the door without saying good-bye.

"Fuck." Trent leaned back on the couch and stared at the blank television screen.

"It went that well, huh?" Logan turned on a basketball game and sat in the chair next to the sofa.

"That woman." He rubbed his forehead and closed his eyes.

"Wake up, man. Pizza's here."

Logan's voice roused Trent from sleep. He opened his eyes to find himself still on the couch, in the same position he'd been in when he closed his eyes. "Sorry about that. How long was I out this time?"

"No worries. About half an hour." Logan jerked his head toward the kitchen, so Trent followed him to the breakfast table. "Feeling any better?"

"Much."

"Here." He set a plate with three slices of pizza in front of Trent. "All the meats."

"The only way to eat pizza." He took a bite and savored the zesty blend of sausage, pepperoni, and bacon on his tongue. Now that he thought about it, he hadn't eaten since breakfast.

And Tina had worked in his house all damn day, and he hadn't offered her so much as a glass of water. What an ass.

Logan poured two glasses of Coke and joined him at the table. "How's the house coming along?"

"I think the place might be haunted."

Logan raised his eyebrows and leaned forward. "Really?"

"Nothing violent like your ghost." The spirit that haunted Logan's house when he moved in had nearly killed Allison out of jealousy. "Just some weird noises and stuff moving around. Tina freaked out on the third floor, and we haven't been up there since."

"Why'd she freak out?"

"She got locked in the room. Said she saw something, but she didn't elaborate. I've been trying to play it off like it's nothing so she doesn't get scared, but I'm pretty sure it's something. Can you swing by one day and check it out? See if it's safe enough for Allison to do her thing?"

Logan chuckled. "She's already planning to go out there this weekend. She told me all about it."

Trent fisted his hand on the table. "Damn it. I told Tina to wait until I talked to you before she brought Allison in."

"Those two are the most head-strong, stubborn women I've ever met. Don't think for a second that you have any control over what they do."

"It's infuriating."

"And damn sexy."

"True." Logan was right about that. As much as her actions irked him, Trent had to admit her strength and persistence turned him on. He loved a strong woman, and Tina was one step away from being Wonder Woman in his eyes.

"Everything else going okay?"

"It's all good. We'll get the big stuff done in the next few days. I'll be back at the office next week."

"And Tina?"

He let out a long sigh. "Man, she put me in the friend zone."

"Ouch."

"Tell me about it. One minute, we're making out in the study. Then we go upstairs and she tells me she wants to be friends."

"Any idea why?"

"Hell if I know. That woman sends so many mixed signals, I don't know which way is up anymore. I can't be friends with her."

"Why not?"

"Because every time I look at her, I…" He clenched his jaw and shook his head.

Logan chuckled. "I know the feeling."

"What would you do?"

He took Trent's plate and carried it to the sink. "Since I've only been in one relationship in my entire life, I'm not the best person to be giving you advice."

"Maybe not, but you're in the only one that matters."

"True. You think Tina's the one?"

"I think so. I want her to be." He ran a hand down his face. He might as well admit it. "I know she is. Without a doubt. And all this back and forth is such a waste of time."

"Well, man. My advice is this: if she wants to be friends, be friends. Slow down. Give her time to realize on her own that she can't live without you. It's what Allison did for me when I was scared, and look at us now."

Slow down. He was chomping at the bit to make that woman his own. But it made sense. If she wanted to be in the friend zone, he'd keep her there. He'd be the best goddamn friend she ever had.

---

Tina finished off her burger and did her best to steer the conversation in every direction but Trent's. Allison played along, listening to her ramble on about nothing, nibbling on her club sandwich and being a good sport like the best friend she was. Tina dragged her to Molly's Place every time she needed a distraction, and while Allison grumbled from time to time, she was always there for her. Always. Tina felt lucky to have such a good friend, but she could see by the look on Allison's face that she was done playing along.

"All right." Allison smoothed the napkin in her lap and rested her elbows on the table. "You've been grumbling under your breath all evening, and that fake smile isn't fooling anyone. Spill."

Tina widened her fake smile and shoved the last French fry into her mouth. "There's nothing to spill. I just needed some girl time."

Allison crossed her arms. "I'm not buying what you're selling, girl."

Tina scanned the crowd, avoiding her friend's gaze. A familiar face smiled at her from across the room, and she returned the gesture. What was his name again? Jason? No...Jake. The volunteer firefighter. Last time she hooked up with him, he didn't have a lot going on in the real job department. But his sexy firefighter body might be just what she needed to get her mind off the lawyer.

She waved at Jake and turned her gaze to Allison. "I haven't had sex in more than a month. I think that's my problem. I need to get laid."

Allison rolled her eyes. "Seriously? You dragged me out to dinner, and you're going leave me here so you can go home with some random guy?"

"He's not random, and I'm not leaving you here. I'll take you home first. Let's go dance."

"I don't want to dance."

"Please? I need to relieve some stress. Maybe dancing will do the trick."

Allison sighed and shook her head. "All right. But only because I love this song."

"Yay!" Tina took Allison's hand and wove her way through the tables to the bar at the front of the restaurant. A Top Forty cover band played their own version of Pharrell's "Happy," and she and Allison joined the mass of people on the dance floor. She caught Jake's eye and winked, and he set down his beer and sauntered toward her.

All those muscles and tanned skin. This was exactly the distraction she needed. The band switched tunes to a slow, sultry version of Awolnation's "Sail," and Jake wrapped his arms around her waist. "Mind if I join you?"

"Sure." She slid her hands to his shoulders and glanced at her friend.

Allison pursed her lips and let out a sigh. "I'm going to get a drink. Do you want anything?"

"I'm good."

Jake pulled her closer to his hard, warm body, and she held him tighter. If she remembered correctly, he was pretty good between the sheets. Maybe a night with him would satisfy her feminine urges so she wouldn't be lusting after Trent every time she looked at him.

He pressed his lips against her ear and inhaled a deep breath before whispering, "I missed you, Tina."

She closed her eyes as the words danced in her ears. He missed her. He'd told her that himself before she'd pushed him away. "I missed you too, Trent."

Jake chuckled. "Did you forget my name, or is Trent your boyfriend?"

Her heart thudded, and she pulled away. "Who said anything about Trent?"

He tried to hold her close again, but she stepped back. "You did, sweetheart. You just told Trent you missed him."

"Oh, no." She pressed her fingers to her lips. She did call him Trent, didn't she? Damn it, Jake's chiseled body was supposed to take her mind off him, but all it did was make her want the sexy lawyer even more. "I'm so sorry, Jake. I didn't forget your name."

He grinned. "No worries. My place or yours?"

"I'm sorry. I can't." Heat flushed her cheeks, and she lowered her gaze to the ground and sulked toward the bar. She didn't need to sleep with a man tonight. She needed to go home, take a cold shower, and sort out her emotions so she could get back to living her life.

Turning to give her would-be distraction one last good-bye wave, she found him already dancing with another woman. She shook her head as she approached her friend. "I'm ready to go."

Allison took a big gulp of her drink and left the half-empty glass on the bar before she followed her to the car. Tina slid into the driver's seat and leaned her head back against the head rest.

What was her problem? Why couldn't she get Trent off her mind? This was *so* not like her. Not at all.

Allison closed her door and buckled her seatbelt. "What happened with Jake?"

Tina lifted one shoulder in a dismissive shrug. "I decided I'm not in the mood for a man tonight."

"You're never not in the mood for men." She rested a hand on Tina's shoulder, her tone turning serious. "It's time to talk about it."

"I don't want to talk about it."

"What happened with Trent today? There was so much tension between the two of you, I could hardly breathe when you came in."

Why was she trying to hide her emotions from her best friend? Even if Allison weren't psychic, Tina always told her everything. But she was so mixed up, she didn't know where to begin. She chewed her bottom lip and let out a long sigh. "He started acting bitchy for no reason in the car on the way to your house. I don't know what's wrong with him."

Allison twisted in her seat to face her. "Really? You can't think of any reason at all?"

"His house burned down, and he didn't tell me. We spent the entire day together, and he didn't even mention it until I had to bring him to your house."

"And you're mad at him for that?"

Gripping the steering wheel, she kneaded the soft leather. "Well, yeah. He should've told me." A heaviness formed in her chest. Was she mad, or utterly disappointed?

"What happened before that?"

She stared out the windshield at a couple kissing on the sidewalk. "Nothing."

Allison tilted her head to the side and flashed a *you're not fooling anyone* look.

Tina slumped her shoulders. The only person she was fooling was herself. "He kissed me earlier in the day, and later I told him I thought we should just be friends."

"I thought you liked him."

"I do, Allie. That's the problem. I like him way too much, and I don't want to end up like my mom."

Allison shook her head. "You're not going to end up like your mom. You're stronger than that."

"I will if I let myself fall for him. I'm already starting to change myself. I ordered a salad for lunch the other day. I don't eat salad."

"Does Trent eat salad?"

"No."

"Did he mention he wanted you to eat healthier?"

"No, but it was right after I kissed him. When he told me not to do it again."

She laughed. "Tina, you're being ridiculous."

"Allie, you know my mom. She fell in love with every man she dated, and she completely lost herself. And she died inside a little bit every time someone left her." She traced her finger along the stitching in the beige leather seat. "I don't want to die inside."

Allison folded her hands in her lap. "You are a confident, independent, kick-ass woman. No man in his right mind would even attempt to change you, and I have a feeling Trent likes you exactly the way you are."

"But what if he doesn't? I'm thirty now."

"That's what this is about, isn't it? Did you find another gray hair?"

Tina straightened her spine. "It was a strand of silver glitter, thank you very much."

"Exactly. And you're only getting better with age."

"But Trent is hot and rich. He could have any woman he wanted."

"And you always get any man you want. How convenient that you both want each other."

"I guess you're right." She started the engine and pulled out of the parking lot. Trent was obviously interested in her. Even without the kissing, every time he looked at her she felt like she'd melt under his heated gaze. He wanted her now, but what about in a few months or years? What would happen when her hair held more glitter strands than black ones?

And he was keeping something from her. His excuses for Allison driving him, his car being in the shop but still sitting in the driveway, the kitchen fire. Something else was going on with him. "I'm going to ask you something, and I want total honesty, okay?"

Allison drew a cross over her heart. "Always."

"Why did you drive Trent to the house this morning?"

She inhaled deeply and stared out the window. "What did he tell you?"

"Truth, Allie."

She pressed her lips together and let out her breath. "He wasn't feeling well from the day before, so I drove him."

Her stomach sank. "What's wrong with him?"

Allison groaned. "He'll have to tell you that himself."

"Why won't you tell me?"

"Because he's a client now. You know I can't discuss a client's private information with anyone. Not even my BFF."

"You and your stupid morals. I don't think there are any laws governing Reiki healing."

"Please understand."

She sighed. "I do…So it wasn't food poisoning?"

"No."

"Is it life-threatening? Is he going to die?" Her heart dropped at the thought. Could he have a debilitating disease and not want her to know?

Her friend patted her shoulder. "It's not life-threatening. I'm sure he'll be fine."

"But you're not even going to give me a hint?"

Allison shook her head and looked at her with sad puppy eyes. "Do you still love me?"

"I don't know. You're kind of a bitch sometimes."

She laughed. "That's *why* you love me."

"True."

CHAPTER TWELVE

The next few days went by in a dizzying blur. Tina met Trent at the Victorian manor each morning, and she did her best to keep her mouth shut about whatever ailment Allison was treating him for. It hurt that he'd lied about being sick and his car being in the shop, and the fact that he didn't trust her enough to confide in her about his illness stung.

Then again, she hadn't exactly given him a reason to trust her. She'd drawn him in and shut it down twice now. She couldn't blame him for holding back.

Except for the creepy room on the third floor, they'd cleaned the house from top to bottom. They seemed to have a silent agreement that they'd avoid that room until Allison gave them the all clear. Trent had stocked the fridge with snacks and drinks, and the movers had finally brought in all the staging furniture. This old Victorian house was starting to feel like a home.

And the more time Tina spent in this place, the more she felt like she belonged here. Belonged with Trent. Would it be so terrible to be in a relationship? Trent was nothing like the men her mother had paraded through their house when she was growing up. He was strong, confident, and kind. And her own strong will didn't seem to bother him one bit. Even when he'd tried to act annoyed that she'd started the renovations on the house without him, he obviously wasn't too perturbed.

She chewed her bottom lip and admired the fluid way his body moved as he sauntered into the living room. Though she'd never seen him naked, she could tell by the way his clothes fit he was solid muscle underneath. Built, but not too built. And that smile...She melted inside every time he grinned at her. What was she going to do about this man?

He dropped onto the new, white sofa and turned on the TV. "It's a shame all this furniture is a rental. It looks good in here."

She sat down a few inches away and tried to ignore the way her heart pounded when she was near him. She needed to do *something* about this man. "I'm a little sad you have to sell the place. It's a great house. It'll be a good home for someone."

"It will. It already feels like a home." He gazed at her with a strange intensity, his dark eyes pulling her in. She felt herself sway toward him, and she couldn't stop. Sitting here with Trent, in this living room, in this house...everything about the moment felt right. If she kissed him again, she'd have to mean it this time. There'd be no turning back. If her lips touched his one more time, she'd have to be sure she was in it for good. She could be in it for good, couldn't she?

His gaze slid to her mouth, and he smiled. "Logan and Allison will be here at one." He shot to his feet and pulled his phone from his pocket. "Want to order a pizza while we wait? I'm starving."

*Damn.* She sat up straight and brushed her hair from her shoulder. "Sure. Sounds great."

"All the meats?"

"Is there any other kind?"

He grinned and punched in the order. "You're my kind of girl."

Her heart fluttered. "Am I?"

"I mean...We have similar tastes. We like the same kind of food. The way you decorated this place is perfect." He shrugged and slipped the phone into his pocket. "We get along. I guess that's what I mean."

She tried to hide her disappointment with a smile. "Yeah, we do."

"When one of us isn't trying to kiss the other one."

She stood and stepped toward him. "The kissing was nice though." So nice, she might like to do it again. Who was she kidding? She *needed* to do it again.

He stepped back. "Meh. It was okay."

She paused, about to be offended, but the playfulness in his eyes made her laugh. "Meh? Did you just call me a *meh* kisser?"

He winked. "I said the kiss was meh. Not that you were."

She fisted her hands on her hips. "That sounds like a challenge to me, and I never back down from a challenge. You want a *wow* kiss? I can show you a *wow* kiss."

"I'm sure you could." He bumped his shoulder to hers as he sauntered past her to the kitchen. "Too bad we're just friends."

*Too bad, indeed.*

The doorbell rang at exactly one o'clock, and Tina

padded into the foyer to answer it. She swung open the door as Trent moved to stand beside her, like they were a couple welcoming their dinner guests into their home. It was a feeling she wouldn't mind getting used to.

"Wow, guys, I love what you've done with the house." Allison pulled Logan through the door and hung her coat on the rack. "The way Tina described the place, I was expecting a house of horrors."

Tina hugged her friend and flashed a smile at Trent. "I put him to work."

"I think *I* put *you* to work, actually." He grinned back, and her heart melted again. He'd always had a charming smile, but something about the way he looked at her lately had her pulse thrumming in her veins.

Trent had held up his end of their pressure-free friendship gloriously. On Tina's end, she'd done nothing but fall harder for him.

Logan looked at his watch. "We don't have a lot of time. The housekeeper will let the caterer in, but I'd like to be home *before* the guests arrive."

Allison linked arms with Tina and led her away from the guys. "You are coming tonight, aren't you? This will be Logan's first party since I moved in, and I need you there."

Tina laughed. "Of course I'm coming. A few months ago, I had to drag you to parties like this. Now you're playing hostess. Who would've thought?"

"I know. It's still hard to believe sometimes. I just wanted to be sure because…well, Trent is staying with us now."

"So he'll be there."

"Yes."

She widened her grin and caught Trent's gaze. "Good."

His dark eyes smoldered as he stepped toward her.

"Are you ready for this? You're not going to freak out this time?" He laughed, but it sounded more nervous than humorous.

"I won't if you won't." She pulled a lightbulb from a drawer and handed it to him. "But I'm not going in there without a light."

⸻

Trent grabbed a stepladder and grumbled under his breath as he climbed the stairs. He couldn't blame Tina for refusing to go into that room without a light. He didn't want to do it either, but he'd look like a wuss if he handed the bulb to Logan. He couldn't make his friend do it *for* him, but he could make him go *with* him.

"Why don't you lovely ladies wait in the hall while Logan and I shed some light on this creep show?"

"Sounds good to me." Tina clutched Allison's arm.

Logan ran his finger over the broken door jamb as he followed Trent into the room. "What happened here?"

"I broke it when Tina got locked in." Every hair on his body stood on end as he set the step ladder beneath the light fixture. The walls already felt like they were closing in on him, and the air seemed to grow thicker. At least with the door broken, there was no chance of *him* getting locked in.

Logan stepped deeper into the room. "She got locked in, so you broke the door down?"

"Yeah." He twisted the burned-out bulb from the socket.

Logan chuckled. "Like a knight in shining armor."

"Fuck you."

"What?" He raised his hands in a show of innocence.

"You saved the damsel in distress. That had to earn you a few brownie points."

Trent glanced into the hallway to make sure the women were out of earshot and lowered his voice. "Honestly man, I don't think I'll ever really know where I stand with that woman." Her words certainly didn't match her actions. Maybe he should've let her show him that *wow* kiss when she'd offered. Nah, he'd still be as confused as ever, and he would've had to deal with a massive hard-on too. He'd done the right thing.

He installed the new lightbulb and motioned for Logan to flip the switch.

"That's better." Tina strode into the room with her head held high, but the way she repeatedly clenched and extended her fingers gave away her true feelings. She was already freaking out, and Allison hadn't even done her thing yet.

He moved to stand next to her and put his arm around her shoulders to calm her nerves. In a friendly way.

*Yeah, right.*

"You'll be fine," he whispered into her ear.

"Thank you." She shivered, leaning into his embrace, and his stomach tightened. He fought the urge to wrap his other arm around her and pull her to his chest. She'd asked for friendship, and that was all he planned to give her…until she asked for more.

Allison crept into the center of the room and turned in a circle. "It's really stuffy in here. Can you open the window?"

Logan slid the glass pane up and pushed on the shutters, but they didn't budge. "They're painted shut."

"This is the only room that isn't finished," Trent said.

"After Tina's experience in here, we wanted to wait until you guys could check it out."

"I don't blame you," Logan said. "There's a ton of energy pulsing through this room, and it can't possibly all belong to you guys."

Allison took Logan's hand. "Can you shut it out?"

The corner of his mouth twitched. "Anything for you, baby."

Allison took a deep breath and closed her eyes.

"Wait," Tina said. "Don't you need salt and crystals and stuff? Isn't this dangerous?"

She opened her eyes. "Most of the time, communicating with spirits is completely safe. We needed salt with Logan's ghost because she didn't like me being there, but it's easier for me to communicate without that barrier. And Logan's gotten good at creating a shield. He can block things out, while I open up, creating a nice balance."

Trent shook his head. "I'm not sure I understood a word of that."

"Trust me, man," Logan said. "It works."

"And if I sense any danger here," Allison added, "we'll leave and come back with some defenses."

"Okay." Tina slid her arm behind Trent's back, hooking her thumb in his belt loop on the opposite side. He couldn't recall her ever having done that in the past, but the way she held on to him felt so familiar, a chill ran up his neck.

They were silent as Allison stood in the center of the room. Aside from the deep rise and fall of her chest as she breathed, she went utterly still. "There are some spirits here, but they're not coming through." She reached for Logan's other hand. "Maybe you're blocking too much. Can you rein it in?"

Logan clutched both her hands in his and closed his eyes as Allison's eyes grew wide.

Tina whimpered, and Trent squeezed her tighter. "I see them." She clutched the front of his shirt in her fist.

"See who?" He looked to the wall where Tina and Allison both stared, but he saw nothing.

"There are seven, maybe ten spirits here," Allison said. "They're showing me that they're trapped here. They're chained to the wall."

Tina pressed her face into Trent's shoulder. "Is there some kind of metaphysical key? Can you set them free?"

Allison shook her head. "They aren't literally chained. It's just how they're showing themselves to me. Someone has them trapped here."

The pounding of Tina's heart into Trent's side made his own pulse race. Could these spirits have been what freaked her out the last time she was up here? "Are they dangerous?"

"They can't leave this room. Wait…one of them is showing me that she can for short periods. She sneaks away. She…" Allison squeezed her eyes shut and opened them again. "She appears to detach her hand to break from the chains. That's weird. But that's how she would appear to a living person who could see her. She'd be missing a hand."

Trent rubbed his hand up and down Tina's back. The room still appeared empty to him, but he'd seen Allison in action. If she saw ghosts, they had to be there. "Who has trapped them here? How can we get rid of them?"

Allison's brow furrowed in frustration. "They aren't saying much. Just… 'She knows…Tina knows.'"

"Oh, God." Tina lifted her head. "I don't know. I told her I don't know."

Trent brushed the hair from her face. His instinct to protect her strengthened, and he tightened his hold on her waist. "Told who?"

"The handless ghost. I saw her in my dream, when the shadow monster was chasing me." She jumped as if she'd seen something else.

"What is it?"

"Nothing." She let out a nervous laugh. "I thought I saw a shadow from the corner of my eye. My nerves are shot. I've never been able to see ghosts before."

Allison wrapped her arms around Logan's waist. "Apparently, this one really wants to be seen. And you've tapped into a latent ability."

"When did you dream about a shadow monster?" Trent's pulse kicked up another notch. Why hadn't she mentioned this before?

"When haven't I? It's been happening all my life."

"I've had the same dream. I'm being chased by a dark, rolling shadow. Sometimes it's chasing you." And if she'd been having the dream, did that mean it was real? Or could the ghosts in this room be giving them nightmares?

Tina looked at him wide-eyed. "Why didn't you tell me?"

"I didn't want to scare you. I—" His knees gave out, sending him toppling to the floor and pulling Tina down with him. *Shit. Not now. Not in front of Tina.*

He held her tight to his chest as the darkened corners of the room in his peripheral vision filled with thick, black shadows. He could not black out this time; he had to protect her.

She lifted her head and glanced from side to side. "Please tell me you see it," she whispered.

"I'm not sure what I see." Was it the shadow from his

dream? Or was it his vision tunneling, threatening to pull him under into another sleep attack?

"Are you okay?" Allison rushed to his side and knelt on the ground while Logan slammed the heel of his hand into the shutters, breaking them open and flooding the room with daylight.

Trent blinked and loosened his hold on Tina. He could still move. "I think so."

"Was it the shadow? You saw it, didn't you?" Tina shifted her weight to her arms, but thankfully, she made no move to get off him.

He wasn't sure he'd be steady on his feet yet. "I tried to take a step, and I twisted my ankle. I didn't mean to pull you down with me. Are you okay?"

"I'm fine." She rose to her feet and dusted off her pants. "But I swear I saw the shadow as soon as we started talking about it." She wrapped her arms around herself and glanced about the room. "It's gone now."

Logan offered him a hand up. "You sure it was your ankle, man? It wasn't another—"

He gave Logan a pointed look. "I twisted my ankle. That's all it was."

"This room gives me the creeps." Tina led the way downstairs and lowered herself onto the sofa.

Trent sat next to her and rubbed his forehead. Thank God he didn't pass out up there. He needed to convince Tina she couldn't live without him—not that she needed to take care of him. She seemed to believe his story about twisting his ankle, and as long as Logan kept his damn mouth shut, she'd keep believing it.

Logan sat in the accent chair, and Allison perched on the arm beside him. "You've both been having dreams about a shadow chasing you?"

Tina caught Trent's gaze. "Apparently."

"And neither of you thought to mention it to the other?"

"Trent did once. Sort of," Tina said. "He called me one morning and said he had a dream I was in trouble. He never mentioned it again, so I blew it off. It seemed irrelevant." She shrugged. "I guess we need to learn to communicate better."

"I guess we do." He put his hand on her knee and gave it a squeeze. When she didn't pull away, he left it there. He'd always craved physical contact with her, but watching her act so brave in the face of handless ghosts and a shadow monster made him need her even more. Most women would have run out screaming by now, but not Tina. She was still here, sitting next to him, in a haunted house.

"Tell me the truth, Allie. Is there really a shadow monster? Or are Trent and I somehow having the same psychically connected nightmare?"

Allison bit her bottom lip and glanced between them. "That's hard to say. I didn't sense anything negative when you guys fell. But if it was a nonhuman entity, it could easily hide itself from me. From all of us."

The thought of having any kind of connection with Tina—psychic or otherwise—sent his heart racing. And that option was definitely better than dealing with a real monster. "We're probably having similar bad dreams because we've been spending so much time together. It's been stressful getting this house ready to sell so quickly."

"That's a possibility," Allison said. "But there's still the issues of the ghosts trapped in the attic room and who or what is trapping them there. Have you had any problems in any of the other rooms?"

"No." Tina raised her eyebrows at him for confirmation.

Aside from the coat rack and the experience he had the first time he set foot in the house, nothing major had happened. And those incidents were most likely products of his overactive imagination. "It seems to be concentrated in the third-floor room."

"Well, then." Allison rose to her feet. "I'd like to bring Gage out to do a scientific investigation. He can take some readings and try to stir up more activity so I can get a better read on those trapped spirits. And if your shadow monster is real, Gage is the person to talk to about that." She took Logan's hand and moved toward the front door.

Tina stood and followed her. "I didn't know Gage has psychic abilities."

"He doesn't, but he's fascinated by nonhuman entities. He's probably read everything that's ever been written about them. Just stay off the third floor until we can check it out."

"Sounds like a plan." Trent turned off the lights and locked the front door behind him as he followed his friends onto the porch.

"It might be a good idea to do some research on the house," Allison said. "I feel like you both have a strong connection to this place. I know the house has always been in your family, Trent, so that makes sense. But Tina... maybe I'm feeling the connection between the two of you."

Tina's eyes widened, and an adorable blush spread from the bridge of her nose, across her cheeks. This had to be the first time he'd ever seen her embarrassed.

Allison flashed Tina a triumphant grin and turned to

Trent. "Did your uncle leave behind any documents or diaries?"

"We packed everything up and put it in storage. I have a key to his safe deposit box, though."

"We've got to go, babe." Logan tugged Allison down the steps.

"Maybe start there. I'll see you both tonight." She hugged Tina and whispered something in her ear. Tina rolled her eyes.

"See you at home, Trent." Allison pranced back up the steps, wrapped her arms around him and whispered, "Are you okay to drive?"

"Yeah. I'm fine."

She pulled away and looked him hard in the eyes as if she didn't believe him.

"I'll be heading that way soon." He waved as his friends walked hand-in-hand down the driveway, then climbed into Logan's Mercedes and drove away.

Trent turned to Tina. "Are you going to hang around?"

She pulled her keys from her purse. "Nah. I've got some things to do before the party tonight."

"Right. I'll see you there."

A smile brightened her emerald eyes. "You can count on it."

# CHAPTER THIRTEEN

Tina's four-inch stilettos clicked on the marble steps as she approached Allison's front door. Her red peacoat barely skimmed her knees, leaving her calves exposed to the frigid winter air, and goose bumps pricked at her skin. Thank goodness it wasn't snowing. She pushed open the door, and a gust of warm air greeted her as she slid out of her coat and handed it to the door man.

She smoothed her tight, red sweater over her torso and adjusted the hem of her black pencil skirt. Her outfit wasn't exactly appropriate for the weather, but with the number of heads turning in her direction as she strutted across the room, it had the desired effect. Now, if it would only work on Trent.

"Tina!" Allison pranced across the room carrying two glasses of champagne and handed one to her. "You're late; I thought you weren't coming."

"Would I do that to my BFF? Besides, you're always the one running out on me at these things, remember? Something about all the men being pretentious assholes?"

She glanced at her fiancé. "They're not all assholes."

"Here's to the good ones." Tina clinked her glass against Allison's and sipped the bubbly liquid. "And speaking of good ones. Where's Trent?"

Allison pressed her lips together and gripped Tina's bicep. "Don't read too much into this, okay?"

"Into what?"

She turned her around to face a group of people. "He's got a leech attached to his arm. Maybe you can save him."

A sinking feeling formed in her stomach. Trent wore dark slacks and a gray button-up with the top two buttons undone. He held a clear drink in one hand, and a red-headed woman was attached to his other arm. She looked gorgeous in her tight-fitting, pink dress, and that made it all the worse.

Tina set her drink on a table and crossed her arms. "I guess he's taking this 'we're just friends' thing seriously." A semblance of a sob caught in her throat, and she blinked back the liquid threatening to collect in her eyes. It definitely wasn't tears. Tina didn't cry, especially over men.

"Seriously, babe, I've been keeping an eye on him." Allison patted her back. "He hasn't done anything to indicate he's interested in her. She's just been following him around all evening."

"And he hasn't done a damn thing to shake her off either." She picked up her champagne and downed the rest of the drink before taking another glass from a waiter walking by.

"You know Trent. He's a sweetheart. He probably doesn't want to embarrass her. Just go talk to him."

The redhead whispered something in Trent's ear and giggled, and heat crept up Tina's cheeks. "Hold my drink."

She handed her glass to Allison and marched toward her man. Maneuvering her way through the crowd, she didn't stop until she stood face-to-face with Trent. "We need to talk."

His eyes widened in surprise. "Okay." He patted the leech on the hand. "Excuse me for a minute."

The redhead narrowed her eyes at Tina and crossed her arms. "Hurry back."

Tina could've sworn she heard him mutter, "Don't count on it," but maybe it was her imagination.

He led her into the kitchen and turned to face her, a goofy smile lighting up his face as if he had no idea what seeing him with that woman did to her. "What's up?"

*Well, what now?* She'd had every intention of talking to him about their so-called friendship tonight, but she hadn't yet planned what to say. She took the glass from his hand and sipped the drink, hoping a shot of liquid courage would get her mouth moving. Like herself until the age of sixteen, the drink was virgin. She scrunched her nose. "What is this?"

"Club soda. What did you want to talk about?" He took the glass and set it on the counter.

She could barely hear him over the clanking pans and caterers rushing about to refill their trays. "Somewhere private, please?"

"Follow me." Taking her by the hand, he led her up the back staircase and turned down a long hallway. The loud, incessant chatter of the party diminished to a dull murmur. He opened the second door on the left and pulled her inside, clicking it shut behind her, silencing the hum of voices from below. He stood close. So close his breath warmed her cheek as he spoke. "Is this private enough?"

A queen-size bed with a slate-gray duvet sat against

one wall. A matching chair occupied one corner, and a large, black suitcase sat in the other. "Is this your room?"

"For the time being."

Jeez Louise, she was alone with Trent in his bedroom. Her mouth went dry as thoughts raced through her head in a jumbled mess, and she blurted out the first one that took hold in her mind. "Who is she?"

He furrowed his brow. "Who?"

"Don't play dumb. The woman attached to your arm down there."

He blinked. "The redhead? Honestly, I don't even remember her name. Lucy? Lacey? Something with an L."

Her pulse thrummed in her ears, and she had to force the words over the lump in her throat. "Are you planning to date her?"

A cocky smile curved his lips. "Does it matter if I am?"

"Yes. It does. I don't want you to date her."

"Why do you care who I date?"

"Because I want you to date me." She covered her mouth to hide her own shock. She hadn't meant for the words to fly out like that, but there they were. She'd said it, and all she could do was wait for his reaction.

He took a step back and inhaled deeply, his gaze traveling up and down her body. His reply was taking too long. He opened his mouth a few times, as if to speak, but closed it again. That could only mean rejection. He was trying to find a nice way to say she'd missed her chance.

Finally, his heavy gaze met hers. "Do you mean that? Or are you going to leave me high and dry as soon as things get a little serious?"

"I mean it this time, Trent. I really do. I tried being your friend, and I can't. I want more. I want *you*." Her stomach tied itself into a knot as he stood there staring at her. She held her breath.

He slipped out his tongue to moisten his lips, and the corner of his mouth pulled into a crooked grin. "I don't know, Tina. You promised you could wow me with a kiss. I think I need to see if you can deliver on that promise first."

The knot released, and a flush of warmth spread through her body. "*Wow* is only the beginning of what I can do." She snaked her hands behind his neck and pulled his mouth to hers. She started gently, teasing him with a soft graze of the lips, reveling in the warmth of his breath on her skin. He smelled like citrus, with a hint of after-shave, and she slid her hands into his hair to pull him closer.

He wrapped his arms around her waist and moaned as he let her in, brushing his tongue to hers. He tasted sweet, like lime, not a trace of alcohol on his tongue. She kissed him long and deep, her body melding to his as she leaned into his embrace, the thrilling sensation of victory tingling in her limbs.

As the kiss slowed, she cupped his face in her hands and pulled away to look into his eyes. "Well?"

A drunken smile spread across his lips. "Hallelujah."

"No kidding." She had to have this man. Right here. Right now. She kissed him again as she unbuttoned his shirt and ran her hands up his stomach. He was all smooth skin and hard muscle, just like she'd imagined, and she couldn't wait to see the rest of him. To touch him. To taste him. To feel his hands on her naked body.

He caught her by the wrists and held her hands against his chest. "Once we do this, we can't undo it. Are you sure it's what you want?"

"I'm positive. But is it what *you* want?"

He shrugged out of his shirt and tossed it aside. "Woman, I've wanted you since the day I met you. Come here." He pulled her close, showering her in kisses, undressing her slowly.

As her clothes fell to the floor, the air chilled her skin, but the warmth of his touch lit a fire inside her. Trailing her fingers down his stomach, she unbuttoned his pants and pushed the rest of his clothing down his legs. He moaned and kicked his pants aside.

The feel of his strong arms wrapped around her, the contrast of his soft skin and hard body pressed against her. She'd been an idiot to deny herself this man for so long. He was sheer perfection with his dark hair, brilliant smile, and muscular everything. And the way he looked at her… like no one had ever looked at her before. Passion and lust filled his eyes, but the way he held her gaze as he caressed her almost made her forget to breathe.

He lowered her to the bed and finally released her gaze as he trailed his lips down her throat. He cupped her breast in his hand, and she gasped as her nipple hardened beneath his touch. He slid his other hand down her stomach to caress her center, slipping one, then two, fingers inside her.

She arched her back and moaned as he found her mouth again, tangling his tongue with hers as she writhed beneath his touch. A sense of urgency overcame her. She needed him now. To feel him inside her. To finally give in to the passion she'd been denying herself. "Trent?"

"Hmm?" He nuzzled her neck, nipping at the delicate skin, sending shivers running down to her toes.

"I need you inside me."

He froze. "Fuck."

"That's the plan, isn't it?"

"I don't have a condom." He rose onto his elbow, sliding his hand over her hip to pull her closer. "I didn't think I'd need any while I was staying here."

"Oh." She looked at him, his smoldering eyes so impassioned, so full of need, she thought she might explode. She'd never been with a man without using protection. If he were anyone else, this moment would end here. Now. But with Trent…This was about so much more than a good time. She'd never needed anyone like she needed this man right now. "It's okay with me. I promise I'm clean."

He furrowed his brow, his gaze becoming even more intense. "I am too. I wasn't worried about that, but are you on birth control?"

"What single thirty-year-old isn't?"

He inhaled deeply, gliding his fingers down her cheek. "You're so beautiful."

"Make love to me, Trent."

He moved on top of her, holding his weight on his hands, and she spread her legs so his hips fit between them. Wrapping her fingers around his length, she guided him to her folds. With his tip pressed against her, she gripped his shoulders and closed her eyes.

"Look at me, Tina." He pressed against her slightly, and electricity shot through her womb.

She opened her eyes and met his heated gaze as he slowly slid inside her. Never breaking eye contact, he filled her completely. And she was completely there, with him. Part of him. Enjoying not just the physical sensation of his body moving with hers, but an intimacy and closeness she'd never felt with anyone before.

Lacing his fingers through hers, he raised her arms

above her head as he moved his mouth over her neck, kissing, licking, nipping at her ear. "God, this feels so right."

She wanted to respond but only managed to make a small mewling sound from her throat. This did feel right. *Trent* felt right. He released her hands, and she clutched his back as his rhythm increased. Body to body, mouth to mouth, they moved in unison, two becoming one in a tangle of limbs and emotions.

So many emotions.

His masculine scent. The sheen of his sweat-slickened skin. The way his muscles contracted with each thrust of his hips. She couldn't hold back. Her orgasm coiled in her core and released in a tidal wave of ecstasy, consuming her, drowning her fears in the essence of this man. He was with her, in her, and she'd never felt closer to anyone in her life.

He moaned as he found his own release, burying his face in her hair as his body slowed, and he relaxed on top of her.

This was the only man for her. Deep down, she'd known it all along, and she'd been an idiot to fight it. She wouldn't fight it anymore.

Trent inhaled her delicious floral scent and rolled onto his back, tugging her to his side. Making love to Tina was more than he could have ever imagined, and he was not letting her go this time.

She propped her head on her hand and rested her other hand on his chest, a sexy smile playing on her lips. "Was that *wow* enough for you?"

He chuckled and slid his fingers into her hair, pulling

her down for a kiss. "Sweetheart, that was the best sex of my life."

"I have to agree." She traced her soft fingertip over his lips. "But that was better than sex. I'd say we made love."

His heart pounded at her words. She'd been the toughest catch he'd ever gone after, and she was well worth the wait. "You knew I wasn't interested in that redhead downstairs, didn't you?"

She bit her bottom lip and gazed at his chest, her confident exterior slipping away to reveal her vulnerability. It was a side of Tina he'd never seen, and he loved it as much as he loved the rest of her.

She traced the outlines of his muscles with her finger, still refusing to make eye contact. "I wasn't sure. She was pretty."

"I didn't notice." He hooked his finger under her chin, turning her gaze to meet his. "You are the only woman for me."

"That's good to know." She rested her head on his shoulder, draping her leg across his.

He lost track of time as they lay there, holding each other. It could have been hours, but it felt like mere minutes as Tina sucked in a sharp breath and raised her head.

"Oh, shoot."

"What's wrong?"

She sighed and rose to a sitting position next to him. "This is Logan's first party since Allie moved in, and I promised her I'd be there for her."

He pushed himself up and leaned against the headboard. "I suppose we should head back downstairs."

"Yeah."

Seeing her sitting there in his bed, gloriously naked, he

fought the urge to climb on top of her and make love to her again. But, damn, he didn't want to fight it. "I doubt they'll miss us."

"Allie will."

He sighed and rose to his feet, offering her a hand to help her out of bed. "Shall we?"

She stood, pressing her soft, warm body to his, and kissed him long and deep. His entire body shuddered, and he couldn't stop the moan from escaping his throat. "If you keep that up, I'm going to keep you here all night."

She grinned and picked up her clothes. "Promise?"

She started dressing, but all he could do was stare. She was so beautiful, so perfect. The graceful way she moved. The way her long, dark hair fell over her shoulders as she bent down to pick up her shirt. And she was so loyal to her friend. He mentally added that endearing trait to the list of things he loved about her.

She caught him staring and laughed. "You probably need to get dressed too."

"Right." He picked up his own clothes and dressed. "We could always check in. Make sure everything's okay, and then come back here."

She stepped into her high-heeled shoes and smoothed the wrinkles from her skirt. "That sounds like an excellent idea." She moved toward him. "But there's something I need to tell you first."

"Oh?"

"If we're going to do this me-and-you thing, I'm all-in. One hundred percent. I don't want to see anyone else."

His heart pounded. A weird, sickening, fluttering sensation flitted through his stomach, making him feel nauseated and elated at the same time. "I can't even imagine being with another woman."

She placed a soft kiss on his cheek. "I've never been in a real relationship before. But if this is what it feels like, I think I'm going to like it."

The air felt as if it were sucked from his lungs, and he couldn't seem to inhale. She was finally ready to start a relationship with him. He opened his mouth to respond, but the words wouldn't come. He couldn't breathe. His jaw fell slack, and he had just enough time to stumble toward the bed before his knees gave out, and the room went black.

---

"Trent? Oh, my God, Trent!" Tina dropped to her knees beside the bed and shook his shoulder. "Are you okay?"

He didn't respond.

"Oh, God. What have I done?" One minute she was confessing her feelings for the man, and the next he collapsed on the bed. She pressed her ear to his chest, and the rhythmic thud of his heart eased her fears. His rib cage rose and fell steadily with his breaths. He was alive.

"Wake up, Trent." She patted his cheek. She shook his shoulder harder.

Still no response.

"Help." Her plea came out as a whisper. "Help. Allie!" She shot to her feet and darted downstairs. Allison stood at the bottom of the steps.

"Allie, help! It's Trent. He passed out."

Allison's eyes widened. "Logan." She touched his shoulder, drawing his attention from his guests, and nodded toward Tina.

"There's something wrong with Trent." She raced back up the stairs, with Allison and Logan on her heels.

Throwing open the bedroom door, she dropped to her knees at Trent's side and placed her hand on his chest. He was still breathing.

Allison knelt beside her and held her hands over his head, breathing deeply like she did when she was healing someone.

"What's wrong with him?"

Allison looked at Logan. "Do you want to tell her?"

"Tell me what?"

Logan shoved his hands in his pockets and strolled toward the bed. "Was he drinking?"

"No, I don't think so."

His gaze slid over the disheveled sheets. "Was he feeling any intense emotions?"

"We slept together. What's going on? Is he okay?" How could they be so calm, when Trent was lying there unconscious?

Logan chuckled. "He'll be fine. Give him a few minutes to wake up. He has narcolepsy."

"Narcolepsy?" She laid a hand on Trent's chest. "So he's just…asleep?"

"Basically. At least he landed on something soft this time."

Allison furrowed her brow and looked at Logan. "Has he ever had this happen after sex?"

Logan lifted one shoulder. "He's never mentioned it, but this was sex with Tina. I imagine that's a completely different story."

"True." Allison fought a smile.

Tina's mind reeled as she tried to comprehend the situation. "Why would it make any difference if it was sex with me?"

Logan laughed. "If you haven't noticed…the dude's crazy about you."

That, she had noticed. She was finally able to admit she was crazy about him too, but why wouldn't he tell her about this? "I don't understand."

"He's had the condition since we were kids," Logan explained. "He's on medication for it, and he hasn't had any episodes in years…until lately. He usually only has sleep attacks like this if he's drinking or if his emotions are really strong. My guess is he was feeling pretty good about what you guys just did, and…"

"Wait." She looked at Allison. "Is this why you drove him to the house the other day? And why I didn't hear from him the day before?"

Allison nodded.

"So you knew." She pointed to Logan. "And you knew." She pointed at Allison. "But he didn't feel the need to tell me?"

Allison rested a hand on her shoulder. "He was worried—"

Trent inhaled deeply, and his eyelids fluttered open. "Shit. How long was I out?"

"Just a few minutes," Logan said.

He turned his gaze to Tina and squeezed his eyes shut. "Damn it. I was hoping you'd never have to see that."

She leaned back on her heels, a spark of anger simmering in her core. "What the hell, Trent? You have narcolepsy, and you didn't want me to know?"

He glared at Logan. "Thanks a lot, man."

"It was kind of obvious, bro." He put his arm around Allison. "Let's give these two some privacy."

Allison gave her shoulder a squeeze. "I'm sorry." She closed the door behind her, and Trent sat up on the bed.

Tina moved to sit next to him and folded her hands in her lap. The flicker of anger dulled to a throbbing hurt deep in her chest. First the kitchen fire, and now this. "Why didn't you tell me?"

He let out a long sigh and took her hand in his. "You are the strongest woman I have ever met. Everything about you is perfect. I was afraid, if you knew I was sick, you'd think I was too weak. I was having a hard enough time catching you when you thought I was healthy. I'm sorry."

Damn, he was good at apologies. She laced her fingers through his. "I don't think you're weak. You fight this silent battle every day, yet you still manage to lead a normal—actually, a really successful—life. Not to mention, you look damn fine doing it."

He laughed and wrapped his arm around her. "Can you forgive me?"

She couldn't stay upset with this man. If she hadn't been such a flake, he might have trusted her with the truth from the beginning. "Of course. And anyway, I'm far from perfect. Why do think I've been so scared to get close to you?"

"I have no idea. I'm quite a catch."

"You certainly are, but growing up, my house had a revolving front door for my mom's boyfriends. She fell madly in love with every one of them, and every one of them wanted to change her. She'd do whatever they wanted. Be whoever they wanted her to be. But ultimately, she could never change enough, and they always left. Over the years, she lost herself. To this day, she can't make up her mind on something as simple as choosing a restaurant for dinner. I'm terrified of ending up like her."

He pulled her into a hug and kissed the top of her

head. "I wouldn't change a single thing about you. You're perfect."

She was the farthest thing from perfect she could imagine, and the sooner he realized her flaws, the better. "I'm bossy."

He looked her square in the eyes. "You have leadership skills."

"I talk too much."

"You're friendly."

"I make decisions for you without consulting you first."

He chuckled. "But you always make the right ones."

"My butt is way too big."

He slid his hand down to her ass and gave it a squeeze. "Are you kidding? I love your curves. Don't worry, okay? I don't want you to change."

Warmth spread through her chest at the sincerity in his eyes. "Okay."

"Stay the night with me? We can put the finishing touches on the house tomorrow and have a proper date afterward."

"That sounds fantastic. But until you stop having these sleep attacks, I'm doing the driving."

He grinned and lowered her to the bed. "Yes, ma'am."

CHAPTER FOURTEEN

Trent put his empty Chinese take-out container on the coffee table and draped his arm across Tina's shoulders. Their plan to finish the house together the day after the party was derailed when Logan needed his help closing a deal. Then, when he saw the pile of paperwork on his desk, he had to focus on his real job and put playing house with Tina on the back burner for the week. It irked him that he hadn't been able to progress their relationship past the sleeping together stage, but Tina seemed fine with the slow pace.

Still, she deserved more than he'd been giving her. "Now that you're finally willing to date me, it seems unfair I haven't had the chance to take you on a proper date."

She poked him with her chopsticks. "You have been working late a lot. I was beginning to wonder if that redhead hadn't caught your eye after all."

"Like that could happen. I only have eyes for you, sweetheart. I am sorry, though. I had to get caught up after missing so much last week."

"I understand. At least we got in a couple of sleep-overs."

His chest tightened as the image of Tina naked in his bed flashed through his mind. She'd been so patient, coming over to his temporary home at Logan's late in the evenings, leaving early in the mornings so he could go to work. But she needed to know he wanted her for more than sex. "Those were nice. I still want to take you out, though. Wine you and dine you."

"And sixty-nine me?" She set her food on the table and crawled into his lap.

Blood rushed to his groin. He definitely wasn't complaining about the sex. "I think that can be arranged."

"I can't wait." She straddled his pelvis and sat on his knees. "And don't worry about taking me out. I've enjoyed every minute I've spent in this house with you. Even when we were pretending to just be friends."

"So have I."

"Don't let my stunningly glamorous appearance fool you into thinking I'm high maintenance. I happen to find sitting on the couch, eating take-out, while the fake fire flickers on the television quite romantic."

He rested his hands on her hips and slid them up and down her delicate curves. He'd never get enough of this woman. "Too bad we can't light a real fire. Make love on the rug in front of the heat of the crackling flames."

"We can if you want to clean out the fireplace when we're done. We have to leave the house pristine to show it."

He chuckled. "No, thanks. We'll stick with the fake one. When's the crew going to be here?"

She slid off his lap and glanced at the clock. "Any

minute now. We'd better clean this up." She grabbed the trash from the table and carried it into the kitchen.

He followed behind, admiring the way her hips swayed as she walked. Her long, dark hair hung loose down her back, and her jeans hugged her round bottom, forming a perfect heart shape with her waist. How did he get so lucky?

The doorbell rang, and he tore his gaze away from Tina's magnificent backside to open the door. Allison stood between Logan and a tall man with sandy-blond hair. "Hi, Trent, have you met Gage?" she said.

"No." He stepped aside so they could enter and shook Gage's hand as he passed. "Don't you usually do your ghost busting with a bigger group?"

"Usually," Allison said. "But Gage is the main one we need for this."

Gage dropped a black duffle bag on the couch. "I'm a one-man show when it comes to tech. Where's Tina?"

"Here I am." She pranced into the living room and threw her arms around Gage's neck. "How are you? I haven't seen you in forever."

Trent clenched his jaw and mentally reminded himself Tina's friendliness was one of the things that attracted him to her in the first place. No need to be jealous...but did the guy have to be so good-looking? He could see why Logan was bothered by him at first.

Gage chuckled. "I've been good. How about you?"

Tina stepped away from Gage and slid her arms around Trent's waist, resting her chin on his shoulder. "Never better."

Allison patted Trent on the cheek. "I'm so happy you two have finally figured out you belong together."

Gage shook his head. "If I'd have known everyone would be coupled off, I'd have brought a date myself. How about a heads up next time?" He winked at Allison and started pulling gear from his bag.

Trent looked at Logan. "What's the plan?"

"I'm going to take some readings around the entire house," Gage answered. "Get a baseline measurement. Then I'll head upstairs and see if I can't stir some shit up."

"What do you need us to do?" Tina said.

Gage shrugged. "Nothing much. I've got some ideas of what the problem might be, based on what Allison told me. Now it's time to find out if I'm right."

Trent looked at Tina. "You mean we could've gone on a real date after all?"

Allison settled into a chair. "We'll need you later. You'll come up when it's my turn to go in. The ghosts seem to be attracted to Tina."

"I can't say I blame them." He led Tina to the couch, and they watched as Gage roamed around the first floor with a light-up device in his hand. Trent turned to Allison. "What's he doing?"

"That's a Mel Meter. It measures electromagnetic fields and temperature fluctuations. When spirits manifest, sometimes they create changes in the atmosphere, and that device can detect them."

Tina laced her fingers through his and squeezed his hand. He didn't need to be a psychic to understand all this ghost talk made her nervous.

"God, Allie, I had no idea being a psychic was so scientific."

"What I do isn't scientific at all. That's why I work with a team."

Gage stopped in the foyer. "I've gotten nothing downstairs. You said you've never had any activity down here?"

"Not really." Aside from the first time he came in the house, he felt completely safe in the entire home, excluding that damn third floor.

"All right. I'm going to head up to where all the activity is. If you don't hear from me in half an hour, I'm probably dead."

"Not funny, Gage," Tina said.

Gage laughed and walked through the foyer toward the staircase. The meter in his hand made a high-pitched chirping sound just as the coat rack tipped sideways. Gage jumped out of the way a split second before it could crash down on top of him.

Tina pulled her knees to her chest and clutched Trent's arm. "Was that a ghost?"

He wrapped his arm around her and rubbed her shoulder. "It's an old house. The floor is probably uneven. It's happened to me before." He wasn't sure what to believe when it came to that damn hunk of wood, but he didn't want to upset Tina anymore.

"I don't know." Gage turned the coat rack upright and ran his meter all around it. "I did get a quick EMF spike right before it happened. Then again, in a house this old, a loose floorboard could have the same effect. Anyway, I'm heading upstairs."

"Be careful." Tina's brow knit with worry.

"I'm sure it's nothing." Trent kissed her forehead.

"You're right. It's probably nothing."

As Gage trotted up the stairs, Allison padded toward

the coat rack. "I thought all the furniture here was new staging furniture. This coat rack feels old."

"It is." Tina followed her into the foyer. "We couldn't bring ourselves to get rid of it. It's kind of creepy looking, but it grows on you after a while."

Logan raised his eyebrows at Trent and mouthed the word *we*.

Trent chuckled and shook his head. Even when they were pretending to be friends, they were already making decisions together like a couple. He stood and made his way into the foyer with the women.

Allison closed her eyes and rested her hands on the wood. She swayed a little from side to side and inhaled deeply, furrowing her brow. When she opened her eyes, she looked at Trent and tilted her head to the side. "That's weird."

"What is?"

"This coat rack is very old. I wouldn't be surprised if it's been here since the house was built. There's a lot of energy stored in the wood, but most of it feels like you."

"Me? I haven't spent more than ten days total in this house." A sinking feeling formed in his stomach. "Is it possessed? Is it draining my energy?"

Allison laughed. "Furniture can't get possessed. There could be a spirit attached to it, but it wouldn't be draining *your* energy and storing it in the wood. Maybe it's because you're related to everyone who's ever lived here. You probably have similar energies."

Gage shuffled down the stairs and stopped on the bottom step. "Did I miss something?"

"Not a thing." Logan joined them in the foyer.

"Damn." Gage shrugged. "Are you sure you saw ghosts up there, Allison? Because I'm not picking up anything.

Sure, it's creepy, but that's nothing a fresh coat of paint and a new rug won't fix."

"I saw them," Allison said. "So did Tina and Logan."

Trent glanced at Logan. "You saw them too?"

"Briefly."

Gage started back up the stairs. "Come on up and see if you can draw them out, because I'm getting nothing on my own."

Tina held tight to Trent's hand as they climbed the steps and came to a stop on the third-floor landing. Her palms were slick with sweat, and she released his hand to wipe them on her jeans. Why was she so scared of this damn room?

She never should have asked Allison to check it out. If her friend hadn't confirmed ghosts did indeed occupy the space, Tina could've sold the house and gotten on with her life. But now that she knew for a fact there were ghosts here, she didn't care to ever step foot inside that room again.

Gage motioned for them to enter, and they all filed in. Tina clutched Trent's hand and stayed as close to the door as she possibly could. Trent flashed her a smile and wrapped his arm around her, but his eyes held an uneasiness that made her own fears worsen.

Allison wandered to the center of the room, her gaze grazing each wall before landing on Tina. "Do you see them?"

Tina shook her head. "No, and I don't want to."

"I don't see them either. Come, help me call to them." Allison reached out her hand, and Tina's stomach dropped to her knees. Her best friend actually wanted her to summon a ghost?

Trent squeezed her shoulders. "Go on. I'll be right here."

She swallowed the sour taste from her mouth and shuffled toward Allison. What the hell was she about to do? She didn't know the first thing about channeling spirits, and the last time she'd watched Allison do it, a ghost had thrown an antique vase at her head. "Is this safe?"

Allison put on her therapist smile—reassuring, but a tiny bit fake at the same time. "If it's not, we'll stop."

"Is Trent safe? Last time…" He'd said he'd twisted his ankle, but now she knew his narcolepsy had made him collapse. Could the ghosts have triggered it?

"Logan will stay with Trent."

"Okay." She took Allison's hands and stared at the wall where she'd seen the ghost.

Allison took a deep breath and lifted her chin. "If there are any spirits in this room, please show yourselves to us."

Tina kept her gaze trained on the wall while Allison did her deep breathing thing, trying to summon the spirits. Something flashed in her field of vision. A brief image of the handless woman raising her stump to her. Then nothing.

Allison exhaled a hard breath and released Tina's hands. "Did you get anything, Gage?"

He shook the device. "Nothing." It made a blipping sound. "Well, wait." He swung the meter around until the chirps grew louder. As he walked toward Trent, the sound grew louder and faster, the lights flashing alternating patterns of red and green. He lowered the device to the floor, and Tina could've sworn a dark mass billowed toward him from the corner.

She squeezed her eyes shut and looked again, but it was gone. The meter stopped beeping. The lights no longer flashed. Gage bumped the heel of his hand against the device and shook his head. "That was weird. I have a theory, though. Anyone want to hear it?"

"I think we should get out of this room." Tina grabbed Trent's hand and pulled him down the stairs. Whatever happened in that room was happening to Trent, and she didn't want him anywhere near it ever again. She'd finally found a man she wanted to be with, and she wasn't about to lose him to a ghost.

The rest of the group followed them down, and they gathered in the living room again. Gage paced in front of the fireplace as they all settled onto the sofa.

"Here's my theory, and you can do what you want with it; it's just a theory." Gage stopped pacing and plopped into a chair. "First let's talk about the ghosts in the attic. They only show themselves when Tina and Trent are around, right?"

"That's right," Allison said.

"So, if Tina and Trent aren't around, they aren't going to bother anyone. And if you're planning to sell the house anyway, your problem is solved. They aren't going to show themselves to anyone else, and you two won't be here much longer."

Trent smiled. "I like the sound of that."

Allison huffed. "I don't like leaving them trapped up there, but if they refuse to talk to me, there isn't much I can do to help them."

Tina bit her lip and looked from Gage to Allison. It

seemed too easy. "You're sure they won't bother the new owners?"

"I don't think they will," Allison said.

"That's good news." Trent patted Tina's knee and left his hand resting on her thigh.

His touch comforted her, but the thought of him selling the house still didn't settle well with her. "As long as Trent owns the house...before he sells it...when we're here, are we in danger?"

Gage shook his head. "Not from the ghosts. They seem to be trapped in the third floor, so as long as you stay away from that room, they shouldn't bother you. Am I right, Allison?"

"It seems that way."

"You said, 'Not from the ghosts.'" Logan leaned his elbows on his knees. "Is there something here that's not safe?"

"This is where my theory comes in." Gage shifted forward in his seat. "I did some research on shadow entities, and I think your dreams could be one of two things. First, like Allison suggested, you two have a strong psychic connection. Add to that the physical connection she didn't tell me about, and I agree with her that the shared dream could be just that. A dream."

"It's not uncommon for two people who are so connected and are sharing a stressful situation to have similar dreams," Allison said.

"If that's the case," Gage added, "once you sell this house and get rid of the stress, your shadow monster should stop bringing you nightmares."

That, Tina could handle. A shared dream due to the stress of trying to get the house on the market so quickly made sense. Plus, the rocky start to their relationship probably only added to the pressure they were both feeling. If she could relegate the shadow nightmare to once every few months like it had been most of her life, she'd be satisfied. "I like that theory."

Trent furrowed his brow. "And if that's not it?"

"You could be dealing with a nonhuman entity that's attached to this house and, more specifically, the family residing here."

Tina's stomach dropped. "A nonhuman entity? You mean, like a demon?"

"Demon. Shadow being. Spirit. Whatever you want to call it. I prefer the term entity because it covers everything."

"But no one lives here." She gripped Trent's hand. "How can it be attached to the family if the owner is dead?"

Gage raised his eyebrows. "The owner *was* dead. Now the owner is Trent, and isn't he related to the previous owner?"

"He was my uncle."

"No." Tina shot to her feet. "No, no, no. There's no demon attached to Trent or to this house. It's the first thing you said. It's stress." It had to be. Accepting the ghosts was hard enough. She wasn't about to let herself believe she'd been hanging out with a demon the past few weeks.

His eyes tight with worry, Trent reached for her hand and pulled her back to the sofa. "Let him finish, sweetheart."

"Anyway," Gage continued, "I found a shadow entity in my research that can trap spirits. Kind of like a soul collector of sorts. That would explain why your attic is full of ghosts who won't leave, and it would explain that spike on the meter that only happened around Trent."

Her stomach rolled. "There's a demon after Trent's soul?"

Gage nervously rubbed the back of his neck. "Man, I hate being the bearer of bad news, but yeah, it's possible."

"But not likely." Allison took Tina's hand in both of hers. "In the five years I've investigated with D.A.P.S, we've only come across a nonhuman entity one time. And I've seen a lot of ghosts. A lot."

Tina pulled her hand from Allison's grasp and leaned into Trent's side. "How did you stop it? What did you do to get rid of it?"

"Each entity is different," Gage said. "To stop your shadow—"

"*If* that's what it is." Allison cut a sideways glance at Gage.

"If you have a shadow entity trapping souls in your attic," Gage said, "stopping it will require a blood sacrifice from the person who summoned it."

"Blood?" Tina's head spun as her own blood drained from her face.

Allison slapped Gage on the shoulder. "Stop scaring them. Really, Tina, nonhuman entities are so rare, and based on the small amount of activity you've had here, I wouldn't worry about it."

She was up for anything to stop the paranormal activity. She'd participate in a séance, use a Ouija board, meditate…whatever it took. But if getting rid of the ghost involved blood in any way, her friends would have to do it without her. "So, what should we do? And please don't mention the B-word again."

"I think you should continue on the path you're on,"

Allison said. "If the shadow is the entity Gage thinks it is, it won't bother anyone who isn't part of Trent's family. And if it really is just stress, it should stop bothering you once the house is sold."

"So we need to sell the house." A sinking feeling formed in her stomach. Her goal since she reunited with Trent had always been to sell the place, but part of her couldn't bear to let it go. This old Victorian manor had brought them together. As silly as it sounded, losing the house felt like she'd be losing part of him.

"I think that will solve your problem," Allison said. "And, just to be safe, Trent probably shouldn't come here unless it's absolutely necessary."

Liquid pooled at the backs of her eyes, but she would not allow it to turn into tears. She held her eyes wide to keep the fluid in check and looked at Trent.

"Hey." He glided the backs of his fingers down her cheek. "You're the number one real estate agent in Michigan. If anyone can sell this place fast, it's you."

Of course she could sell it. She could find a buyer tomorrow and close the deal by the end of next week if she wanted to.

The question was, did she really want to?

If that's what it took to keep Trent safe, then yes. She definitely wanted to.

## CHAPTER FIFTEEN

"I guess I should've gone through all this stuff before we put it in storage." Trent heaved another cardboard box onto the desk and flipped open the lid. "I don't know why I was in such a hurry to sell my uncle's house."

Tina pulled a stack of papers out of the box and shuffled through them. "Maybe it was because you didn't want to spend too much time dealing with me."

He grabbed her hips and pulled her close. "If I didn't want to deal with you, I would've called another real estate agent."

She snaked her arms behind his neck and brushed a soft kiss across his lips. "I'm glad you called me."

His stomach still tied itself in knots, scattering his thoughts, every time she kissed him. Why had he been in such a hurry? If he'd sold the house to a flipper and been done with it, Tina might have flitted out of his life as quickly as she had last time. "Me too. What exactly are we looking for again?"

"Diaries, letters…anything written by or about any of

the previous homeowners that could give a clue as to why the ghosts are trapped in the attic." She pulled from his embrace and rummaged through the box.

"So, you really don't believe Gage's theory?"

Pausing, she let the papers in her hands float down into the box. "I don't want to believe it. Besides, I talked to Allie this afternoon, and she has another theory."

Trent sat on the edge of the desk. "Theory number three. I'm intrigued." Anything was better than a demon going after his soul. Gage exuded enough confidence that Trent didn't doubt his suspicion could be true. Allison's insistence on the rarity of non-human entities helped ease his mind, but still… He'd welcome a thousand different theories as long as none of them involved soul-sucking demons.

"Allie says people can trap spirits too. Sometimes on purpose, but sometimes not. So, it's possible someone who lived there summoned the spirits, and then didn't know how to—or didn't want to—let them go."

"You think my uncle did it." The house did look like a scene from a horror movie when he inherited it. It wouldn't have surprised him if his crazy uncle had summoned a few ghosts to keep him company.

"It would explain why the handless ghost lady told Allie I knew who trapped them. I found that picture of his wife and daughter on his desk. Maybe he was trying to bring them back."

"That makes sense."

"I'm glad you think so because I feel like I'm grasping at straws. The listing is scheduled to go live tomorrow, and I want to solve the mystery of the trapped ghosts before someone else inherits the problem. I've already sold one haunted house in my career, and that was one too many."

He had to smile at her determination. "What if it wasn't Uncle Jack?"

She reached into her briefcase and pulled out a stack of papers. "I've got information on every owner of the house since it was built in 1889. All their last names are Austin. Maybe the first names mean something to you?" She handed him the list.

He scanned the page and dropped it on the desk. "Not really. I never got into genealogy."

"Let's start with the first owners. Cox and Bertha Austin had the house built when they moved here from Virginia. He was a furniture maker, and they came to Michigan when he went into business with his younger brother."

Trent chuckled. "What kind of a name is Cox? Poor guy. I bet he got the shit beat out of him in junior high."

Tina smirked. "It's not so bad. I went out with a guy named Dick Johnson once."

He cringed. "And did he live up to his name?"

"He acted like a dick, so I never touched his Johnson."

"Nice."

She put the lid on the box and lifted another one off the stack. "What about Bertha? That's a hideous name."

He took the box from her and slid it onto the table. "Hey, that's my car's name."

"You named your car Bertha?"

"She's a fine piece of German machinery."

Stifling a giggle, she pulled the lid off the crate. "Uh-huh. Oh, look. This box is filled with pictures. How neat."

"You know what would be even more neat?" He stepped behind her and trailed his fingers down her back.

She cast a skeptical look over her shoulder. "What?"

"You, me, and a can of whipped cream." With a hand

on each hip, he pulled her backside to his front to emphasize his point.

She wiggled from his hold. "That would be messy."

"And fun."

"True. Hey, here's a couple standing in front of the house before it was finished being built. I bet that's Cox and Bertha." She examined the picture more closely. "He looks like you." She blinked a few times. "Wow. He *really* looks like you."

"Let me see." He took the picture from her hand and stared at the image. Cropped to show the couple from the hips up, the faded sepia photograph felt fragile in his hand. Though the paper on which it was printed was thick, the brittleness made it feel like it would disintegrate if he closed his fingers around it. He gingerly laid the picture on the table.

Great-great-great-uncle Cox—or however they were related—did look an awful lot like him. Good thing he took after this guy, and not Uncle Jack. "I can see the resemblance." The likeness interested him, but the woman intrigued him. She seemed so familiar, but he was certain he'd never seen this photo before.

Tina looked over his shoulder. "Bertha's pretty. Too bad her name didn't match."

She was gorgeous, but it was more than that. There was something about her eyes and the way she wrapped her arm around the man's waist. The ease with which they fit together. "She kinda reminds me of you."

Tina snorted. "She has light hair and dark eyes. The exact opposite of me."

"I guess you're right." He gazed at the photo one last time and placed it into the box. They looked like a couple in love—the direction he hoped his relationship with Tina was heading.

"And I am definitely not a fine piece of German machinery."

"No." He slid his hand up the back of her neck and tangled his fingers in her hair. "You are one hundred percent sexy American woman. I've had enough of this stuffy storage room. Let's go grab some dinner and have a sleepover at your place."

"A real date. I like the sound of that."

"Do you have anything special in mind?"

"For dinner or for the sleepover?" She tucked her fingers into his back pockets and pressed her hips to his.

"Both. But we should probably have dinner first, or else we'll never eat. Where do you want to go?"

"I've been craving Buffalo wings. Extra spicy with a side of fries. And they have to have be the bone-in kind. Boneless wings are just chicken nuggets dipped in sauce." She crinkled her nose in disgust.

His mouth watered. "Woman, you are magnificent. Let's go."

---

Tina slid her key into the lock and pushed open her apartment door. Her heart pounded in anticipation as Trent followed her inside and closed the door behind them. Not bothering to turn on the lights, she slid her arms around his neck and pressed her lips to his.

A deep *mmm* sound resonated from his throat, and he pressed his hands against the small of her back, holding her close to his body. He trailed his lips along her neck and caught her earlobe between his teeth. "You're not wasting any time tonight."

The warmth of his breath on her skin gave her goose bumps. His masculine scent made her head spin. She could have this man every day for the rest of her life, and she'd never get enough of him. "I wasted three months avoiding you before. I need to make up for lost time."

"Why did you avoid me for so long? I'm still not sure what I did to scare you off."

She slid her hands down his arms and laced her fingers through his. She'd much rather have been using her mouth to taste this magnificent man, but she could spare a few words to settle his mind. He deserved the truth. "You didn't do anything wrong. You've never done anything that wasn't absolutely right."

"What was the problem?"

She tugged him to the bedroom and gazed into his dark, trusting eyes. He'd been nothing but patient with her from the beginning while she'd played games with his heart. She cupped his face in her hands and stroked her thumb across his cheek. "I told you about my mom, and how I was afraid I'd end up like her."

He nodded. "I wish you would have talked to me about it. I might have been able to calm your fears."

"I doubt it. Not back then. When I look at you, all I can see is forever. I've never felt this way before, and at first, it scared me to death." She pulled him into a hug and rested her head on his shoulder. "I was afraid and stupid, and I ran away instead of facing my fears."

"Are you still scared?"

"A little. But I promise you, I'm not going anywhere this time."

He pulled her tighter to his chest. "Good, because I'm not letting you go."

She lifted her head from his shoulder and smiled seductively. "You're mine, Trent Austin."

"And what are you going to do with me?"

With her hands on his firm chest, she pushed him against the wall and pressed her body to his. His arousal dug into her hip, and she slid her hand between them to caress his hardness. "I'm going to show you what forever with me will be like. I hope you can handle it."

His lips brushed her ear as he spoke in a hoarse whisper. "Should I be scared?"

"Not if you can handle it."

He swallowed hard and cupped her butt in his hands, grinding his arousal against her. Every nerve in her body flared to life, his touch lighting a fire inside her. She stepped away and slipped her shirt over her head to reveal the emerald-green lace bra she'd chosen to match her eyes. As she dropped her pants to the floor, Trent smiled his approval.

Still leaning against the wall, he unbuttoned his shirt and licked his lips. "That has got to be the sexiest set of lingerie ever made, on the hottest woman alive. I'm not sure my knees can hold me."

She rushed toward him. "Are you okay? Are you having an episode?"

He chuckled and pushed from the wall. "I'm fine. But you might be a little breathless after I finish ravishing you."

She caught him by the shoulders and pushed him onto the bed. "Not until I ravish you first."

Straddling his lap, she yanked his shirt down his arms and tossed it to the floor. He wrapped his strong arms around her and kissed her long and deep. Unhooking her bra, he slid the straps down her shoulders, and she ground her center against his hardness, sending tingling electricity straight to her womb. She needed him inside her so badly, her head spun. But she'd wait. She wanted to explore him. To taste every inch of skin, to show him just how much she appreciated his body before she gave herself to him.

She pushed his shoulders to make him lie back on the bed and finished undressing him slowly. Then she started at his neck and kissed her way down his body. The delicious taste of him made her mouth water for more. The feel of his soft skin and tight sinew beneath her hands sent her heart into hummingbird mode.

As her lips neared his navel, his breathing grew shallow. A single bead of moisture collected on his tip, and when she flicked out her tongue to taste him, he sucked in a sharp breath and clutched the sheets in his hands.

She'd never been so turned on in her life. Never gotten so much pleasure from giving. She reveled in the sounds he made. The way he responded to her touch. He moaned as she took him into her mouth, and he rose onto his elbows. She could feel him watching her as she sucked him, and that made it all the more erotic.

She'd planned for this to simply be foreplay, but as she increased her rhythm, and his muscles tightened in response, she had to see it through to the end. To give him all the pleasure such an amazing man deserved.

"Hold on." He rested a hand on her head to slow her, but she didn't want it to end until he was satisfied. "Seriously. Stop. Stop, stop, stop."

He sat up, and she released her hold. "What's wrong?"

"It burns."

"What burns?"

He bit his bottom lip and fanned his crotch. "It feels like my dick is on fire. Fuck."

"Oh, no. The Buffalo wings."

He clenched his teeth. "Extra spicy."

"They were so hot my tongue went numb. The spices must still be in my mouth." Poor thing. She could only imagine what the heat must've felt like down there.

He groaned and squeezed his eyes shut. "Shit. When I said you were hot, I didn't mean it literally."

She stifled a giggle.

"I'm glad you're enjoying this." He stood and tiptoed in a circle, still fanning his dick.

She shouldn't have been laughing. He must've been in pain, but… "I'm sorry. You're just so cute."

"I'm not cute."

"Let's get you in the shower. Hopefully it will wash off."

---

The cold water pelting Trent's dick combined with the burning sensation of hot wing sauce should've cured his erection in seconds. But his view of Tina's naked body, with her full breasts and curvy hips, kept him rock hard. The corners of her mouth twitched ever so often like she was trying hard not to laugh. Hell, once the pain went away, he'd probably laugh about too. Right now, though, it was all he could do to hold back the tears.

He ran his hand over his dick and groaned. "It's not helping."

"Use soap."

He grumbled and lathered himself up, but the burning didn't stop. "Still not helping."

Tina washed her hands in the sink. "You probably still have some sauce on your hands. Let me help." She stepped into the tub behind him, slid the curtain shut, and rubbed the bar of soap across her palms. She wrapped her hand around his shaft and stroked it a few times. "Rinse it off, and we'll do it again. The burning is just on the outside, right?"

"Yeah." He rinsed his dick and let out a breath as the burning started to fade.

She grabbed him again and gave him another few strokes, and this time he could actually enjoy the sensation of her soapy fingers wrapped around him. The tension in his shoulders released, and he couldn't help but let out a moan.

"Is that a sound of pleasure or pain?"

"Both."

"Rinse it again."

"Yes, ma'am." The cold water from the shower soothed his skin, but Tina's supple body pressed against his back lit a fire in his core. The burn subsided to an almost-pleasurable warmth, as if he'd used one of those couple's heated lubricants. This, he could deal with. But when Tina slid her soapy hand down his shaft for a third time, he wasn't about to tell her to stop.

Instead, he closed his eyes and let her stroke. The warmth felt good now. Too good. And her breath against his ear gave him goose bumps.

"You look like you're enjoying this. All better?" She kissed his neck, never slowing her pace.

"Much, much better." The water washed the soap away, leaving only the sensation of Tina's soft skin rubbing against his. "In fact…" He shut off the water and turned to face her. "I think we should go back to bed before things get *too* much better."

She released his dick. "This was our first shower together."

He raked his gaze over her curvy body. "We'll have to have a do-over. You didn't even get wet."

"Oh, I'm plenty wet."

So. Damn. Sexy.

She stepped out of the shower and led him back to the bed. "Lie down, and let's finish what we started."

He climbed onto the bed and lay on his back. "As long as you don't put my dick in your mouth, you can have your way with me."

"I've got a better place to put your dick."

"Why don't you show me?"

"I'd love to." She straddled his pelvis and ran her hands over his body. Her touch ignited every masculine urge inside him, and his dick twitched in anticipation of feeling her wet warmth enveloping him.

She rested her breasts against his chest and nuzzled into his neck as she lowered herself onto his cock. The tightness of her center wrapped around him sent electricity shooting through his limbs.

"I love your body, Trent. You're so sensual and sexy."

He loved her body too. And her heart. And her soul. Hell, he loved *her.* He bit his tongue to stop himself from telling her just that as she rose on her hands and gazed into his eyes. Her silky hair fell over her shoulder, and she smiled as she moved her hips up and down in perfect rhythm.

She sat up straight and ran her hands over her own curves as she rode him. She was so confident. So completely aware of her own sensuality. She knew exactly what she liked, and she wasn't afraid to ask for it.

How the hell did he end up with such an amazing woman?

She dropped her head back and closed her eyes as her ecstasy overtook her. Her legs trembled, and she leaned forward on her hands, her long, black hair spilling around him like a satin curtain. He gripped her hips and plunged himself deeper inside her. She moaned and lowered her mouth to his as his own orgasm rocketed through his body.

Panting and slick with sweat, she collapsed on top of him and slid onto her side. God, he loved this woman. She had his heart in her hand, and all he could do was hope she wanted to keep it. She'd mentioned forever twice tonight. Hopefully she meant it.

He traced his fingertips along her arm. "This kind of forever, I can definitely handle. The first kind…not so much."

She propped her head on her hand and brushed the damp hair away from her face. "I'm sorry I burned your dick."

"It was worth it. It actually felt good after you washed it a few times."

Mischief danced in her eyes. "So next time we have wings…"

"Don't even think about it."

CHAPTER SIXTEEN

Trent pressed the home button on his phone and stared at the last text Tina sent him: *I miss you.* She'd sent the message nearly four hours ago, but those three little words had kept him distracted all morning. The same woman who, only a few months ago, wanted nothing to do with him was now sending him texts to let him know she missed him. A smile tugged at the corners of his mouth. He missed her too.

Since he'd gotten back into the routine of his job, and Tina had listed the house, he hadn't had an episode in over a week. He was even starting to get a little energy back rather than being exhausted and going straight to sleep when he got home. Of course, the excitement of seeing Tina in the evenings probably helped to keep him awake.

The repairs on his own house were coming along, and he'd be able to go back home within the week. With all the stress finally lifting from his shoulders, combined with the new medication taking effect, his condition improved daily. He'd even managed to convince Logan to let him drive himself to work today.

He stared out the seventeenth-floor window at the sparse traffic below. Cars whizzed by on the freeway. No back-ups. No accidents. Ann Arbor wasn't *that* far away. If he took an extended lunch break, he could drive out to the house and surprise Tina. She'd had two showings this morning, and with one more this afternoon, she'd still be there.

Before he could talk himself out of it, he grabbed his keys and headed out the door. He picked up a bouquet of lavender tulips on his way to the parking garage and made his way to the house.

Tina's Mustang sat alone in the driveway, which meant she'd be alone in the house. Though he didn't believe Gage's theory about a shadow demon living in the attic, it still made him nervous for her to be there by herself. Even Allison's theory that his uncle might've summoned the ghosts and trapped them there didn't settle well with him, but what else could he do? Hopefully Tina would sell the house quickly. With any luck, she already had.

He jogged up the front steps and let himself in. Tina padded in from the kitchen, and her eyes lit up when she saw him.

"I wasn't expecting to see you today." She glided into his arms and pressed her lips to his. "Did you leave Logan in the car?"

"I assume he's still at work. These are for you." He handed her the flowers.

"Thank you. They're beautiful." She sniffed the petals and furrowed her brow. "Did Allison drop you off?"

"Nah. I drove myself."

She blinked at him a few times as if trying to choose her words carefully. "Did the doctor say it was okay for you to drive again?"

"I haven't had an episode in over a week." He ran his hand up her arm and gave her shoulder a squeeze. "I'm okay."

"Does Logan know you drove here? He was supposed to be keeping you in line while I'm away." Though she said it with a smile, the look in her eyes told him she wasn't happy about him driving.

"He knows I drove to work this morning. I didn't see him when I left this afternoon." He sighed and ran a hand through his hair. "I'm fine, okay? I wouldn't drive if I didn't think it was safe."

"I know, but...You're not even supposed to be here." She cast her gaze to the floor. "If there really is a shadow demon that wants your soul..."

He hooked his finger under her chin and raised her gaze to his. "You aren't starting to believe that, are you?"

"I don't know."

"Have you had the dream lately?"

"No, I guess I haven't."

"See?" He pulled her into his arms and inhaled her sweet floral scent. "There's nothing to worry about."

"All right." She pulled from his embrace and guided him into the kitchen. "I guess I can forgive you this time. You did bring these beautiful flowers. They'll look great on the breakfast table." She pulled a bouquet of silk flowers from a vase and filled it with water before arranging the tulips and positioning them in the center of the table.

"Don't you want to take them home?"

She paused, a perplexed look falling across her features. "This house is starting to feel so much like home, I guess I forgot we don't live here."

His stomach tightened at her use of the word "we." The thought that she'd even consider living with him had his heart thrumming in his chest. "Aside from the ghosts in the attic, it does have a homey feel, doesn't it?" But Tina could make a storage shed feel like home to him, as long as she was there. "How'd the showing go this morning?"

She bit her bottom lip as a pink blush spread across her cheeks. "I might have screwed that up."

"I doubt that. What happened?"

"They were a nice couple, and they seemed to like the house. But something about them didn't feel right. When I pictured them actually living here, I don't know. It didn't settle well with me. I don't think they were the right family for this house. That sounds crazy, doesn't it?"

He started to say yes, but he paused. He'd been so intent on getting rid of his burden, he hadn't stopped to think about what it would actually feel like to let this house go. It had been in his family from the beginning. His ancestors built it, and no one but the Austin family had ever lived here. In fact, now that he thought about it, he couldn't imagine anyone living here unless it was himself...and Tina.

He shook his head. While it would be hard to let the house go, he could do it. But the woman standing before him...he couldn't live without her.

"Why are you looking at me like that?" Tina stepped toward him. "Are you mad at me?"

"You are the most amazing woman I have ever met. If you didn't think they were right for this house, then they weren't."

She blew out a breath. "Good. Because, sometimes, I feel like I'm going crazy when it comes to this place. Oh, that reminds me. I wanted to show you something." She opened her briefcase and handed him a faded sheet of paper.

"What's this?"

"I couldn't sleep, so I got up early this morning and dug around in the storage unit. I found it tucked inside Jack's address book."

He scanned the handwritten page—all names, some written in blue ink, others in black. "These are the same names from the list of homeowners you found."

She took the paper from his hands. "Some of them are. Some weren't on my list. What do you think the check marks next to the names mean?"

"I have no idea."

"And look at this. Lucy and Emily. That's your uncle's wife and daughter. They're circled in red pen. Why do you think your uncle made this list?"

"I don't know."

"What if these are the ghosts in the attic?"

"You think Uncle Jack trapped his own wife and daughter in the attic?" It sounded even more ridiculous when he said it out loud. Sure, his uncle was crazy, but he wasn't a soul collector. At least, he didn't think he was. He cut his gaze toward the cellar door. Maybe he'd find some bodies in the basement after all.

"There are no check marks by their names. Maybe they're circled because they were next on his list. Maybe he was practicing when he summoned the others. I don't know. Maybe he was so lonely, he was trying to bring the whole family together."

"But only the dead ones." He took the paper from her hand and laid it in her briefcase. This had to stop. "I think you've been spending way too much time here. You should let one of your colleagues handle any showings this weekend, and we can take a trip. I wouldn't mind a few days off. Maybe we can fly down to Mexico and spend some time on the beach."

"You think I'm crazy, but this list goes hand-in-hand with Allison's theory."

"No, I don't think you're crazy."

"Look." She grabbed the list from her briefcase. "Cox and Bertha's names don't have check marks."

"So?"

"And look at the last name on the list." She held the paper up and pointed to the entry. "That says 'Trent.' That's your name."

"So it is." There could have been plenty of reasons why his name appeared on that paper, but he didn't drive all the way out here to talk about theories.

"Why is your name on the list of ghosts in the attic?"

"That's not what the list is." He took the page from her hands, folded it in half, and laid it on the table.

She clenched her hands into fists. "How do you know it's not?"

"How do you know it is?"

She blinked as if coming out of a daze. "I don't. My God, I am going crazy."

"You're not crazy, sweetheart. If I saw your name on a list like this, it would bother me too. But it's probably there because he willed the house to me. Who knows what the crazy old man meant by this, but you know what?" He gripped her hips and pulled her close. "None of this will matter once the house is sold."

She inhaled deeply and relaxed into his embrace. "You're right. I've always loved a good mystery novel, but real-life ones are apparently too much for me to handle. Were you serious about Mexico?"

"Warm, salty air. Sun and sand. I could sure use a vacation."

"Me too."

"I'll book it this afternoon." Some time away from this place would do them both good.

"That sounds fantastic." She pressed a soft kiss to his lips.

An image of Tina lying on the beach in a tiny bikini played in his mind. The sand in her hair. Her skin slick with oil and sweat. "How long until the next showing?"

She glanced at a clock on the wall. "Two hours."

He rested a hand on her hip and slid the other one into her hair. "Is that bed in the master bedroom really a bed? It's not just a cardboard box covered in a duvet, is it?"

She grinned. "It's real."

"Would it be wrong of us to make love in a rented bed?"

She leaned in and pressed her lips to his ear. "We don't have to tell anyone."

Her intoxicating scent and the feel of her warm breath against his skin made his knees weak in a good way. And when she nipped at his earlobe and tugged him to the bedroom, he knew without a doubt this was the person he was meant to spend forever with.

She undid the buttons on his shirt and smiled as it dropped to the floor. "Even though I know what's underneath the wrapping, it still feels like Christmas every time I undress you. This might be my favorite part."

"Hmm…" He pulled her shirt over her head and unhooked her bra. "If undressing me is your favorite part, I need to step up my game."

"Your game is great. I just really like the way you look

naked." She reached for the button on his pants, but he caught her by the wrist.

"So you're saying you'd rather look at my naked body than feel my lips on your skin?" He nuzzled into her neck and trailed kisses down to her shoulder while unzipping her skirt and pushing it to the floor.

She inhaled deeply, running her soft hands up his chest. "No, your lips are great."

"Just great?" He slid her panties down her legs and gently pushed her onto the bed before undressing himself.

"They're amazing." Lying back on a pillow, her soft, black hair fanned out around her like a flame. The afternoon sun filtered in through the sheer drapes, warm light accentuating her perfect features and making her glow like an angel.

His angel.

He climbed on top of her and kissed his way down her throat and across her chest, taking his time with each breast, hardening her nipples with his tongue. When his teeth grazed the sensitive pearl, she sucked in a sharp breath and a tiny whimper escaped her lips. He trailed his tongue down her stomach, her muscles tightening as he neared her navel.

He stopped and looked up her. "Still think undressing me is the best part?"

"Have you looked in a mirror lately? You're hot as hell."

"Hmm...I'll have to work harder." He moved down her body, tasting, nipping, and kissing every inch of her soft, sweet skin.

She spread her legs, and he settled between them, kissing and stroking her inner thighs, up one leg and down the other. When he reached her center, he paused, his lips a scant centimeter from heaven, and let the anticipation build. He could almost feel the desire emanating from her. Her need for him to touch her. To taste her.

She arched her back, bringing herself closer to him, and whispered, "Please."

He pressed his lips against her, and she held her breath. As he slipped his tongue out to taste her, she exhaled a satisfied hiss.

Holy hell, this woman was sexy. He couldn't hold back anymore. He lapped at her sensitive nub, bathing it in the warmth of his tongue, reveling in the sweet taste of Tina. She moaned as he slipped his fingers inside her, writhing and wiggling as he brought her closer to ecstasy.

Everything about her intoxicated him. The taste of her skin. Her scent. The sounds she made as she climaxed, gripping his shoulders and pulling him to her.

"Make love to me, Trent. I need you inside me."

He rose onto his hands and pressed his tip against her. "Are you sure you wouldn't rather just look at me? I'm hot as hell."

She grinned wickedly and hooked her heels behind his thighs, drawing him toward her. "I take back what I said before. *This* is my favorite part."

He groaned as he filled her, warm wetness sheathing him, squeezing him, as he made love to her. Their bodies fit together effortlessly. Their movements seemed flawlessly choreographed as if they'd made love thousands of times, yet each time felt new, like it was the first. Everywhere she touched him—the pressure, the friction—was sheer perfection. He loved this woman with every fiber of his being, and he'd make love to her every day for the rest of his existence if she'd let him.

"Oh, Trent."

The rasp of her voice. The warmth of her breath on his skin. It was enough to send him over the edge. He quickened his pace, and she matched his rhythm beat for beat, clutching his back and crying out again as another orgasm overtook her. His head spun, and he squeezed his eyes shut as a tidal wave of ecstasy crashed through his body.

He collapsed on top of her, gasping for breath as the elation subsided, a drunken calmness remaining in its wake. He rose up on his elbows and gazed into her bright green eyes. "I love you, Tina."

She bit her bottom lip, as if she were unsure of how to respond. "Allison always says if something is meant to be, it will be. That if the universe wants something to happen, it will happen, no matter how hard you try to stop it. I think she's right."

He rolled onto his back, and she snuggled into his side, draping her leg across his waist. She loved him. He could see it in her eyes. Feel it in the way she touched him. She didn't have to say the words. Not yet. Hell, he probably shouldn't have said them yet either. It was too soon. God, if he'd screwed this up...

She lifted her head and kissed his cheek. "Be patient with me."

"I'm not going anywhere."

"Except to Mexico."

"Only if you're coming with me." She was still holding back, but he could wait. She'd just said herself that if the universe wanted something to happen, it would. And he knew without a doubt that spending forever with Tina was definitely meant to be.

He lay there with her for a while, relaxing in the comfort of her embrace. He must've dozed off because, when he opened his eyes, Tina stood next to the bed, fully dressed, watching him with a sweet smile on her face.

He stretched his arms over his head and pushed into a sitting position. "This rental mattress is really comfortable."

"It is. I almost fell asleep too. But the buyer will be here in half an hour."

"We better make the bed, then." He got dressed and helped Tina straighten the comforter before she walked him to the door.

"Do you want to come over after work tonight?" The hopeful look in her eyes tightened his chest. Thank God, he hadn't scared her away.

He pulled her into a hug. "I would love that. I'll be there around seven."

She opened the door and brushed her lips to his. "Please drive safely."

"Always."

He waved goodbye as he got in his car and pulled out of the driveway. What the hell was he thinking telling her he loved her so soon? She'd been skittish about their relationship from the beginning, and if he'd used his brain, he would've waited for her to say it first. Instead, he'd let his damn emotions carry him away. He'd rushed into it, like he seemed to do with everything. If he'd jeopardized their relationship, he'd never forgive himself.

*Way to go, man.* He was such a jack ass. He knew better than to move too fast with her. If she started over-thinking…Sweat beaded on his forehead just thinking about what she might do. A sudden heaviness formed in his head, and his jaw fell slack.

*Oh shit.* He barely had time to curse himself before his arms seized up and jerked the steering wheel hard to the right. He needed to stomp the brake, but his legs wouldn't move. His entire body was paralyzed. He couldn't even close his eyes as his car skidded off the road and plowed straight toward a pine tree. Everything seemed to move in slow motion as the front end of the car crumpled with the impact. His body jerked forward and then to the side. His head smashed into the window. The glass shattered, but the pain felt like his skull had shattered too.

Something thick and warm oozed down his face, but he couldn't lift his arm to wipe it away. He couldn't tell if he was upright or lying on his side. A vague awareness of being lifted from the car registered in his consciousness. Of lying on his back in the dirt. Sirens. Voices shouting. His vision tunneled. Darkness closed in around him.

Nothing.

Then a face appeared in front of him. A body formed. A woman stood before him, and she lifted her arm to him. He reached out to take her hand, but all she had was a stump.

Tina stayed on the second floor while the potential buyers ventured up to the third. What the hell was her problem? The man of her dreams told her he loved her, and all she could do was spout off some metaphysical crap she'd heard Allison say.

Why couldn't she say the words? She certainly felt the feelings. She loved Trent. She could finally admit that to herself, but something about having to say it out loud had made her freeze. She was an idiot. As soon as she saw him again tonight, she'd say it. She'd be a fool not to.

"Is the owner planning to do anything about the third

floor? It's quite musty up there, and the door is broken." The blonde woman held her husband's arm as they descended the stairs.

Tina flashed her a tight-lipped smile. "I'm sure he'll be willing to put a fresh coat of paint on the walls and move out the old rug."

The woman looked at her husband. "I like this house."

She seemed snooty. Not at all the type of person who deserved a home like this. Tina couldn't read people's energy the way Allison and Logan could, but something about the couple felt off. They didn't belong here.

"One thing I should warn you about, though," Tina said. "The neighbors are really loud. A group of college boys. A fraternity, I think." She shrugged. "Something to consider." That was a lie, but the snooty buyers didn't need to know that.

The woman made a sour face and led her husband down the stairs. Tina showed them out and fell into a chair in the living room. Why did she love this house so much? What would the payments be on a mortgage for a place this big? If she could afford it, she could buy the damn thing herself, monsters and all. Board up the third floor and forget about the ghosts. Or maybe figure out why they were trapped there after all.

Then again, she intended to keep Trent in her life. And he wanted to get rid of the house, so she couldn't very well buy it herself and expect him to be happy about it. She would have to let *someone* buy it, but it had to be the right family. It had to *feel* right first.

She sighed and rubbed a hand down her face. Trent was right. She needed to let this place go. Some time on a beach with Trent and his rockin' body would be just the distraction she needed.

Her phone rang, and she dug it out of her purse and checked the screen.

"Hey, Allie. What's up?"

"Tina." Her voice was thick with tears. "You need to come to the hospital. It's Trent."

CHAPTER SEVENTEEN

*H*er heart sprinting in her chest, Tina darted down the hospital hallway to room Five-C. She couldn't stop her hands from shaking, and the sandwich she'd had for lunch threatened to make a reappearance with every step she took. Pausing at the doorway, she reached a trembling hand toward the knob and dragged in a ragged breath.

This could not be happening. She would open the door and find they were mistaken. Trent would not be lying unconscious on the bed. It would be someone else. It had to be.

She pushed open the door and stepped inside.

Her stomach tied in a knot.

Trent lay, bruised and bandaged, on the bed, half a dozen different contraptions humming, beeping, and dripping around him. He didn't acknowledge her when she entered the room. Didn't make a move to greet her as she rushed to the bedside and took his hand in hers.

"Trent?" She forced his name over the lump in her throat.

"He's in a coma."

Tina lifted her gaze to find Allison standing on the other side of the bed, her hands hovering above his head in her healing position. Logan sat in a chair in the corner, and he rose to his feet and stepped toward Allison.

Confusion clouded her thoughts. A coma? It wasn't possible. Trent was a strong, capable, take-charge man. Stuff like this only happened to guys like him in the movies. This was real life…but this situation could not be real. Pressure built in the back of her eyes as she stared down at him. "How?"

"Our best guess is he had a sleep attack while driving," Logan said. "Ran off the road and plowed into a tree."

"He had just stopped by the house to surprise me. Is he…" Her bottom lip trembled, and her eyes stung. She couldn't even ask the question. There was no question. "He's going to wake up soon." He would. He had to.

Allison wiped a tear from her cheek and dropped her arms to her sides. "He hit his head pretty hard. He has a concussion, but they can't find anything else wrong with him. The doctors…" She inhaled deeply as Logan rubbed his hand across her back. "The doctor said if he was going to wake up, he should have done it by now."

Tina sucked in a shallow breath as the heart rate monitor beeped a slow and steady rhythm. A clock on the wall ticked away the seconds, and the humming of the machines seemed to grow louder as she tried to grab on to one of the hundreds of thoughts racing through her head.

She clenched and released her fists and looked at her best friend. "You can save him, Allie. You have to."

"I'm trying, but the energy block he had before has gotten denser and bigger. I've never encountered anything like it before." She raised her eyebrows in a sympathetic look. "It's okay to cry."

Tina closed her eyes and released her breath. A flood of tears poured down her cheeks, and for the first time in as long as she could remember, she didn't fight the flow. She traced her fingers down Trent's cheek and ran her thumb over his soft lips. Just a few hours ago, love had danced across those lips. And now he might never wake up.

"He shouldn't have been driving." She glared at Allison. "Why did you let him drive?"

Allison blinked. "Why did *I* let him drive? Tina, he seemed fine. He hadn't had an episode in over a week."

Nausea churned in her stomach. "But you knew he wasn't fine. He still had that energy block in his head, didn't he?"

"Yes, but lots of people have blocks." Allison took a step back. "Are you blaming me for this?"

Her entire body trembled, and she clutched the bed rail to hold herself upright. "He was staying with you. You should have been taking care of him. You shouldn't have let him drive."

Allison's mouth dropped open. "You let him drive too. This happened after he saw *you*."

The truth in her words slammed into Tina's chest like a sledgehammer. She *had* let him drive. She'd gotten onto him for doing it when he arrived, but she hadn't tried to stop him when he left. She could have convinced him to wait. To stay with her until the last buyers left, so she could have driven him back to work. She could have prevented it. He would be sitting in his desk chair at the office right now if she would have thought to make him stay. "Oh, my God. This is my fault."

"Ladies." Logan pulled Allison toward Tina and wrapped his arms around both of them. "Don't fight about this. We *all* could have tried a little harder to convince him not to drive. But the truth is, Trent's a grown man who makes his own decisions. If he insisted on driving, there's not a damn thing any of us could've done about it."

Tina nodded and wiped her eyes. "I'm sorry, Allie." It was everyone's fault and no one's at the same time. She looked at Trent lying motionless in the bed. Finding somewhere to place blame was a lot easier than dealing with the fact that the man she loved might never wake up.

"I'm sorry too," Allison said.

"Where's his family?"

"Snowed in," Logan said. "A blizzard hit New York yesterday. Airport's closed."

"So we're all he has." She stepped from under Logan's arm. "He told me he loved me."

"Oh, sweetie." Allison rested a hand on her shoulder.

"I didn't say it back." A sob bubbled up from her chest and lodged in her throat. "Now he might never know I really do."

And it was all because she'd been too chicken to say the words. If he never woke up…If she never got the chance to tell him how she really felt…A fresh flood of tears streamed down her cheeks, and she covered her face with her hands.

"You can tell him now." Allison walked her toward the bed. "Sometimes, people in comas are aware of everything going on around them."

Logan nodded and wiped a tear from his cheek. "He's probably heard every word we've said and wishes he could tell us all to shut the hell up."

She picked up Trent's hand and laced her fingers through his. "You think he can hear me?"

"It's worth a try. We'll give you a minute. Come on, Logan." She tugged her fiancé out the door, and it shut behind them.

Tina sat on the edge of the bed and rested a hand on Trent's chest. His heart beat slow and steady beneath his skin, and his ribcage rose and fell with each peaceful breath. He was only sleeping. This was just an extended bout of narcolepsy, and any minute now, he would wake up and smile his adorable smile and pull her into his arms.

"I'm so sorry, Trent." She put her other hand on his chest and smoothed the hospital gown down his stomach. "When you told me you loved me, I just…I froze. I've never experienced love before, and I didn't know how to react at the time. Of course, now that it's too late, I know exactly what I should have said."

She scooted closer to him and brushed the hair back from his face. A line of pink marred the white bandage on his forehead. She let his hair fall back over it. "I should have said, 'I love you too.'" Her stomach tightened, and more tears flowed from her eyes. "I do, Trent. I love you. I love you so much, sometimes it feels like I might drown. And it scares me to death to feel so strongly, but I'm done fighting it. I'm done holding back."

She leaned forward, resting her head on his chest, clutching the sheet in her fist. "I love you. You're everything I've ever wanted. All I'll ever need. You're the only man I'll ever want, and if you would just wake up, I would tell you that I'm yours forever."

She sobbed into his chest, her tears dampening his gown as she heaved in a ragged breath. "I'm sorry, Trent. I'm sorry for breaking up with you all those months ago.

I'm sorry for playing hard-to-get and wasting so much time. So much time that we could have been happy together. If I'd known this was coming, I wouldn't have wasted a single second. If I'd known this was coming, I would've told you I loved you from the start. Because, deep down, I've always known you were the one for me. I was just too scared and stubborn to admit it."

She lifted her head and peered down at his face. Peaceful. Serene. She could imagine his lips curving into a smile. His strong arms holding her tight. But still he didn't move. He breathed and his heart beat, but that wasn't enough. "You're supposed to wake up now. That's how it always happens in the movies. I spilled my guts to you, and now you're supposed to wrap your arms around me, tell me you heard every word, and we'll live happily ever after."

She pressed her lips to his. They were still warm, soft like she remembered them. But he didn't respond. Not even the slightest movement to let her know he felt her presence. She ran her fingers over his lips and kissed him again. "Not even for true love's kiss?"

She could barely breathe. The pain in her chest felt like it would split in two. A heaviness in the room pressed down on her. Suffocating. Drowning. "Please wake up. You can't leave me. Not now. Not when I'm finally ready to love you."

She stared at him, willing him to move. To smile. To open his eyes. Anything. "Damn it, Trent. Wake up. I need you." She buried her face in his chest, gripping his gown like a lifeline. *He* was her lifeline. She might as well be a ghost trapped in the attic because her existence was meaningless without him. "Please, God. Don't take him from me. I need this man."

She tossed her head back toward the heavens and let out a raspy moan. "I need him. Do you hear me? He's mine, and you can't take him."

Turning her gaze to Trent, she released her grip on his gown. "Please, God. I'll do anything. I'll take his place if you'll let me." She lowered her head to his chest, pressing her ear over his heart to listen to the promise of the rhythm. To fill the hollow ache in her chest with the sound of life...of hope...beating through his veins. "Please. He's my everything. Don't take him from me."

CHAPTER EIGHTEEN

The sound of muffled voices pulled Tina into consciousness. She squeezed her eyes shut against the pounding in her head and swallowed the dryness from her throat. From the position she lay in, she definitely wasn't in her bed, but it had to have been a dream. When she opened her eyes, she'd find herself drooling on her desk at the office. Anything would be better than the reality she refused to accept. She wasn't at the hospital. Trent wasn't in a coma.

She fluttered her lids open and blinked her eyes into focus. Harsh fluorescent lighting cast a sickly-green glow on the stark white walls. Her heart sank.

She was living a nightmare.

The vinyl recliner squeaked as she pushed into an upright position and worked out the cramp that had formed in her shoulder from keeping her arm on Trent's bed all night. If he was even remotely aware of what went on around him, she wanted to be sure he knew he was never alone. She'd have squeezed into the bed with him and slept by his side if the nurses would've let her.

They'd tried to kick her out when visiting hours ended last night, saying only immediate family members were allowed to stay. Like hell, she would leave. With his family snowed in six hundred miles away, it hadn't taken her long to convince them she wasn't going anywhere. They'd have to knock her unconscious and drag her out before she'd leave him alone.

She stretched her arms over her head and nodded at Allison and Logan, who stood at the foot of the bed. They both looked like they hadn't slept all night, and Logan's eyes were so tight with worry, Tina could only imagine the hell he must've put himself through last night. Logan's OCD had gotten better in the time she'd known him, but he was by no means cured.

She stood and took Trent's hand in hers. "Rough night?"

Logan half-smiled. "Probably no rougher than yours."

"Every square inch of floor in our house has been swept, vacuumed, washed, and waxed." Allison rubbed Logan's back. "But we made it through. How are you?"

Tears pooled in her eyes, and she shook her head. There were no words. Nothing could describe the way the emptiness had sliced open her chest and torn out her heart.

"Oh, sweetie." Allison pulled her into a hug. "I'm going to do everything I can to heal him. And I know the doctors are doing what they can too."

"The doctors aren't doing anything." She pulled a tissue from a box and wiped her nose. "A nurse comes in every few hours and looks at the monitors, but that's it."

"He's scheduled for another brain scan this morning," Logan said.

"And you and I have some work to do," Allison said.

"Work?"

"Your handless ghost friend visited me last night."

Tina dropped into the chair and rubbed her forehead. "I swear I don't know what she's talking about. I've never seen that woman before. Not that I could recognize her if I had. Her face was so blurry and weird. All I can think is that Trent's uncle trapped her there, like we talked about before."

Allison shook her head. "She didn't even mention being trapped this time. It's hard for her to stretch so far from the room, and she only appeared to me for a few seconds. But she said you could help Trent."

A spark of hope ignited in her chest, but confusion quickly squelched it. "How does she know about Trent?"

"His heart did stop beating for a few minutes after the crash," Logan said. "Maybe his spirit—"

"Don't." Tina shot to her feet. "Don't even say something like that. Trent didn't die, and he's not going to." Logan was Trent's best friend. How could he even entertain the idea of Trent…She shook her head. She would not allow her thoughts to go there.

"If there is a way you can help him, don't you want to?" Allison said.

"Of course I do." She sat on the edge of the bed. "What else did she say?"

"That's it. She faded away as soon as I started asking questions."

She gazed at Trent's face. The swelling had receded, leaving only a dark purple bruise beneath his left eye. "How am I supposed to help him if I have no idea what to do?"

Allison looked at Logan, and he nodded. "We're going back to the house. To the third floor."

"Like hell, we are. Something freaky happens every time I go into that room. And I'm not leaving Trent alone."

"He won't be alone. Logan will stay with him."

Tina gave Logan a wary look. "Allison and I are going to the creepy attic alone, and you're okay with that?"

He shook his head. "Not really. But Gage is meeting you there."

"And you're okay with *that?*"

He sighed and drooped his shoulders. "Gage has always had Allison's back. He'll keep you safe." He shrugged. "Or I'll kill him."

Allison stepped toward Trent and hovered her hands above his head. "He's already threatened Gage with his life if one of us gets hurt. Though, I hope he wasn't really serious." She eyed Logan, and he shrugged again.

"Why go back? All the ghost has ever said is that I know or that I can help. What makes you think she'll say anything this time?"

Allison moved her hands over Trent's heart and took a deep breath, pausing before she answered. "I think Trent's condition might be caused by something supernatural."

Tina blinked at Logan. "But you said he's had narcolepsy since he was a kid."

"He has."

"But it didn't flare up again until he inherited the house," Allison said.

Tina rubbed the back of her neck. "I thought it was stress causing the flare up."

"That's what I thought at first, but some entities are capable of intensifying conditions that already exist, without ever having to make their presence known."

Her stomach churned. She closed her eyes and let her

breath out slowly. "Please tell me you don't think it's the shadow demon. Because, I have to say, I preferred your theory of Trent's uncle trapping the ghosts. I can deal with humans. I'm growing more accustomed to spirits. I can't handle demons, Allie."

Allison sighed. "Honestly, I don't know. Some really strong ghosts can do it too. But whatever it is, if we can stop it…If we can save Trent's life, I'll do whatever it takes."

Tina dropped her arms by her sides. After her dreams and the things she'd seen in the attic…it was time to stop denying it. "I'm going to fight a demon."

"Or a ghost. We won't know until we get there. Go home and take a shower. I'll pick you up in forty-five minutes."

She gazed down at Trent and brushed her fingers across his face. "What if he wakes up and I'm not here?"

"Believe me, you wouldn't want him seeing you looking like that," Allison said. "A toothbrush would do you some good too."

She ran a hand through her tangled mess of hair and looked at Logan. "You'll call me with any news? Even if his pinky finger twitches, I want to know."

"I've got your number on speed dial."

Allison hovered her hands above Trent's head. "I'll be there as soon as I'm done with his healing session."

"Okay." She bent down and pressed her lips to Trent's. "I love you. I promise I won't be gone long. And if it is a shadow demon doing this to you, I'm going to send that thing straight to hell where it belongs."

Tina sat in the passenger seat of Allison's Prius as they rolled up the driveway toward the old Victorian home. The new blue paint and crisp white trim gave the house such a quaint, pleasant feel—a stark contrast to the sinister soul-sucking demon possibly lurking inside. She narrowed her gaze at the third-floor window and ground her teeth. Whatever was doing this to Trent—whether it was a shadow demon or an evil ghost—she planned to thoroughly kick the entity's ass and make sure it never stepped foot in that house again.

How she was going to do that was another issue entirely. That's where Gage and Allison came in. If it was a ghost, Allison could get rid of it. But if it was a shadow demon, hopefully Gage could tell her what to do.

And she would do *anything* to get her man back.

They pulled up next to Gage's Jeep and found him sitting on the front porch steps, chewing on the end of a piece of red candy. He stood as soon as they got out of the car and met them on the front lawn.

"Sorry we're late," Allison said. "His treatment took longer than I planned."

Gage wrapped Tina in a tight embrace. "No improvement, then?"

All she could do was shake her head in response. If she tried to talk about Trent's condition, she'd break down again. And right now, he needed her to stay in ass-kicking mode. His life depended on it.

She swallowed the sob that tried to creep up from her chest and marched up the steps. "There's an entity up there that's messing with my man. Let's go kill it."

Gage picked up his duffel bag and followed her to the porch. "You can't actually kill something that's already dead...or was never alive to begin with."

She unlocked the door and squeezed the handle. "You know what I mean."

"Sure, I do. But it's not going to be that simple." He followed her inside and dropped his bag on the table.

"He's right, Tina." Allison set her bag next to Gage's and pulled out a canister of salt and an ostrich egg-sized quartz crystal. "First we have to figure out exactly what's causing the problem."

"I don't care what's causing the problem. I just want it gone." The first tear spilled down her cheek, and she squeezed her eyes shut to stop the rest of them from flooding her face. She had to hold it together for Trent. He needed her to be Wonder Woman, and damn it, she was going to pull through for him.

Allison put her hands on Tina's shoulders. "We are going to get rid of it, but we need to be careful. One step at a time, okay?"

Tina nodded.

"First we're going to go up there and try to make contact with the spirit that visited me last night. That's all. Right now, we're gathering information. Then we'll form our plan of attack."

"Just tell me what to do."

Allison handed her the salt canister. "Hold this, and follow me."

As they reached the top of the steps, Gage dropped his bag outside the door. "I'll go in first and take a baseline reading." He grabbed his Mel Meter and pinned them with a hard look. "Don't come in until I give you the all clear. And stay away from the stairs. In fact, why don't both of you go sit in that far corner and wait for me to come out? I value my life, and I don't need your boyfriend bashing my face in because you fell down the stairs."

Allison crossed her arms. "Logan isn't going to hurt you, Gage."

"I'm not taking any chances." He disappeared through the doorway.

Tina clenched the cardboard cylinder of salt in her hands. She slipped her fingernail beneath the metal spout, sliding it open and pushing it closed as she tried to keep her breathing under control. "What do we do now?"

Allison rubbed her hand on Tina's back. "Give him a few minutes. Then we'll go in and try to make contact."

She shook the half-empty canister in her hands. "You're using salt this time."

"This could be dangerous. When we go in, I'm going to pour a ring of salt around us. It's important you stay inside it. If you don't—"

"I remember."

Gage stuck his head through the doorway. "All right, ladies. I'm getting nothing, as expected. Come on in."

Tina clutched Allison's arm and swallowed the sour taste from her mouth as she entered the attic. Every hair on her body stood on end as she followed her friend to the center of the room. Her palms went slick with sweat, and the salt canister slipped from her hand. She caught it before it spilled on the rug. "Here, Allie. You better hang on to this."

Allison took the salt and set the crystal by the window. "The spirits aren't showing themselves to me, but we can try to call to them. Let me pour a salt ring, and we'll give it a try."

Tina inched her way toward the door. "Does it have to be in the center of the room? Wouldn't it be safer to do it closer to the exit? Just in case?"

Allison closed her eyes and took a deep breath. "I feel

more strongly about this spot, here in the middle. The energy seems denser here." She kept her eyes closed and tilted her head to the side. "It almost feels like a gateway. This could be where your ghost friend passes through when she stretches out of her prison."

"Hold on." Gage wedged his shoe under the rug and lifted the edge. "How long has this rug been here?"

Tina shrugged. "No clue. It was here when we got the place."

"Have you looked under it?"

"Aside from Trent breaking the door jamb, we haven't done a thing with this room. Every time we're in here, something freaky happens."

He grabbed the edge of the carpet with his hands. "Help me roll it up." He looked at Allison. "It could be a portal."

Allison paled, a look of dread flashing in her eyes before she raced to Gage's side and helped him roll up the rug. Tina clutched the heavy fabric and together, they folded the rug over on itself, revealing a strange circular pattern scratched into the wood floor beneath. Swirls and strange geometric patterns bordered the outer edge of the circle, and a roughly-sketched pentagram occupied the center of the space.

Allison took a step back and covered her mouth. "Oh, my God. How could I have missed that?"

Tina eyed the strange design, and a sickening feeling formed in her stomach. "What is it?" But she knew exactly what it was.

Gage stepped toward it and ran his hand over the pattern. "It's definitely a portal. It wasn't done correctly, though."

Tina backed toward the door. "Get away from it, Gage."

He chuckled and knocked on the floor. "It's not like it's going to suck me in." He tapped his fist against his chest. "I'm too solid for that."

Allison poured a ring of salt on the floor and pulled Tina into it. "Come inside the salt ring anyway. Just in case."

He sauntered toward his bag, pulled out a thick, leather-bound book, and flipped through the pages. "I'll be fine." He ran his finger across a page and nodded. "Whoever scratched this design into the floor was summoning human spirits. See here." He pointed to the design on the floor. "These symbols represent the elements, and this one is for soul energy. But they got this one wrong. I'm not sure what they were trying to draw, but that might be why the spirits are trapped here."

Goose bumps rose on Tina's skin. A chill cascaded down her spine as a heaviness grew in the air. Something was happening in this room, but her friends seemed oblivious. "Allie, do you see the ghosts?"

"Nothing is showing itself to me. What do you see?"

Her heart sprinted in her chest, and her mouth went dry. "Nothing. I'm just freaking out a little."

Allison took her hand. "Take a deep breath."

She tried to rake in a breath, but the air was thick. Stagnant. Stale. Her nostrils twitched as the faint scent of something rotten crept into her senses. "Do you smell that?"

"Just the musty scent of an old attic."

Tina scrunched her nose. "I smell something rotten."

"Get inside the salt circle, Gage," Allison commanded.

"Hold on." He set some sort of device in the center of the portal. "I don't smell anything."

"Oh, God." The darkness in the corner of the room moved. A roiling, black fog billowed, folding in on itself as it thickened. "Please tell me you see that."

Allison shook her head. "What do you see?"

Her legs trembled. Her hands shook. How could they not see the giant shadow undulating in the corner? A dense, buzzing energy filled the room. The shutters slammed shut. Then the door. The lightbulb sparked.

The room went dark.

"Oh no." She blinked hard, but it didn't go away. The dark mass grew, rolling across the floor toward them. "Do you see it now?"

"No, but I feel it," Allison said.

The shadow crept closer. A spark of anger burned in Tina's chest. If they were going to beat the damn thing, her friends needed to be able to see it. She turned toward the billowing mass and shouted, "Show yourself to them."

Allison gasped.

Gage stumbled and fell on his ass. "Holy shit." He crab-walked backward toward his bag while the device on the portal went crazy, flashing lights and letting out a high pitch squeal.

The shadow lengthened, wrapping itself around the device and chunking it into the wall with a *crack*. A deafening silence followed as the air seemed to be sucked from Tina's lungs. The shadow grew, thickening into an inky blackness as it rose into a spiraling, vertical column.

"Gage, move!" Allison shouted, but he sat frozen to the spot.

It oozed toward him and reached out a spindly tendril of fog, wrapping around Gage's neck. He clutched his throat, clawing at the shadow, but his fingers passed right through the fog. A horrid gurgling sound emanated from his esophagus as the shadow lifted him from the ground and hurled him across the room. His shoulder slammed into the wall, and he dropped to ground.

"Gage!" Tina darted toward him and grabbed his arm, pulling him to his feet. Allison caught his other arm, and they both tugged him toward the door. He stumbled, taking Allison down with him.

The shadow swirled, rolling toward Tina like a freight train. She braced herself for impact and prepared to scream, but it stopped a foot in front of her. The onyx mass folded in on itself, forming into an almost human-like figure. Its featureless face regarded her as she tried to will her legs to move.

In her peripheral vision, Allison rose to her feet and gasped. The shadow turned toward her, lashing out a tendril to grab her by the arm. Tina screamed and yanked her from the shadow's grasp. Gage scrambled to his feet and pulled open the door.

A flood of light from the hallway cut through the room, and with a hiss, the shadow shrank back to the corner. Tina clutched Allison's hand as the three of them lingered in the doorway. The shadow stayed in the corner, but the heavy, electric energy still buzzed around them.

"Well, ladies, I think we found its weakness." Gage strolled into the room like a crazy person and picked up his and Allison's gear. Pulling a flashlight from his bag, he shined it into the darkened corner, and the shadow receded into the wall. Gage chuckled, flashing the light into each corner before sauntering toward the door.

"Weakness or not, I want out of this room." Tina led the way down the stairs, the buzzing energy dissipating the farther they retreated from the attic. By the time she reached the ground floor, no trace of the shadow monster remained, but her heart still raced in a panic.

She fumbled with the knob on the front door, her sweat-slicked palms sliding across the brass. "Piece of shit, open up."

"It's okay." Gage peered up the stairwell. "I don't think it could reach us down here, even if it were dark."

Tina flung open the door and pulled Allison onto the porch. "Get outside, Gage. Now."

"Oh, all right." He shuffled onto the porch and pulled the door closed. "But it seems to be tied to that room."

Tina leaned over the porch railing and heaved in a raspy breath. The crisp winter air stung her eyes, tightening her lungs as she fought to catch her breath. "What the hell just happened?"

Allison sat on the bottom step and dropped her head in her hands. Gage put his hand on the doorknob.

Tina stopped him with a sharp look. "Don't even think about it."

"But—"

"Don't." She shook her head and walked down the steps to face Allison. "Are you sure we're safe out here?"

She stared at the ground. "Gage is right. It can't manifest in the light, and it's tied to the room. More specifically to the portal." She lifted her head. "The portal I should have picked up on the first time I was here. I'm so sorry, Tina. I've never been more wrong about something in my life."

Tina sat beside her. "It's okay. The carpet covered the portal. If I hadn't been so scared of the stupid room, I'd have removed the rug a long time ago, and then we would have found it."

"But I sensed it." Allison wrung her hands. "Every time I went into that room I was drawn to the center. I should've realized there was something there. Gage, you were right about the shadow entity all along, but I didn't believe it."

"Don't be so hard on yourself." He dropped onto the step next to Allison. "This is only the second non-human entity I've ever encountered too. I probably wouldn't have believed it either, if I hadn't done so much research on the damn things."

"None of us wanted to believe it." Tina wrapped her arm around her friend's shoulders. "The important thing now is that we know what it is. We know what we're up against, so we can fight it. Right, Gage?"

"Absolutely. The problem is, we're going to need Trent to do it. Vanquishing a shadow entity like this requires a blood sacrifice. It's got to be the blood of the person who summoned it, and since it's always been Trent's family living in this house, I can only assume it's his blood we'll need."

Tina's chest tightened, her stomach churning at the mere mention of blood. "He's in a coma." Tears threatened to spill again as she uttered the words, but she held them back. She had to be strong.

"Is his dad around? His blood would work too."

Allison shook her head. "His parents are snowed in. It could be days before they can get out here."

He lifted his shoulders. "We'll just have to hope he wakes up soon, then."

"Wait, Allie, you said the demon was keeping Trent in a coma. If it can't reach us out here, how can it reach him there?"

"I don't think it's keeping him in the coma, but he was in this house right before the accident."

"He never went upstairs."

"The shadow can't manifest in the light," Gage said. "Meaning it can't turn into that smoldering smoke monster and kick anybody's ass. It can still have other effects, though. Its power gets weaker the farther from the portal it stretches. But if Trent already had this condition, it definitely had enough power to aggravate it, even if he was downstairs."

She rose to her feet and paced through the yard. "If the demon wants Trent's soul, and it can obviously attack people when they're near its nest, why didn't it kill him when he was up there?"

Gage stood and leaned against the handrail. "Because evil suckers like that thrive on suffering. The more he suffers before he dies, the more power the entity gets from his spirit when it traps him."

Her breath caught. "He's not going to die."

"I know. I was just saying."

She clenched her hands into fists so tight, her nails dug into her palms. "Well, don't *just say* anything about Trent dying. It's not going to happen."

"I'm sorry."

She turned to Allison. "So, there's a chance he could wake up on his own, even before we kill this shadow thing?"

"It's possible. I still can't figure out exactly what it did to his brain. It disrupted something in the way his body handles sleep, but I can't seem to unblock it. Maybe if we could send the shadow entity back through the portal, its hold on him would release."

"But we need his blood for that," Gage said.

"What if we got some of his blood and brought it here? He's in a hospital. Surely we could manage to sneak a few drops when no one was looking. Bring it here in a vial or something. Would that work, Allie?" Though how she'd keep the contents of her stomach where it belonged in the process, she wasn't sure.

"Dealing with demons is not in my wheel house." She looked at Gage. "What do you think? Would it work?"

He took a deep breath and rubbed at the scruff on his chin. "I honestly don't know. It's worth a shot."

"That's what we'll do then. We'll try to get a little of his blood. Then we'll bring it back here, and Gage can lead us through whatever ritual we need to do to get rid of the thing." She stopped pacing and rested her hands on her hips. She had a plan. Something she could put into action and do something about. Anything was better than sitting around waiting for Trent to wake up…or worse.

"There's something else, though." Allison stood and smoothed her sweater down her stomach. "When the shadow stopped and looked at you, I was able to get a reading on it. It knows you, Tina."

"I've spent the past month working on the house. Apparently, we've been spending a lot of time together, and I didn't even realize it." She shivered at the thought that that thing had been watching her all this time. Invading her dreams. Hurting the man she loved.

"And you've been dreaming about it your whole life. I don't think those dreams were any sort of premonition. I think you've dealt with this entity before."

## CHAPTER NINETEEN

*L*ogan rose to his feet as Tina and Allison entered the hospital room. Dark circles ringed his reddened eyes, and fresh tears pooled above his lower lids. "You just missed the doctor."

Tina rushed to Trent's side and took his hand in hers. She traced her fingers down the side of his face and brushed her thumb over his lips. Still warm. Still soft. There was no way he was close to death. She sat on the edge of the bed and rested her hand on his chest, watching it rise and fall with his breaths. "What did he say?"

"The scan was completely normal. No evidence the crash caused any permanent damage to his brain."

A knot in her chest released. "The concussion?"

"Healing like it should. They can't find any reason why he hasn't woken up." He gave Tina's shoulder a squeeze. "So they're not sure he will."

Not waking up was *not* an option, and if one more person suggested it, she might not be able to stop herself from punching them. Straightening her spine, she squared her gaze on Logan. "He will. We know why he isn't waking up." She told him about the shadow entity and what Gage discovered in his research. "We just need to figure out how to get some of his blood, and then we'll destroy the shadow and bring Trent back."

"In theory," Allison said. "I still think there's more to it than that. I'd like to get a better reading on you, Tina, and how you're connected to the house…to the shadow."

"That doesn't matter. We have to get Trent back first."

Logan cut his gaze toward the door. "The doctor said he's sending in a nurse to draw blood for more testing. Maybe we can convince her to draw an extra vial for us."

That sounded way too simple. "I doubt a nurse is just going to give us his blood. It's probably illegal. Definitely unethical."

Logan shrugged. "She will if the price is right."

"I don't like that idea." Allison stepped around the bed and hovered her hands above Trent's head. "I don't want the nurse to risk losing her job. Couldn't we distract her and take some when she's not looking? I'd feel more comfortable if *we* were the wrong-doers."

Tina chuckled. "I feel like we're the cast of *Scooby Doo* making an overly elaborate plan to stop the shadow monster."

Logan sat in the vinyl recliner. "Only, in our episode, we won't be ripping a mask off the monster at the end and finding out it was really crazy Uncle Jack's even crazier brother all along."

Tina tapped her finger against her chin. "Still, this could work." She looked at Logan. "Fred, when the nurse comes in, you flirt with her to distract her." She turned her gaze to Allison. "And Daphne, you swipe a vial of blood while he has her under his spell. Got it?"

Allison shrugged. "I always considered myself more of a Velma, but okay."

Logan crossed his arms. "Fred doesn't date Velma, and I'm not being Shaggy."

"This is definitely a job for Fred." Tina leaned down and placed a kiss on Trent's lips. It was a hair-brained idea, but it was the only one she had. She'd make it work.

Logan eyed her skeptically. "Where will you be while Allison and I are doing all the work?"

"Over there in the corner, trying not to pass out."

The door clicked open, and Tina rose to her feet as a nurse wheeled a cart into the room. She'd never seen this one before. Fresh out of college, with lanky arms and curly red hair, he couldn't have been more than twenty-two years old.

*He.*

His dark-green scrubs hung on his shoulders like they were a size too big. He stood only a few inches shorter than Logan, but his muscle mass hadn't quite caught up with his height. Tina pressed her lips together to suppress a smile. They guy had an uncanny resemblance to Shaggy.

As the nurse approached the bed, Logan lifted his arms and mouthed the words *I'm out.*

*Fantastic.* She couldn't count on Allison to be the distraction. When it came to flirting, her best friend was definitely more Velma than Daphne. Hell, Scooby would be a better candidate for the job. It was up to Tina. Which meant she'd have to get close to the blood.

Her stomach churned as she moved away from the bed to give the nurse access to Trent's arm. His cart held crates of vials in various sizes and a stack of labels with bar codes. He typed something into the computer and scanned one of the labels.

Allison widened her eyes and jerked her head toward the man as if to say, "Get on with it."

She swallowed the sour taste from her mouth and stepped toward the nurse. "Hi there. What's your name?"

He fumbled with the scanner and nearly dropped it on the floor. "Uh, Steve." He set the scanner next to the computer and applied a label to a vial.

"My name's Tina."

His Adam's apple bobbed as he swallowed.

"Why do you have so many different sizes of containers?" She ran her hand over the top of a box of vials and batted her lashes at Steve.

Obviously unaccustomed to flirting, his mouth opened and closed a few times before he formed words. "Different tests require different amounts of sample."

She rested a hand on his shoulder. "Wow. How do you keep it all straight? You must be really smart." She cringed inwardly. Hopefully, if Trent really could hear them, he also heard the plan and knew this was just a distraction.

"Tina, stop flirting with the man and let him do his job." The smile behind Allison's voice was evident, but luckily, Steve was too nervous to catch on.

"It's not my fault, Allie. Whenever I see an attractive man, I can't help but flirt." *Jeez, Louise, I sound like a bimbo.* She dropped her arm to her side and took half a step away.

"It's okay." Steve glanced into her eyes but quickly shifted his gaze to the vial in his hand. He cleared his throat. "I'll just…get on with it."

Steve attached the first container to Trent's IV, and a gush of redness flooded into the glass. Tina's head spun at the sight.

She bit her bottom lip and squeezed her eyes shut. "How many of those do you have to draw?"

He looked at the computer screen. "Four. Are you okay? You look a little pale."

"I'm fine. I just get a little nervous around attractive men."

He glanced at Logan and furrowed his brow.

"That one's spoken for, so he doesn't count." She managed a grin, and Steve smiled in return.

He put the first vial into a rack on the cart and started to draw the second sample. All the blood in Tina's head seemed to plummet to her feet as the offending liquid pooled into the container. Her stomach lurched, and she covered her mouth with her hand.

Steve put the second vial on the cart and turned toward her. "You don't look well."

"I'm okay." Her knees buckled.

The nurse caught her by the arm and lowered her into a chair. He pulled a small flashlight from his pocket and shined it into each of her eyes. "Either you're sick or you can't stand the sight of blood. Which is it?"

Her stomach twisted, and she swallowed before the saltines Allison had forced her to eat this morning could make a reappearance. "Blood."

He laughed and straightened his spine. "I'm almost done. Do you want to wait in the hall?"

"I'll stay. I just won't watch."

"If you insist." He turned back to his cart and paused. "I could've sworn I already drew two samples."

Allison shook her head, her expression as guilty as a teen caught sexting with her boyfriend. "I only saw you do one." She cut her eyes to the left and gave him a tight-lipped smile. Man, she was a terrible liar.

He sighed and shook his head. "I guess I did then."

Steve picked up another vial and drew more blood, and Allison slipped the stolen sample into her purse. A bead of sweat rolled down her forehead, and she wiped her palms on her jeans. The poor girl looked like she'd pass out herself.

"All done. You can look now." Steve stood by his cart, staring at Tina as if waiting for her to say something else.

"Okay. Well, you have a nice day, Steve."

He nodded his head and mumbled, "You too," as he wheeled his cart out the door.

Tina sat up straight and tentatively scooted to the edge of the chair. Thankfully, the room didn't spin. Her meager lunch stayed in her stomach. "He was sweet. I feel bad for flirting with him."

Logan chuckled. "Don't. You probably made his day."

Allison picked up her purse. "I texted Gage. He's going to meet us at the house."

"And bring lights? A lot of them?" The concern in Logan's voice was evident.

Allison wrapped her arms around his waist. "We'll be safe. I promise."

He closed his eyes for a long blink. "I want to come with you."

Tina shook her head. "Someone has to stay with Trent. If he wakes up…"

"Then you stay. I'll go with Allison and Gage. You can't handle the blood anyway."

"No way. Allie says the shadow knows me. And it's personal. I'm going to kick its ass and send it back to hell for what it's done to Trent."

Allison pulled from his embrace and cupped his cheek in her hand. "And given what Gage has researched about this type of entity, you would be in more danger than Tina or me. It magnifies pre-existing conditions. You've worked so hard to get your OCD under control. I would hate to see it intensify because of this thing."

He clutched her hand and held it to his chest. "It could still hurt you both."

Tina swung her purse over her shoulder. "I'm as healthy as a horse and mad as a honey badger. It's not getting a piece of me."

"As long as we keep it from manifesting, it won't hurt us. And Gage promised to bring plenty of light to keep it in check." She kissed his cheek. "Trust me?"

"Always. But I still worry."

"I'll call you as soon as we're done." She looked at Tina. "Ready?"

Tina cast one more longing glance at the man she loved and squared her shoulders toward the door. "Let's do this."

---

Tina sat in Allison's passenger seat, clenching and unclenching her fists, watching the veins in her wrist protrude and recede with each movement. This ritual required blood, and she'd nearly fainted watching it fill the vial at the end of Trent's IV. Would she be able to stay conscious when Allison poured it onto the portal to complete the ceremony?

She'd figure something out. She'd close her eyes or turn her back to the portal when it happened. Trent needed her, and there was no way she'd let him down.

She looked at her friend. "You still have the blood?"

Allison patted her purse. "I can show it to you if you don't believe me."

"That's okay." She wiped her sweaty palms on her jeans. "I'm scared, Allie. I was terrified when we helped the ghost in Logan's house cross over, and she was just a human. This thing is an evil…God knows what it actually is. I'm scared shitless."

"We could wait. Give Trent a little more time to wake up on his own. See if we can figure out your connection to the entity."

"No. I can't sit around doing nothing. I want to get rid of this thing." She glanced in the rearview mirror and let out an impatient sigh as Gage's black Jeep approached from the road. "Finally."

Tina clambered out of the car and marched toward his Jeep. She yanked the door open before he cut the engine and fisted her hands on her hips. "What took you so long?"

He grabbed a backpack from the passenger seat. Without responding, he shoved the bag into her arms, slid out of his seat, and paced to the back of the vehicle to get another larger bag. "I was gathering supplies. And I stopped by the library."

She followed him around the car. "Seriously? You decided to pick up the latest Dean Koontz novel on your way here?"

He rolled his eyes. "Hardly. I've read them all."

Allison met them in the driveway. "Is something wrong?"

"No. I wanted to double-check my research. Make sure we're performing the right ritual, so we don't end up inviting something even nastier over to our side." He marched toward the front porch, and Allison followed.

Tina couldn't make her legs move. "Wait. That could happen?"

Gage paused on the steps. "If we do it wrong, it could."

"Allie?"

Allison stood beside Gage. "I'm not going to sugar-coat it, babe. This could go terribly wrong."

"Jeez Louise." She slung Gage's backpack over her shoulder and trudged toward the porch. What had she gotten herself into? If someone had told her their plan could backfire and they could end up inviting another monster into their realm…Well, what difference would it have made? She had to help Trent, and this was the only way she knew how.

She looked at Gage. "And you aren't the slightest bit scared?"

"Nah. I've never been afraid to go after what I want." He cast a glance toward Allison. "But I do know when to quit if the goal is unattainable. If this doesn't work, my advice is to board the place up and never step foot inside again."

"It's going to work." She brushed past her friends and unlocked the front door. Stepping into the foyer, she hung her coat on the rack and patted the top of the stand. "Don't worry. I'll bring him back to you soon."

Gage stepped through the door, followed by Allison. "I'll go in first and get the lights set up. There won't be a dark corner or crevice anywhere in the room when I'm done."

"But we'll *all* be inside a salt ring, just in case." Allison glared at Gage.

"You don't have to tell me twice," he said. "I've experienced what this thing can do." He handed them each a sheet of paper. "This is the incantation. We'll all say it in unison. Hopefully three are more powerful than one."

"The number three holds a lot of power," Allison said. "It's sacred in many belief systems."

Gage nodded. "Then we'll each pour one drop of Trent's blood onto the portal."

Tina whimpered. She wasn't sure she could handle looking at it in the vial, much less pouring it herself. "Allie…"

"It's okay. I'll pour the three drops myself. Tina's scared of blood."

Gage stifled a laugh. "Okay then. Three people doing the incantation. Repeat it three times. Three drops of blood on the portal, and that should do it. Wait here. I'll call you up when I'm ready."

He took his backpack from Tina and bounded up the stairs. Allison rested her hands on the coat rack and closed her eyes.

"Trent loves that gnarly piece of wood." Tina laid her hand on top of the rack. "I thought it was ugly at first, but I kinda like it now."

Allison opened her eyes and gave it a quizzical look. "I still don't understand how a piece of wood could have absorbed so much of Trent's energy so quickly. And yours too. I feel you both, but I don't see you."

"If the shadow has been affecting Trent's narcolepsy without him knowing it, could it also have been draining our energy somehow? Maybe storing it in the wood?"

Allison furrowed her brow. "I honestly don't know. This whole ordeal is so incredibly bizarre. I feel useless."

Tina wrapped her arm around Allison's shoulders. "You're my BFF, Allie. You'll never be useless to me."

"All right, ladies," Gage called from the second-floor

landing. "This place is brighter than a high school football stadium on a Friday night in Texas. Come on up."

Tina swallowed and stepped toward the stairs. Never in her wildest dreams would she have believed she'd be doing this. She gazed up the staircase. "Well, let's go kick some demon ass."

"Look out!" Allison shouted.

Tina turned to find her friend righting the overturned coat rack. She grabbed her jacket from the floor and tossed it onto the sofa. "Did it fall over again? The arms must be off-balance."

Allison shook her head. "It didn't fall. Your ghost friend pushed it."

Tina sucked in a sharp breath, jerking her head to the left and right, but she didn't see the handless woman. "Is she still here?"

"I think she pushed the coat rack to stop us. When I caught it, she looked at me and said, 'Please don't.' Then she disappeared."

"Why on Earth would she want to stop us from vanquishing the demon that has her trapped?"

Allison rubbed her arms. "I don't know, but I have a bad feeling about this."

"So do I, but we have to help Trent." They were about to battle a shadow demon. If she had any feelings about it that weren't bad ones, she'd have to be crazy. The nausea gnawing at the pit of her stomach was natural, the intense feeling of dread squeezing her chest expected. She linked arms with her friend and tugged her toward the stairs. "Let's get this over with."

Gage met them at the top of the steps. "Do you have your scripts?"

Tina held up her paper. "What language is this?"

"It's Latin. Everything is pretty much pronounced how it's spelled." He turned to Allison. "Don't try to do anything with the ghosts yet. We have to get rid of the shadow before you can help the rest cross over."

Allison nodded. "Got it. No ghosts." She faked a smile, but the uneasiness in her expression made Tina's stomach tighten. If Allison wasn't confident they could defeat the monster, how could she be?

Gage held up a container of salt. "Let's go."

Squinting against the brightness of the once-dark room, Tina crossed the threshold into hell. That's how it felt, anyway. Gage had set up an industrial-strength lantern, emitting 360 degrees of super-bright light, in each corner of the room. Two other intense lights sat on either side of the portal, illuminating the entire space. She stood near the portal next to Gage while Allison poured a ring of salt around the three of them.

"I'm not sure how much good this will do against a demon," Allison said. "I've only ever used it against human spirits."

"Hopefully we won't need it," Gage said. "Do you have the blood?"

Allison held up a clenched fist, the purple tip of the vial protruding between her thumb and forefinger.

Wooziness made Tina sway on her feet. She had to get this phobia under control. Maybe if she convinced herself it was tomato juice, she could stop the world from turning on its side. It wasn't like it was coming out of a person. It was just a thick red liquid inside a glass container. Tomato juice. That's all it was. A cocktail ingredient in their arsenal of demon vanquishing gear.

She took a deep breath and straightened her spine. "What do we do?"

"Give me a minute to connect with the portal. Then we'll recite the incantation and seal it up with the shadow inside." Allison closed her eyes and rocked gently as she did her psychic thing.

A static electricity built in the air, and Tina's arm hairs stood on end. A heavy dread settled deep in her stomach, and it took all her will power to keep her feet planted to the floor. Her instincts told her to run. Though she couldn't see the damn thing, she could *feel* it was there. And it wasn't happy it couldn't manifest.

"It's definitely open," Allison said. "There's a void in the middle of the room. Let's recite the chant and force the entity back inside."

Tina read the words. They seemed to roll off her tongue in a steady rhythm, though she had no idea what they meant. The pressure in the room grew heavy, suffocating, as they called on the shadow and commanded it into the portal.

They finished the first recitation and started the second. The air buzzed around her. Hot. Electric. An emptiness formed in the center of the portal, like a vacuum. The temptation to step toward it overwhelmed her, and she slipped her hand into Gage's, hoping he'd hold her in place.

He gave her hand a squeeze and nodded as they began the third and final repetition of the incantation. The electric sensation in the air strengthened until it felt like ten thousand charged needles pressing into her skin. Sweat beaded on her forehead. She squeezed her eyes shut against the pain.

As they recited the final word, the electric piercing stopped. Every negative feeling inside the room was sucked into the portal, and the air grew light and soft.

Tina opened her eyes and looked at Allison. "That's it? It's gone?"

Allison pulled the cap off the tomato juice and held her hand over the portal. "We have to seal it with three drops of blood, and it should be gone."

Blood.

Allison tipped the vial, and the first drop splashed onto the wood floor. Tina's stomach lurched. The second drop seemed to fall in slow motion and landed next to the first with a splat. Her knees buckled. Gage caught her by the waist, and she buried her face in his chest as the third drop fell to the floor.

"You all right?" He led her to the wall and propped her against it. "Do you need to sit down?"

"It's done." Allison capped the vial and slipped it into her pocket.

Tina swallowed the sour taste of bile from her mouth. "I'm okay. Are you sure it's gone?"

"I don't feel it anymore. Do you?" Allison said.

"No." Laughter bubbled from her throat. "We did it. We vanquished a demon." She threw her arms around her friend and hugged her tight. "We should call Logan. Maybe Trent's awake already."

"Uh, ladies?" Gage held a device in his hand. "Something's not right here."

As soon as the words left his lips, a pulse of energy shot through the room, slamming into Tina's chest and knocking her off her feet. The air *whooshed* from her lungs as her back slammed into the wall. She slid to the floor. One by one, the lights in the corners popped and dimmed in a shower of sparks. Gage grabbed a lantern by the portal and hauled Tina up by the arm. "Definitely not right."

Allison took the other still-lit lantern and barreled out

the door. Gage followed her out, but Tina stayed glued to the spot.

Whether it was fear or anger that kept her from running, she wasn't sure. Maybe it was a little of both. They'd done everything right. Gage had double-checked his research. This demon should have been back in hell.

It billowed in front of her, rising up into a vertical mass of fog. Angry heat coursed through her veins, and she threw out her fist, scattering the smoke. "You can't have Trent. He's mine."

The fog reformed. Thicker. Blacker. The heaviness in the air pressed into her.

"Tina, come on," Allison yelled from the doorway. "You can't fight it like that."

"I will stop you." She took two steps back before turning on her heel and sprinting for the door, but something caught her foot. She went down inches from the exit. Gage pulled her hands, but the shadow had her by the leg. Her boot slipped off, and she scrambled to her feet, darting through the door.

They raced down the steps and onto the front porch. Tina leaned against the railing, but Allison dropped the lantern on the steps and marched toward the car.

Gage put his hand on Tina's shoulder. "Are you okay?"

She watched her friend get in the car and buckle her seatbelt. "What happened?"

"I think we pissed it off. Royally."

"No kidding. What's wrong with her?"

He picked up the lantern and let out a sigh. "She experiences this shit differently than you and me. No telling what she saw in there."

"Why didn't it work? Is it because we didn't *all* pour the blood onto the portal? Everything seemed to be going fine until then." If her stupid fear was the only thing keeping Trent in that coma…

"It's possible. But it's more likely that the blood has to come straight from the source. That Trent needs to recite the incantation and spill his own blood."

"Shit."

"Yeah."

Allison started the engine and honked the horn. Tina hugged Gage. "I'll call you."

"Take care of her."

"Always." She limped toward the car in one boot and a one stocking-foot. The shadow was trying to take her boyfriend, and now it had her favorite boot. There would be hell to pay.

## CHAPTER TWENTY

*A*llison didn't say a word on the drive back to the hospital, no matter how many times Tina tried to get her to talk. Tina followed her through the parking garage and into the hospital elevator. Allison pushed the button for the fourth floor and grumbled under her breath.

Tina threw her hands in the air and let out an exasperated breath. "What, Allie? Why won't you talk to me?"

Allison clenched her fists. "I knew this wasn't going to work."

"How did you know?"

"Because I felt it in my gut." She squared her gaze on Tina. "And every time I ignore my gut feelings, something bad happens that could have been prevented."

"Nothing bad happened." The elevator doors slid open, bringing in a gust of chilly, sterile hospital air. "Our plan didn't work, but we can try again."

Allison let her breath out in a huff and marched down the hall, stopping outside Trent's room. "You could have been killed. We all could have. And if you'd listened to me, rather than rushing in like some vigilante ghost-busting cowboy, it could have been avoided."

Tina clenched her jaw and glared at her friend. How dare she fault Tina for trying to save the man she loved? "Put yourself in my shoes, Allie. If Logan were lying unconscious in that bed right now, what would you do? Would you be calm and rational? Or would you be doing everything in your power to help him, whether it put your own life in danger or not?"

Allison closed her eyes and took a deep breath. "Rational thinking does seem to fly out the window when our loved ones are in danger, doesn't it?" She flashed an apologetic smile and held out her hands. "May I?"

"Sure." Tina placed her hands in Allison's. It had been ages since her friend had read her like this. She watched as Allison's eyelids fluttered shut and she swayed slightly from side to side. The energy around her felt like a magnet, pulling Tina in.

Funny. She'd never felt anything when Allison read her before.

Allison opened her eyes and smiled sadly. "I'm sorry I snapped at you. I would feel the same way if Logan were the one in a coma." She wiped a tear from her cheek and wrapped her arms around her.

Tina had managed to hold it together all morning, but that one tear sliding down her best friend's cheek opened the floodgates. Her throat felt as if she'd swallowed a wad of cotton, and the tearing pain in her chest ripped open even more. "I love him so much, Allie."

"I know."

"What are we going to do? I can't live without him. I don't know how I've made it as long as I have."

"Hey." Allison put her hands on her shoulders and looked her in the eyes. "We're going to fix this."

"How?" Hopelessness consumed her. Guilt gnawed at her heart. She felt useless. She'd let Trent down, and she had no idea how to help him now.

This whole ordeal was her fault. Trent had wanted to sell the house to a flipper, to get rid of it as soon as possible, and she'd talked him into hanging onto to it. All to make a few more bucks. If she'd listed it when he'd asked her to, none of this would have happened. If she had listened to him instead of being so stubborn…

"I want to do a past-life regression with you." Allison opened the door and motioned for Tina to follow her into the room. "I think you have a connection to the house. Your energy is way too strong there for the short amount of time you've spent in the place."

"Wait." She paused in the doorway. "You think I lived there in a past life?"

Logan tossed a magazine on a table and rose to his feet as they shuffled in. "How did it go?"

"Not good." Allison gave him a kiss and turned to Tina. "I do. It's the only way to explain the energy I feel and the way the shadow feels about you."

Logan narrowed his eyes. "How does the shadow feel about her?"

A sinking feeling formed in Tina's stomach. If she was one of the former residents in another life, that would mean…*Oh, no.* "If I lived there before, that means I'm related to Trent."

Allison shrugged. "Distantly, maybe."

Logan chuckled. "Tina and Trent are related?"

"That's gross, Allie." Tina rubbed her arms to chase away the icky feeling forming in her veins. "I don't want to know if I'm related to him. What if we're cousins or something?"

Allison shook her head. "It would be so distant, it wouldn't matter."

Logan ran a hand through his hair. "Will you girls please stop ignoring me and tell me what's going on?"

Allison told him what happened at the house. "And I think Tina is connected to all this in a much deeper way than we originally thought. So we're going to do a past-life regression to see if she can remember anything."

"Shit." He pulled Allison into a hug and kissed the top of her head. "On that note, do you mind if I go grab some dinner?"

"Sure." Allison looked at the clock. "Be back in an hour? We should be done by then."

He raised a hand to Tina. "Good luck."

"I'm going to need it." She plopped into the chair next to Trent's bed and laced her fingers through his. Feeling the warmth of his skin and watching the rise and fall of his chest sent a flood of reassurance through her body. He was only sleeping, and she *would* figure out how to wake him up. "Tell me what to do."

Allison pulled a chair across from Tina and settled into it. "This isn't stage hypnosis. In fact, it's not hypnosis at all. You'll be in complete control of yourself the entire time. If it gets too intense, all you have to do is open your eyes, and you'll be back in the present. Now take five slow, deep breaths with me."

Tina closed her eyes and inhaled deeply as Allison counted.

"In two, three, four, five. And out two, three, four, five."

She repeated the breathing count four more times, and warm, liquid relaxation flowed through her body.

"I'm going to take you into a meditative state, but in order to do that, you need to be completely relaxed. We're going to start with your feet and work our way up."

Allison guided her through relaxing every muscle in her body, from her toes to the top of her head. When she reached her fingers, Tina relaxed her grip on Trent's hand but kept her palm resting in his. Wherever Allison was about to take her in her mind, she needed Trent's touch to ground her to the present. To the time that really mattered.

"Now, I'm going to count backwards from ten. As I do, I want you to picture the house in your mind and imagine the numbers floating away, evaporating into vapor."

As Allison slowly counted, Tina imagined the house. She pictured the façade, with its cheerful blue paint and crisp white trim. A little girl with blonde ringlets and a yellow dress giggled as she ran up the front steps into the house.

Tina could barely focus on the numbers as she followed the girl into the foyer and hung her scarf on a familiar coat rack by the door. The rest of the furniture she hadn't seen before, but it held a strange familiarity that made no sense at all. Was she really seeing something from a past life? Or was her mind only telling her stories? Keeping her eyes closed and her body relaxed, she gently parted her lips to speak. "Allie, how do I know if what I'm seeing is a past life or if it's just my imagination?"

"How are you seeing things? Can you see yourself… your body…there in the image? Or does it seem like you're looking at things through your own eyes, like you're actually there?"

Tina took a deep breath and focused on the image. In her mind, she glanced around the room. The only person she saw was the little blonde girl, lying on the floor, playing with a wooden doll. She raised her hands in front of her face and focused on the ring adorning her left hand. A brilliant round diamond perched atop a gold setting shaped like the petals of a flower. On either side of the stone, the band formed the shape of a bud with intricately designed leaves accenting it. The little girl giggled, pulling Tina's attention away from the ring, and darted up the stairs.

"I think I'm seeing through my own eyes. I can't see my face."

"You're in a past life. Look around. What does the house look like? The furniture? Can you figure out the time period?"

She walked into the living room and turned a circle. "The furniture is an old style. Thick upholstery. Heavy, dark wood. But not creepy-looking like the furniture from Trent's uncle. It's pretty, and it looks brand new. Like it hasn't been used much. And it doesn't look very comfortable." Hadn't she seen it in a dream?

"That sounds typical for the time period when the house was built. Now, I want you to focus on the people. Is there anyone else in the house?"

"There's a little girl. About four years old, maybe."

"Focus on her. Does she feel like anyone you know?"

Tina walked to the staircase and peered up to the second floor. "Mabel." The name danced on her lips as if she'd said it thousand times, but how did she know the child's name?

The girl appeared on the landing. *"Mommy?"*

Tina gasped. "I was her mom."

"And you know her name," Allison said. "This is good. Stay there. Who else lives in the house with you?"

She tore her gaze away from Mabel and scanned the room. "No one else is here."

"Single moms living in big, Victorian homes weren't common in the 1800s. You probably had a husband. Focus on a male presence and tell me what you see."

The little girl ran down the hall, and Tina focused on the front door. A male presence. Mabel had to have a father. She inhaled deeply and tried to concentrate, relaxing her body and thinking only of the memories.

The door swung open, and a man walked in. He wore a tailored suit with an ascot tie, and… "Oh my God."

"Do you see a man?"

"I've seen him before. In a photograph. He's the original owner of the house." The man regarded her and hung his coat on the rack. The rack she remembered watching him carve.

"Do you know his name?"

"It's Cox. Cox Austin." Her heart sprinted. "So my name must be Bertha." Was it possible? The reason Tina loved the house so much was because she lived there in a past life. And the man she was married to… "He looks so much like Trent." Tears pooled in her eyes to see this man standing before her. Alive. Awake.

"Who does he *feel* like? He looks like Trent because they're related. Can you get closer to him? Feel his energy?"

In her mind, she walked to the man. He smiled and swept her into his arms, placing a tender kiss on her lips. *"How was your day, my love?"*

Tina breathed in a shaky breath. The taste of his lips. The way his arms felt wrapped around her. "He feels like Trent. Allie, he *is* Trent."

Her heart raced in hummingbird mode, and her mouth went dry. This couldn't be possible, yet it explained so much. Her feelings for Trent. The way they got along as if they'd known each other forever. How comfortable she felt with him in that house. "What does this mean?"

"Aside from explaining your connection to Trent and the house, not much. We need to go deeper. What is your relationship with the shadow? Where did it come from?"

She didn't want to think about the shadow. Right now, just for a moment, she had Trent in her arms again. "Can I stay here and hold him for a while?"

Allison let out a slow breath. "I know it's hard, babe, but you have to let him go. That version of Trent isn't real. And the real one needs your help."

In Tina's mind, she released her hold on the man she loved and wandered up the stairs. She tried to focus on the shadow, but she found herself in the child's room, sitting in the rocking chair. A wave of despair crashed down on her as she rocked the cold, lifeless body in her arms. A sob bubbled up from deep in her chest, lodging in her throat, as tears streamed down her cheeks. "She's dead. Oh, God."

"This is just a memory." Allison's voice sounded like a distant echo. "Put it on a movie screen in your mind. Separate yourself from it."

She did as her friend said, and moved the image of the dead child in her arms to a screen. The despair eased to sadness, but she couldn't stop the flow of tears. "Measles. She died from measles, Allie. We have vaccines for that now."

"Was the shadow involved? Focus on the shadow."

She concentrated on the monster. Facing the devil himself would have been better than reliving the death of her little girl. The air seemed to be sucked from her lungs as the memory flashed through her mind. The depression. The desperate need to see her daughter again. The failed séances and futile attempts at contacting her spirit through natural means that led to the botched ritual that opened the portal to the shadow.

As a lifetime of memories tumbled through her mind, she fought to catch her breath. How could she have done such a thing? No amount of desperation was excuse enough for the evil she'd unleashed. Her body shook. Her head pounded. It was too much to bear.

"Tina." Allison clutched her hand. "I'm going to bring you back now. I'm going to count from one to ten, and I want you to count with me. Come on...One... Two...Three..."

Tina forced the words through the dryness of her throat. "Four...Five...Six." Her voice came out as a croak.

"Seven...Eight..." Allison's voice grew louder. "You're becoming aware of your body. You can wiggle your fingers."

She squeezed Trent's hand and sucked in a breath. "Nine...Ten..."

"Open your eyes now. You're in the present, Tina. Wake up."

She tentatively opened her eyes, squinting against the harsh fluorescent lights. As her pulse slowed to a normal rate, the queasiness in her stomach subsided and she found her voice. "It all makes so much sense now. Allie, I know where the shadow came from. It—"

Trent's fingers wrapped around hers, and her heart

leapt to her throat. She jerked her head toward to the bed, her mouth gaping as his eyelids fluttered open.

He raked in a ragged breath and coughed. "Well, that was a wild ride."

His raspy voice sounded like a symphony to her ears.

Tina squealed and jumped to her feet, cupping his face in her hands. She gazed into his eyes—his *open* eyes—and ran her hands down his neck, across his chest, and back up to his face. "Trent. Oh, my God." She nuzzled her face into his neck, inhaling his warm, masculine scent as she clutched his shoulders. "You're awake."

The feeling of his arms sliding across her back to pull her into a hug made another round of tears spill down her cheeks. "Oh, Trent. I love you." She pulled away to look into his eyes. "Before anything else is said…I love you. I'm sorry I didn't tell you before, but I do. I love you."

He tucked a strand of hair behind her ear. "I know. I heard every word. I love you too."

Another sob bubbled from her chest, but now her tears were from elation. She pressed her lips to his, and this time he kissed her back. The knots in her stomach slowly began to untie, and the hollow pressure that had become a permanent fixture in her chest released its hold. She would never take those soft, full lips for granted again. She'd never take *him* for granted. She laid her head on his shoulder and let out a satisfied sigh. Trent was awake, and he was hers.

He ran his fingers through her hair and wiped a tear away from her cheek. "I don't think I've ever seen you cry."

"Don't get used to it. It doesn't happen very often." She lifted her head. "What happened? How are you awake?"

His laugh morphed into a dry cough. "I have so much to tell you, but could you get me some water first?"

"Of course." She pulled a half-empty bottle from her purse. "It's not cold, but I can ask the nurse for some ice."

"This is good." He took the bottle and drank the rest of the contents.

"I hate to be the one to break up your reunion," Allison said. "But I'm going to tell them he's awake." She slipped out the door.

Tina tossed the bottle in the trash and returned to her position on Trent's chest. She had her man back. Her revelation from the regression, the damn shadow monster…it could all wait. Right now…this moment was all that mattered.

"You know," Trent tightened his arms around her. "I had to become one for a few minutes for it to happen, but I finally saw a ghost."

## CHAPTER TWENTY-ONE

*T*rent didn't get the chance to explain anything before the doctors rushed in and swept him away for more testing. Another brain scan. An EKG. More blood drawn. He was beginning to feel more like a medical experiment than a human being.

Of course, the scan and the EKG came back normal, though it would be hours before the readings became official. At least they removed all the tubes they'd stuck in unspeakable places. All he had left was the IV in his arm, and that he could handle. It was nearing midnight by the time they wheeled him back to his room.

Tina sat curled up in the vinyl chair next to the bed. Her raven hair spilled across her face, and his fingers twitched with the urge to feel its softness. Though he'd drifted in and out of a dream state for God knew how long, every time Tina had touched him, she'd pulled him back to reality. He may not have been able to make his body respond, but his mind had been fully aware of every word she'd said. Her tears. Her cries to God to bring him back to her. Her despair had torn his heart to pieces, and there hadn't been a goddamn thing he could do about it.

She inhaled a sharp breath and popped her head up. Confusion clouded her eyes until her gaze landed on him. She smiled. "Is it time to go home?"

He moved from the stretcher to the bed and pushed the button to raise himself into a sitting position as the nurse typed something into the computer. "He's going to have to stay put for a while until we get all the results back. If everything looks good, he may be released tomorrow."

An orderly rolled the stretcher from the room, and the nurse followed him out the door.

Tina sat on the edge of the bed and held his hand, drawing it up to her mouth to kiss his fingers. Dark circles ringed her tired eyes, and her disheveled hair looked sexy as hell. But he knew Tina, and she must have been exhausted to not take notice of her own appearance.

"You should go home and get some rest. Between watching me sleep and fighting demons, you must be tired."

She looked at him like he was crazy. "Like hell I should. I'm not leaving unless they drag me out."

So persistent. So strong. Damn, he was a lucky man. "Then lie down with me." He scooted to the other side of the bed and lowered it flat.

Tina settled in next to him, resting her head on his shoulder, draping her leg across his. "Are you comfortable enough?" She rubbed her hand over his chest and inhaled deeply. "I don't want to keep you from sleeping."

He'd stay awake for the rest of his life if he could have Tina in his arms like this. "I doubt I'll be doing much sleeping. I've been out for…how long was I out?"

"About a day and a half." She yawned deeply and relaxed into his side.

He chuckled. "That explains why I'm not tired. That past life thing you did with Allison was intense. I didn't know you could take someone back with you like that."

Her only response was the steady rise and fall of her chest as she slept.

Pressing his lips to her forehead, he inhaled her delicious scent. It could wait. What mattered now was that Tina was in his arms again and he actually had control of his body so he could hold her.

He lost track of how long he lay there with her snuggled into his side. He counted six times a nurse came in to check on him, each one shaking her head disapprovingly at Tina curled up next to him. But no one forced her to move. He could've held her like this for the rest of his life —preferably not in a hospital bed—and cherished every second of it. Though a tiny spark of fear that he wouldn't be able to wake up again burned in his chest, the heaviness of his lids eventually overwhelmed him. He reluctantly closed his eyes and drifted to sleep.

He woke as Tina slid out of bed, and he turned onto his side and reached for her. "Where are you going?"

"I'm going to borrow your bathroom and clean myself up. I'm a mess."

Eye-level with her backside, he couldn't help but smile as she strode to the bathroom. The things he planned to do to that woman the second he got her home...

She paused by the door. "Allison just texted. She and Logan are on their way. We can talk about our new plan of attack once they get here." She slipped through the door and closed it behind her.

Trent sighed and raised his bed to a sitting position.

All the things he wanted to do to Tina would have to wait. He fiddled with the buttons on his bed, raising it up and down as the second hand on the clock ticked away. Lifting his arms over his head, he stretched the soreness from his muscles and rolled his neck. Damn, it felt good to move. A decent meal and a romp between the sheets with his favorite real estate agent would feel even better.

Tina emerged from the bathroom with a clean face, her once-tangled hair flowing in silky waves over her shoulders. A smile brightened her eyes when he caught her gaze, and his heart gave a squeeze.

She furrowed her brow and approached the bed. "Did you hear what I said to Allie about my past life?"

"I sure did, Bertha. I guess I'll have to find a new name for my car."

She frowned. "Your car is totaled."

He raised his eyebrows in feigned surprise. "Bertha didn't make it?"

She laid a hand on his shoulder. "I'm sorry. You gave her a good life while she was here."

"I did take good care of her, didn't I?"

"And at least now we know why you gave her such a hideous name...Cox." The corner of her mouth twitched as she pressed her lips together, suppressing a smile.

"Come here, Bertha." He tugged her to his chest, and she playfully swatted his shoulder.

"Don't call me that." She pulled away and laughed, but her face turned serious as she looked into his eyes. "I didn't tell Allison everything yet. About the shadow. About what I did...What *Bertha* did."

"I know. I saw your vision. I think you took me with you when you regressed." He cupped her face in his hand and stroked her soft cheek with his thumb. "And then you brought me back. You pulled me out of the eternal dream state I was stuck in and woke me up."

She held his hand to her face. "More than a hundred years later, and here we are again."

"Together at last."

"Forever."

He slid his gaze to her plump, pink lips, and his mouth watered with the urge to kiss her. "I would love to make out with you right now, but I haven't used a toothbrush in two days."

She pulled a small plastic container from her purse. "I just used it, but if you don't mind catching my cooties, you're welcome to freshen up."

"If you have cooties, I think I've already caught them." Swinging his legs over the side of the bed, he rose to his feet. He expected the room to spin as he stood, but other than a little bit of stiffness from lying down so long, he felt fine. Great, actually. He slipped the plastic claw-like monitor off his finger and took the toothbrush from Tina. "I'll be right back."

"I'm not going anywhere."

The minty toothpaste worked wonders on the cat-litter taste that had occupied his mouth since he woke up. He splashed some water on his face, careful to avoid the bandage, and tousled his hair. He had definitely looked better, but with no hair brush and wearing a pale blue hospital gown, this was as good as it was going to get. At least now he could actually kiss his woman without his breath knocking her out. And man, was he planning a good, long kiss.

He opened the bathroom door, and Logan pulled him into a bear hug. And now the kissing would have to wait. He held back his disappointed sigh as his friend held him by the shoulders. The sheer happiness in Logan's eyes filled Trent's heart with gratitude. Every time Tina had left his side to fight the demon, Logan had been there for him.

"It's good to see you up and moving, man." Logan gave him another squeeze before Allison slipped between them.

"How are you feeling?" She kissed him on the cheek.

"Never better."

Tina took his hand and pulled him close. "Watch out, Allie. I haven't even gotten to kiss him yet. Not a real kiss anyway." She snaked her arms around his neck and pressed her lips to his.

She was warm and soft and he couldn't help but open up to let her in. So what if they had an audience? This was the reunion kiss he'd been waiting for. Her tongue brushed his, and heat coursed through his veins. God, he loved this woman.

Logan chuckled behind him. "Nice ass, man."

Tina slid her hands down his back, pulled open the hospital gown, and gripped his bare butt in her hands. "And it's all mine."

"Shit." He pulled the gown closed and dropped to the bed. "Sorry about that, Allison."

Allison shrugged. "It is a nice ass."

"Ha ha. You're all hilarious." His ears burned as he slid back onto the mattress and covered his lap with the blanket.

"They haven't released you yet?" Logan sat in a chair in the corner, and Allison moved to the other side of the bed.

"Nah. Still haven't gotten all the test results back. I thought about telling them it was a shadow demon causing all the trouble, but I figured they'd throw me in the psych ward if I told them the truth."

"The truth probably wouldn't be helpful in this case." Allison hovered her hands above Trent's head and closed her eyes. "Your block is back to normal. The way it was before the accident."

*Damn.* He slumped his shoulders. "So I'm not cured?"

"I'm afraid the only way to cure you is to vanquish the demon."

"Shit. Damn demon."

"I agree." Allison sat on the arm of Logan's chair.

Logan rested a hand on her knee. "What's the plan?"

Tina settled onto the edge of the bed next to Trent and pressed her lips together. He could only imagine how difficult this must have been for her to suddenly have to relive such a tragedy.

He took her hand. "Do you want to tell them about your regression? Then I can probably fill in the blanks with what I learned while I was out."

Tina inhaled deeply and blew out a hard breath. "I know where the shadow came from. Bertha summoned it."

Allison furrowed her brow. "Why would she do that?"

"The little girl. Mabel."

Trent squeezed her hand as the memories flooded his mind. The torment. The anguish. Though it didn't even happen in this lifetime, the raw emotions clawed at his soul as if the tragedy had just occurred.

Tina's lower lip quivered. "Bertha was distraught when Mabel died. She started calling in psychic mediums to summon her daughter, but Mabel's spirit had already moved on. No one could make contact with her."

Allison nodded. "That's common with children. Unless they've been through something traumatic, they haven't experienced enough in this realm for anything to hold them here. Child ghosts are very hard to contact."

He rubbed his hand across Tina's back, his heart aching at the way her voice trembled. She leaned into his side. "Well, Bertha decided to take matters into her own hands. She started studying witchcraft, searching for ways to manipulate energy to force her daughter back to our side."

"She made the portal," Allison said.

"She did. And like Gage said, she did it wrong. She messed up one of the symbols, and instead of pulling a human ghost through the gateway, she summoned the shadow. The defective symbol was supposed to represent the Austin family. To call to them. Instead, it bound the shadow to them." She sniffled.

Trent wrapped his arms around her, hoping his embrace provided enough comfort for her to continue. "It's okay."

Tina nodded. "She freaked out and was afraid to tell her husband what she'd done, so she tried to fix it herself. She attempted to close the portal, but all she managed to do was bind the shadow to the gateway in the third-floor room. She covered the drawing with a rug, and the shadow has been collecting the spirits of everyone who's lived in the house since." She leaned her head against Trent's shoulder as if merely telling the story exhausted her.

Logan scratched his head. "Then why didn't the shadow take Bertha and Cox's spirits too? If they were able to be reborn, they aren't trapped in the attic, right?"

"That's right," Allison said. "Do you know how they managed to get away?"

Trent hugged Tina tighter and continued the explanation for her. "The shadow did its thing in the beginning, preying on their preexisting conditions, namely Bertha's maddening depression. The poor woman went nuts, and they moved to Virginia to be closer to her family. She died shortly after they moved. Cox sold the house to his brother, and that line of Austins are the ones who are trapped in the attic."

Logan arched an eyebrow skeptically. "And you got all this from a past life regression?"

"There's more," Trent said. "After my accident, when my heart stopped beating for a few minutes, I died."

"No, you didn't." Tina pulled away and looked him hard in the eyes. "You did not die. Don't even say that."

The anguish in Tina's gaze tore at his heart. Though he was certain he'd crossed over to the spirit world, he couldn't bear to see his lover in pain. He brushed a strand of hair away from her face. "Then maybe I was hallucinating, but I talked to the ghost lady without a hand. Turns out, she's my great aunt Lucy. Jack's wife. Her heart condition and her daughter's aneurism…the shadow used their illnesses to kill them and trap their souls.

"Jack became a recluse in his depression. He eventually found the portal and figured out there was a demon in his house." Trent looked at Allison. "Apparently, he had his own psychic abilities, and he was able to communicate with the shadow. He made a deal with the devil, so to say."

Tina sucked in a sharp breath. "That's why your uncle left the house to you. He knew you were Cox."

"Exactly. Remember when I said the handful of times I'd seen him in life, he'd been so creepy I was afraid of him? Turns out those creepy vibes were because he was reading us all, trying to find Cox and Bertha. The shadow promised him if he delivered our spirits, when Jack died, he'd get to see his wife and daughter again."

Allison pressed her fingers against her temples. "So when you said it felt like someone was whispering in your ear, telling you to call Tina to help you sell the house…"

"That, I don't know. Uncle Jack had never met Tina, so I don't know how he could have known it was her."

Tina clenched her fist. "The shadow knew. I've had dreams about that thing since I was a little kid. It must have put the idea in your head."

His stomach ached with regret. "I'm so sorry I got you involved in this."

She shook her head. "Don't be. I'm part of it, and I still would be, whether you got me involved or not." She laced her fingers through his. "And if you hadn't called me, I might have spent the rest of my life living fifteen minutes away from the man I'm meant to be with and not even realizing it."

Trent's chest burned as anger ignited inside him. He'd put his friends' lives in danger. Every time one of them stepped foot inside that house, they could've been killed. Hell, maybe the shadow had ahold of one of them now. What if Tina had a latent heart condition she was unaware of and the shadow was slowly destroying her body like it was trying to do to his?

He shifted forward to rest his feet on the floor. He'd been in this bed far too long while his friends had been risking their lives for him. "It's too dangerous for you to go back there. For any of us to. We need to board the place up and forget about it."

"We can't do that." Tina stood and faced him. "We have to vanquish it. It took my favorite boot. You know how I feel about those boots." She fisted her hands on her hips.

Trent rose to his feet, and the gown gaped in the back, the draft sending a chill up his spine. He reached behind to close it and sat back down. "Where the hell are my clothes?"

Logan lifted a backpack from the chair. "I brought you some. But you should wait and see if they're going to release you."

"They're going to release me. They can't hold me here against my will." Fisting the gown shut at ass level, Trent marched toward the bathroom, snatching the bag from Logan's hands along the way. "And then we're going to bulldoze the place to the ground and burn the scraps."

He slammed the door and fumbled with the ties on his gown. Ripping it off, he shoved his legs into his jeans and finished getting dressed. There was no way in hell he'd allow his friends to endanger their lives for his family curse. He'd destroy the place and be done with it. Then he'd take Tina to Mexico, marry her on the beach, and they'd live happily ever after. End of story.

He peered at his face in the mirror. Peeling the bandage from his forehead, he found the cut had been glued rather than stitched shut. A clear layer of film covered the angry, red mark above his eyebrow, but no trace of blood remained. He let his hair fall over his forehead, concealing the cut, and tossed the bandage in the trash.

As he opened the door, a hushed silence fell across the room. His friends' straight faces told him they'd been scheming, but he couldn't let them go back to that house.

"Feel better now?" Logan asked.

"Much." But the tension in the room thickened like pudding.

Tina wrapped her arms around him and slid her hands down to his back pockets. "I preferred the easy access of the gown, personally."

Her flirtatious smile and sensual touch were almost enough to distract him from his plan. Almost. "I'll give you all the access you want as soon as we get home. But now, I need my phone so I can call a demolition company."

Tina bit her bottom lip and looked at Allison. "Tell him what you told us, Allie."

"Destroying the house isn't going to destroy the portal. The etchings in the wood—even the wood itself—are only symbolic. Just like the ghost of your Aunt Lucy isn't really missing a hand. It's how she presents herself because, since she's attached to the space, part of her stays behind even when she stretches away to leave."

Allison sank into a chair and folded her hands in her lap. "The portal is made of energy. And the energy will remain whether the house is there or not. Which means the shadow will still be in our dimension and it will still have a hold on you."

*The hell it will.* He was done playing with monsters. "A hold on me how? I'm awake now. Tina brought me back with her when she woke from her regression. She pulled me out of the dream state I was stuck in. She saved me from the shadow."

Tina brushed his hair off his forehead. "But the shadow is still affecting your brain. Allie still feels the block."

"So, I'll have to deal with sleep attacks every now and then. I've dealt with them before. I'd rather live the rest of my life with my narcolepsy flaring up than risk your lives any more than I already have."

Allison gave him a sympathetic look. "Your life won't be very long if we don't stop this thing. It's going to kill you. And then it will kill Tina."

His heart gave one solid beat in his chest before lodging itself in his throat. Of course the monster would go after Tina. She wasn't an Austin, but she had been in a past life. It was one thing for him to have to deal with the demon for the rest of his life, but there was no way in hell he'd let that thing go after his woman. "You think your ritual will work if I provide the blood myself?"

"It has to," Allison said. "We got it inside the portal before. We just couldn't seal it. Hopefully, with you there reciting the words and providing the blood, it will work." She chewed her lower lip, the uncertainty in her eyes less than reassuring. "Did you ever check out what was in his safe deposit box?"

"We only went through the stuff in storage. Other than the list Tina found with my name on it—which apparently *was* a list of ghosts in the attic—there wasn't anything of use."

Allison nodded. "It's worth checking into before we go back."

The door swung open, and a doctor with white hair and a matching lab coat entered the room. "Good news, Mr. Austin. Your tests came back normal, so we're going to release you." He paused and raked his gaze over Trent's clothes. "But apparently, you already knew that."

Tina squeezed his bicep. "We were hopeful."

The doctor scanned his tablet and pressed a few buttons on the screen. "Someone will be in shortly with your release papers. You'll need to check in with your own doctor tomorrow, and if you feel anything out of the ordinary, let us know."

"Will do, doc. Thanks." Though a demon messing with his brain probably wasn't what the doctor meant.

The door opened again, and as the doctor slipped out, a male nurse shuffled in. Tina stiffened, dropping her arms to her sides, and the nurse's face reddened as he lowered his gaze to the floor. Trent didn't need to read the guy's nametag to know this was Steve, the one who drew his blood yesterday.

Steve cleared his voice. "Uh, Mr. Austin, I have your release papers. If you could sign there." He handed Trent a stack of papers and a pen.

Trent pressed his lips together, fighting his smile. "Thanks."

Tina rested her hand on the small of Trent's back. "Hi, Steve." Her voice was small, full of shame or embarrassment. He wasn't sure which.

"Hey." Steve barely lifted his fingers in a pathetic wave before turning his gaze to Trent. "There's a prescription for pain meds in there if you need it."

"I appreciate it, man." He passed the pen and signature page to the nurse.

Steve cast one last uncomfortable glance at Tina and scurried out the door.

Trent chuckled. "Well, that was awkward."

"I…it was…" Tina's brow knit in humiliation. "You didn't happen to be listening when we took your blood, did you?"

"I did. You were really laying on the charm. Should I be jealous?"

She clutched his ass and pulled his hips to her. "You've got nothing to worry about."

"Good." He slid his arms around her and pressed his lips to hers. Even he wouldn't have fallen for Tina's pathetic attempt at flirting with the nurse. He almost felt bad for the guy.

Allison cleared her voice, and he reluctantly released his hold.

Tina looked at her. "Well, Velma, the mystery is solved. Let's load up the Mystery Machine and go bust the bad guy."

Logan crossed his arms. "She can be Velma if she wants, but I am still not being Shaggy."

Trent laughed. "Don't look at me. I'm way too hot to play that role."

Tina rolled her eyes. "You can both be Fred, but I'm going need a shower before we go."

"Me too." Trent lifted an eyebrow at Tina. After spending nearly forty-eight hours asleep, feeling her soft, soapy hands all over his body would be just the welcome back to reality he needed.

"Well, then." She ran her hands up his chest. "Want to come home with me?"

Blood rushed to his groin, tightening his jeans. Thank goodness he'd changed out of that hospital gown. "That sounds like an excellent idea."

Allison cleared her voice. "I think an even better idea would be for me to go home with Tina, and Logan can take you back to our place to get ready. I'd like to vanquish this entity while it's still daylight."

Tina stuck out her bottom lip. "Oh, Allie, you always ruin the fun." She sighed and stepped away from him. "She has a point though."

"And you guys can stop by the bank to check out the

safe deposit box on your way." Allison picked up her purse.

He didn't like it. Those women had a tendency to take matters into their own hands, and his overwhelming need to protect them both had his nerves on edge. "All right. But no one steps foot inside that house without me. If you get there before us, wait in the car."

Allison gave him a mock salute. "Yes, sir."

He held Tina with a firm gaze. "I'm serious, sweetheart. We're in this together, so we fight it together. Promise you'll wait for me?"

She kissed his cheek. "I promise."

## CHAPTER TWENTY-TWO

*T*ina sat behind the wheel of her Mustang and focused her gaze on the chip in her light pink nail polish. As soon as all this was over, she'd have to treat herself to a spa day. A deep-tissue massage, a mani/pedi, and a hair cut would get her back into shape. Not that Trent seemed to mind when she was a mess.

A glance in the mirror in the hospital room had nearly caused her to faint; she'd looked so hideous. But with the way Trent looked at her, she never would've known she'd been so disheveled. His eyes held so much love and passion. No one had ever looked at her the way he did.

"How did we get so lucky, Allie?"

Allison inhaled deeply and opened her eyes.

"Oh, sorry. Were you meditating?"

"Not really. I was just thinking the same thing. These guys were meant for us."

She smiled. "And when the universe wants something to happen, it happens."

"Exactly."

She picked at her chipped polish. "I'm worried about

him going in there. If the shadow wants him dead, how are we going to stop it?" An image of what the shadow had done to Gage flashed through her mind, and her throat tightened. "Can't he just yell the incantation from the front yard or something?"

"I wish we all could. But we need his blood to seal the portal, and we already know it won't work if it doesn't come straight from him."

The sensation of a thousand spiders crawling across her skin made her shiver. Her stomach turned at the mere thought of seeing blood coming from Trent…or anyone. "I want to be there for him. I want to protect him. But if I pass out when he cuts himself…"

Allison took her hand. "So don't watch. Logan will be shielding him. I'll make sure he stays in the salt ring. Gage is bringing new bulbs and batteries for all the lights, and now that we know what to do, we can work quickly. You can do this, girlfriend. I have faith in you."

She could, couldn't she? Wonder Woman could do anything she set her mind to, and so could Tina. She took a deep breath, the nauseating fear churning in her stomach turning to a solid chunk of resolve. "You're right. I can. I have to, so there's no point in worrying about it."

Logan's Mercedes pulled into the drive, followed by Gage's Jeep. Tina sprang from her seat and threw herself into Trent's arms before he could shut the car door.

"Whoa." He chuckled. "I missed you too."

"I love you. If anything happens to you in there…"

"Hey." He gripped her shoulders and pushed her away to look in her eyes. "I promise we are going to make it through this. We have a trip to Mexico to plan, remember? You're not going without me."

"Damn right I'm not." She intended to spend the rest

of her life with this man, and nothing—demon, ghost, or otherwise—could stop her. She slipped her hand into his, and they met the others on the porch. "Did you find anything in the safe deposit box? Uncle Jack wasn't hiding a shadow buster in there all this time, was he?"

The corner of his mouth twitched. "Nothing like that, unfortunately. Just some old jewelry and a few gold coins. Valuables that had been passed down for generations."

"Damn."

Trent squeezed her hand. "Everyone knows what to do?"

"Same as before," Gage said. "Only faster and more effective."

Tina placed her hand on Logan's shoulder. "You promise you'll shield him?"

Logan cast a wary glance at his fiancée.

"He needs you more than I do," Allison said. "I'll be fine."

Logan nodded. "I'll do my best."

"All right, gang." Tina slid the key into the lock and pushed open the door. "Let's get this over with." She stepped into the foyer, and her heart slammed into her throat. Everything looked the same. The pristinely-decorated living room sat undisturbed to her right. To her left, she caught a glimpse of the cheerful yellow kitchen, but a heaviness in the air she'd never noticed before enveloped her as she tip-toed deeper into the home.

She eyed the coat rack as she passed it, expecting it to topple over at any moment. Though the antique piece of wood didn't budge, she opted to lay her coat across the back of the couch. The others followed her lead, leaving their belongings in the living room while Gage hauled his bag of supplies up the stairs.

Trent stepped toward her and took her hand, but he stumbled. She caught him around the waist before he could hit the floor.

Logan clutched his shoulder. "I guess you need that shield now, my friend."

Trent let his breath out in a huff. "I'm okay."

"No, you're not." Tina's throat thickened. "It's already affecting you. There has to be another way." She grabbed his arm and pulled him toward the door.

He held his ground while Logan's grip on his shoulder remained. "There is no other way." He tugged her to his chest. "We'll do this together."

"Okay." She pinned Logan with a hard stare. "Don't let him go."

"I won't."

"Lamps are burning and so is daylight," Gage called from the top of the stairs. "Let's get this show on the road."

"He's right." Allison started up the stairs. "If it's already getting to Trent, we need to move fast."

Dread turned Tina's blood to ice, but she followed her friend, with Trent and Logan right behind.

"I think you can let me go now, man," Trent said as he slipped his hand into Tina's.

"Physical contact makes it easier for me to share the shield," Logan said. "So, I'm either going to hold your shoulder or hold your other hand. Your choice."

The pressure in the house seemed to thicken the closer they got to the top of the stairs. Nausea churned in Tina's stomach as she forced herself to place one foot above the other. "Any way you can shield all of us?" Her voice cracked with nervousness.

Logan shook his head. "I'm not even an expert at shielding myself. Shit still slips through sometimes."

"That's reassuring." Tina stopped outside the door and squeezed Trent's hand.

"He has more control over his ability than he realizes," Allison said. "And he's getting stronger every day. I've never met anyone who could extend his personal protection to another person."

Allison crept into the room and motioned for the others to join her. Tina stuck close by Trent's side, her leg muscles tightening, involuntarily preparing to bolt at the first sign of trouble, until she spotted her boot lying in the corner.

Scratch marks were etched into the leather, and the heel had broken off. She gritted her teeth as the heat of anger flushed through her body. "Bastard. I didn't know it had claws."

"I'm sure it can do worse, and I don't want to waste time getting to know it." Allison poured a ring of salt around them all. "This is a circle of protection. Nothing may harm us inside this circle."

Static electricity built in the air, and a pounding formed in Tina's head. Something told her a simple ring of salt wouldn't do much good against a soul-trapping demon. "Do you think the shadow plays by the rules?"

Allison set the salt container on the floor. "Probably not, but it's worth a try."

Gage handed everyone a paper with the incantation, and they all recited the words. Halfway through the first recitation, the floor began to rumble beneath Tina's feet. Negative energy buzzed in the air, and though the walls didn't move, she couldn't shake the sensation they were closing in around her. The pounding in her head grew harder. Harder. Until it felt like her brain would bust through her skull.

She clutched her head with one hand and tried desperately to focus on the words swimming on the page before her. The room seemed to spin as she glanced at each of her friends. The strained looks on their faces said they felt the effects too. "It knows what we're doing."

Allison touched her elbow. "Finish the incantation."

Tina forced the words through her tightening throat to finish the first chant with the others.

An emptiness formed in the center of the portal. Hollow. Magnetic. If she threw herself into it now, would the skull-splitting pounding in her head stop? Could she end the torment by sacrificing herself to the shadow? If she gave in…if she let it take her, maybe her friends would be safe. She leaned toward the gateway.

"Don't even think about it." Allison tightened her grip on Tina's hand, and a pulse of energy shot through her arm, slamming into her chest.

Tina shook herself, coming out of the trance and planting her feet firmly on the floor. "Thanks, Allie."

They started the second incantation, and the first light in the corner shattered. The shadow billowed in the small strip of darkness, its tendrils reaching out toward the light, only to be jerked back again as soon as it touched it.

Allison's eyes grew wide. "The spirits are here. Oh, God, it's tormenting them."

Flashes of images appeared to Tina. Fractions of seconds gave her glimpses of the ghosts howling in pain. "Don't listen to them. Don't listen to them, Allie."

Allison squeezed her eyes shut and clutched her head. "He won't stop hurting them. He wants them all. They say… No…oh, God. I see Jack with the shadow. If we give him Trent, he'll get to see Lucy and Emily again. He can't see them now. The shadow's keeping them apart. It's..." She dropped to her knees. "Stop. Please stop screaming."

Tina's heart wrenched at the pain in her best friend's eyes. She was helpless against Allison's visions. What could she do?

"Allison." Logan knelt, clutching her to his chest. "Don't channel, baby. Block them out. Let's finish the incantation."

"Oh, shit." Trent's knees buckled beneath him.

Tina caught him by the arm and lowered him to the ground. His entire body fell limp, but his eyes remained open. "Trent! Talk to me. Are you okay?"

No response.

"Trent!"

The shadow demon churned in the corner. Trent stared emptily at the ceiling.

Tina held his face in her hands. "Please say something, baby."

"Is he breathing?" Gage dropped to his knees and rested a hand on Trent's chest. "He's alive. Who's got the blade?"

"Here." Logan slid a razor blade across the floor.

Gage picked it up. "We need to finish the incantation."

"We need to get Trent out of here." She looped her arms beneath his and started to tug him toward the door.

"We need his blood first." Gage grabbed Trent's hand and dug the blade into his flesh. Thick, red liquid pooled on the cut and oozed across his palm.

The room spun. Tina's vision tunneled, and her stomach lurched. She stumbled to her knees. Dear lord, this was it.

They'd lost.

Allison pinched her hard on the back of the arm.

"Ouch!" Tina blinked. The room stilled.

"You are not passing out on us now." Tears filled Allison's blood-shot eyes as she rose to her feet and handed Tina the paper. "Read."

Tina held Trent's good hand and turned away from the blood to read the third and final repetition of the incantation. The emptiness in the portal expanded like a vacuum, sucking the static energy into its center. All the air in the room seemed to go with it. She couldn't breathe.

Gage counted, "One…two…three drops of blood from the Austin bloodline. That should do it." He dropped Trent's hand and rose to his feet. "So why is nothing happening?"

"And why is Trent still not moving?" Logan scooped him into his arms and started toward the door.

"Wait." Tina tightened her grip on Trent's hand.

The floorboards rumbled. The vacuum reversed, flooding the room with an electric charge so thick and heavy, she could hardly move. The pressure intensified until her ears rang and her skin buzzed. The single darkened corner grew darker. The shadow began to reform.

It didn't work. The portal didn't seal.

Tina shot to her feet.

Three drops from an Austin. From the bloodline of the person who opened the portal. That should have sealed it.

She clutched her pounding head.

But an Austin *didn't* open the portal. Bertha did. And she was only an Austin by marriage.

"We need to get him out of here." Logan moved toward the door.

"Wait." She grabbed his elbow. "We need to do the

incantation one more time." And pray she'd be able to accomplish what she was about to do.

"His blood didn't work," Allison said. "We need to get him away from the shadow's influence."

"His blood didn't work because it's not *his* blood that we need. It's mine."

"Of course." Allison picked up the razor blade. "If Bertha didn't have any more children after Mabel, then Trent is only related to her by marriage."

She swallowed the grapefruit-sized lump in her throat. "And I *am* Bertha. I have her soul."

"One more time. Quick," Logan said. And they all recited the chant.

The shadow fought, the push and pull of energy in the air creating a dizzying, nauseating effect. Tina needed to spill her blood on the portal and end this before everyone blacked out.

Allison held up the razor. "Do you need me to do it?"

Tina took the blade. "If Bertha did it all herself, I should too." She held her arm over the portal and squeezed her eyes shut. As she pressed the edge against her hand, sharp pain sliced through her palm, and something warm rolled across her skin. *Don't think about it. Don't think about it.*

"And three," Allison said.

The hollowness in the center of the room expanded, making the entire chamber feel like a void. A pulse of energy rippled out from the portal. Every light in the room exploded into a shower of sparks.

"Into the hallway," someone shouted, and Tina felt herself being tugged into the light. Logan lay Trent on the rug and pressed a cloth against his hand. A burning sensation drew Tina's attention to her own hand. A trail of bright red blood oozed from her palm to her wrist.

Her stomach lurched. The room tipped on its side.

---

Trent lay there, staring at the ceiling, as his friends bustled around him. He'd heard everything that went on in the attic, but his paralyzed view of the rafters above gave him no visual clues to whether or not they'd won. Had they defeated the shadow? Or were they in the hall because the monster still churned in the darkness?

"Oh, Tina," Allison said. "Therapy works wonders for problems like this." Her voice sounded calm. Almost amused, without a hint of panic. Her shoes made a shuffling sound on the carpet as she approached him. She hovered her hands above his head, and a warm, liquid melting sensation spread through his skull.

He squeezed his hands into fists and released them. He wiggled his toes and bent his knees. Allison's face appeared above his, and she smiled. "The energy block in your head is gone. Can you get up?"

"Yeah." He pushed himself into a sitting position. Logan knelt beside Tina, taping a bandage to her hand. Gage moved in and out of the room, carrying his lights and equipment and arranging it into a bag, grumbling something about how much lantern bulbs cost.

"This is a liquid bandage." Allison reached for his hand. "It will sting a little, but it'll stop the bleeding faster."

He winced as she applied the liquid to his skin with a tiny brush. Tina still sat with her back to him. She hadn't spoken his name. Hadn't so much as cast a glance his way.

Was she disappointed in him for collapsing? Had she finally decided his illness was too much of a weakness?

Allison taped a bandage over his sealed wound and leaned toward his ear. "She has her back to you because she's afraid she'll pass out again if she sees the blood on your hand."

"Oh." The tightness in his chest released.

"Sorry." Allison rose to her feet. "I'm not trying to read you, but my nerves are kind of raw right now."

"It's okay." He stood and examined the bandage on his hand. Not a trace of blood remained.

Allison stepped to Logan and slid her arm around his waist. "It's all cleaned up, Tina. I think you're safe."

Tina scrambled to her feet and raced toward him. He caught her in his arms as she slammed into his chest and showered his face in kisses. She laughed and draped her arms over his shoulders. "We did it. Do you feel that? It's gone. Close your eyes. Can you feel the energy?"

He closed his eyes and focused on the air around him. If there was some magical energy floating in the atmosphere, he was oblivious to it. "I don't feel anything."

"Exactly." She rested her head on his shoulder, pressing her body to his and holding him tight.

His mind flashed back to the first time they'd embraced in this hallway, after Tina's encounter with the shadow. She'd felt so right in arms then. She felt even more so now. His strong, independent woman had stopped a shadow demon from stealing his soul. She'd saved his life. And his afterlife.

"What about the ghosts?" Gage zipped his bag and set it near the stairs. "Did they jet when the demon left?"

"Some of them did," Allison said. "Do you have my crystal?"

Gage rummaged through his bag and pulled out the egg-shaped stone.

"Some of them are going to need our help. I can do it on my own, but it would be easier if we all did it together."

"Wait," Tina said. "We're going to open another portal?"

"This one will be exit only," Allison said. "But there are a lot of ghosts, and I could use some grounding energy."

Tina clung to Trent's arm as they crept back into the room. No electric buzzing in the air greeted them. His arm hairs didn't stand on end. The walls didn't feel as if they were closing in. Instead, the room felt like…a room.

Tina relaxed her grip and let out a slow breath. "This room feels so normal. Normal in here feels weird."

Allison set the crystal on the floor by the wall and motioned for them all to join her. Trent stood between the women, holding each of their hands to complete the circle. "Don't we need salt?"

"These spirits are anxious to leave. I don't think they're going to cause us any problems." Allison took a deep breath and stared at the wall. "Everyone focus on the crystal and imagine a white light coming down from the sky. This is a portal to the other side. Any spirits still residing in this house should step into the light and cross over."

Tina gasped. "I see them. Do you see them?"

Trent looked at the wall. He could imagine the light around the crystal, but he didn't actually *see* it. He didn't see anything but a rock and a wall. He shook his head.

"There's your Aunt Lucy," Tina said. "She's waving. Oh! And she has her hand back."

"She wants to thank you both," Allison said. "She's

sorry about scaring you with the coat rack. Since neither of you could see her in the beginning, it was the only way she knew to communicate."

Trent chuckled. At least it wasn't all in his imagination. "I thought I was going crazy there for a while. No worries, though. I'm glad we could finally help."

"Jack is here too," Allison said.

He gritted his teeth as anger burned in his gut. The man had been out to get him his entire life. He'd almost succeeded. "Tell him to get his ass into the light and never come back."

"He wants to apologize. And he says he hopes that one day you'll love someone enough to understand why he did what he did."

The anger in his chest cooled to a mild disdain. He wanted to think that, if faced with the same circumstances, he'd make better decisions and not endanger other people. But he could definitely empathize with the man. He squeezed Tina's hand. "I already do."

He stood there for a while longer, watching Allison, Tina, and Logan looking in the direction of the wall, their eyes focusing on something…but nothing he could see. He gazed at the woman he loved, in awe of her newfound ability. "Can you really see them all?"

"In flashes. They come in and out, but yes. I see them. I thought it would be scary, but it's actually amazing."

Gage chuckled. "Don't feel bad. I can't see a thing either. I can show you how the equipment works. Sometimes that's just as cool."

"That's all of them." Allison released his hand. "And you're very grounded, Trent. If Tina ever decides to explore her ability, she'll need you."

Tina kissed him on the cheek. "I'll always need you."

He pulled his woman into a tight hug and looked over her shoulder at Allison. "So that's it? The house is clean? I can sell it now?"

"I'll do a general energy cleanse in each room, just to be sure. But I'm confident you won't be having any more trouble with spirits or shadow demons. Right, Gage?"

"According to my research, the portal disappears after a blood ritual like that. I think you're good to go."

CHAPTER TWENTY-THREE

"*I* had no idea you were such a good cook." Tina put the last of their dinner dishes in Trent's new stainless steel dishwasher and closed the door. She couldn't remember the last time she'd used her own stove. Most of the meals she ate in her apartment were either microwave or take out.

"It's not hard to master the BLT." He put the frying pan away and dried his hands on a pale-yellow dish towel. "Bacon, Lettuce, Tomato, Bread." He shrugged.

"But you do it with such style."

He tossed the towel onto his shoulder. "I felt like I needed to reclaim my kitchen. I started the fire cooking bacon…"

"So naturally, bacon had to be the first thing you cooked when it was rebuilt."

He winked. "Naturally."

She took the towel from his shoulder and hung it on a steel hook next to the extra-deep, sparkling porcelain sink. Pale yellow and slate gray tiles formed an alternating pattern on the backsplash that accented the granite countertops perfectly. "You'll have to give me the number of the contractor you used. They did an amazing job. Probably added ten grand onto the resale value."

He grinned and grabbed her ass, pulling her hips to his. "That's good to know." He lowered his lips to hers, kissing her long and deep. Goose bumps rose on her skin as he glided his fingers along her bare arms to slip them into her hair. "Speaking of reclaiming things...does all that burning sage and meditating that Allison did in the house really work? All the old energy is gone?"

Her thoughts scattered as she trailed her lips up his neck and nipped at his earlobe. "It's very hard for me to concentrate on talking when you're touching me like this." She slid her hands into his back pockets, and his arousal hardened against her hip.

He shivered, releasing his hold on her. "Sorry. Let's talk first."

"Do we have to?"

He took her hand and led her to the living room. "Is all the old energy really gone?"

She slipped her hands beneath his shirt, brushing her fingers across his muscular stomach. He was so warm. So sexy. His masculine scent drew her in, making her mouth water with the need to taste him. She couldn't keep her hands off him. "It's what Allison does. If she says it's gone, it is."

"And it works on everything?"

She sighed and dropped her hands to her sides. The look in his eyes told her there'd be no fun time until the conversation ended. "Furniture. Walls. Floors. Sure. Why?"

"Does it only work on wood? Or does it work on metal too?"

"It works on everything. Is something wrong?"

A seductive smile curved his lips as he reached into his pocket and pulled out a small metal object. He held it in his palm and offered it to her.

She picked up the familiar ring, admiring the intricate metal work and the sparkling diamond nestled in the center. "This is Bertha's wedding ring. How did you get this?"

"I found it in Uncle Jack's safe deposit box, and I recognized it from your past life regression. I assume, since Bertha didn't have any children to pass it on to, it went to Cox's brother's side when they died, and it's been passed down for generations. Allison cleared the old energy from it while you were outside."

The diamond sparkled under the recessed lights in Trent's living room, the gold flower buds glistening as she turned the ring over in her hand. "It's beautiful."

"Will you wear it?"

"Oh, I can't do that." She handed it back to him. "It was Bertha's *wedding* ring. It wouldn't be right for me to wear it."

His brow furrowed as he examined the ring. "But you *are* Bertha. Or you were at one time."

"I know. But it's her wedding ring. I can't."

He closed his hand around the jewelry and nodded. "I understand. I'll buy you a new one then."

Her heartbeat seemed to pause before slamming into her chest. "Wait. What?"

He shrugged. "If you don't want to wear this one, I'll buy you a new ring. We can go shopping together if you like."

She blinked, opening and closing her mouth, trying to

make her mind form a complete thought. "Are you…are you proposing?"

He chuckled. "Apparently, I'm not doing a very good job of it."

Pressure built in the back of her eyes, and a high-pitched giggle bubbled up from her throat. "Why didn't you say so? I didn't want to wear it because it was a *wedding* ring. If I'd known you were asking me to marry you, I'd be wearing it *now*."

"Well?" He held the ring toward her.

Of course she would marry him. But if she was going to say yes, he would have to do a better job of asking. She crossed her arms and shifted her weight to one foot. "You're going to have to ask me properly, mister."

He grinned and knelt on one knee. "Tina, I love you more than any man has ever loved a woman in the history of the world. I want to spend the rest of my life with you. And if I get another life after this one, I won't rest until I find you, so I can spend that one with you too. Will you marry me?"

She smiled as he slid the ring onto her finger. "Now that's a proper proposal."

He stood and wrapped his arms around her waist, pressing his forehead to hers. "Now give me a proper answer."

"Yes, Trent. I will marry you. In this life, and in the next." Gripping his shoulders, she jumped, linking her legs around his waist. He caught her by the butt and carried her to the bedroom as she kissed him.

They fell to the bed, his hands roaming her body, caressing her, sending electricity coursing through her veins. He slipped her shirt over her head and undid the front clasp of her bra, spreading it aside and cupping her breasts in his hands. The heat of his tongue bathed her sensitive nipples until they hardened like pebbles beneath his touch. His lips scorched her skin as he worked his way down her stomach and removed her pants.

She scooted to the center of the bed, her gaze never straying from his magnificent body as he slowly undressed for her. A beam of moonlight cut through the darkness of the room to illuminate his sculpted features as he stood before her, gloriously naked and erect. Like a statue perfectly carved from stone. But with the softness of a bear as he climbed onto the bed and wrapped her in the protective cage of his arms.

"You are the most beautiful woman in the world. Inside and out." His breath against her ear made her shiver, and as she wrapped her fingers around his length, his entire body shuddered.

"I'll take you inside now, if you don't mind."

He inhaled deeply and rolled on top of her. "Mmm…I don't mind at all." He held her gaze as he entered her, staring deep into her eyes, penetrating the depths of her soul. "I love you, Tina."

"I love you too." How easily the words came, passing from her heart across her lips as if she'd loved this man all her life. They fit together like they were made for each other. Certainly, they were.

Skin to skin, soul entwined with soul, their bodies joined as one.

"Oh, Tina." His raspy voice vibrated through her chest as he moved inside her. Delicious friction sent thrilling tingles shooting from her center down her legs and straight up to her heart. She tangled her fingers in his soft, dark hair and lifted her hips to meet his thrusts. Her orgasm crested like an ocean wave, crashing through her body with searing pleasure.

He shuddered inside her, a masculine growl vibrating from his chest as his own orgasm overtook him. His breath came in short pants, hot against her neck. As his muscles relaxed, his breathing slowed to a soft, rhythmic motion. Resting inside her, he lay utterly still, and she basked in his delicious, musky scent. She would never understand why she fought her feelings for this man for so long. He was everything she would ever need.

Several minutes passed, and he didn't move. A cold tendril of fear wound its way up her spine as her heart sank in her chest. The intense emotions. The passionate love-making. Had he been taken under by another sleep attack?

"Trent?" She rubbed her hands over his sweat-slickened back. "Are you awake?"

"Mm-hmm." His lips vibrated against her ear. "I just feel so good, I don't want to move."

A wave of relief washed through her chest. "You don't have to. We can stay like this all night."

"How about forever?"

"Works for me." She tightened her arms around him and kissed his shoulder. A promise of forever used to be her greatest fear. Now, she wouldn't take anything less.

He rose onto his elbows, a drunken smile lifting the corners of his mouth. "With the new kitchen, how much do you think my house is worth now?"

"I'd have to do a little research to be sure. Why? Do you want to sell it?"

"It's a great house for a single guy, but we'll probably need more space eventually."

"That's true. My apartment won't work for a couple either."

He kissed her mouth, her cheek, her neck. His lips brushed against her ear as he whispered, "Or a family."

She couldn't fight the smile tugging at her lips. "We definitely need more space."

He brushed a strand of hair from her forehead. "I think we need to find somewhere to call our own. Together."

"I think I know just the place."

## EPILOGUE

*T*ina wasn't kidding when she'd said she was low-maintenance. Based on Logan and Allison's extravagant wedding, Trent had expected her to want a similar ceremony. Something fancy in an expensive hotel downtown. Hundreds of guests. Live music at the reception. But when she'd suggested a simple affair with their closest friends and family, and the backyard of their Victorian manor as a backdrop, he was reminded exactly why he loved this woman. She was made for him. No doubt about it.

She wore a simple, white satin gown with a slit up the side that provided him a glimpse of her long, sexy leg with every step she took toward him down the aisle. She swept her dark hair up in a pile on top of her head, accentuating her slender neck and shoulders. A few raven strands hung loose around her face, framing her emerald eyes. Her entire body seemed to glow with the love emanating from her gaze. He was marrying a goddess.

He met her at the end of the aisle and took her hand in his, reminding himself to keep his knees slightly bent so he didn't pass out. He hadn't had an episode since they'd vanquished the shadow demon six months ago, but he'd seen enough *America's Funniest Home Videos* episodes to know he wasn't taking any chances.

Tina handed her bouquet to Allison and smiled as she slipped her other hand into his. Her palms were dry while his were slick with sweat. His heart threatened to beat a hole through his chest, and she appeared calm, confident, relaxed. What had he done to deserve such an enchanting angel as his wife?

She didn't make him write any fancy vows or memorize any lines. The ceremony was short; he repeated the few words the minister told him to, slipped the ring on her finger, and kissed his bride.

Sweet and simple. Like life should be.

As they turned around to face the small audience, the minister introduced them as Mr. and Mrs. Austin. His mom dabbed at the tears in the corners of her eyes, and his dad gave him an approving nod.

Tina's mom wiped the tears from her cheeks with the back of her hand and pulled Trent into a tight hug. "You take care of my baby."

He patted her back as Tina grinned. "Yes, ma'am. I will."

"I'm so glad she found you."

"All right. Let the man breathe." Tina pried her mom's arms from around his neck and hugged her tight.

"I'm so happy for you, sweet pea," her mom said.

"Me too, Mom. Let's go eat. I'm starving."

They feasted on grilled steaks and baked potatoes and spent time chatting with all of their guests. As evening approached, their acquaintances slowly trickled away, leaving behind only their family and closest friends.

Allison admired Tina's ring for the umpteenth time and pulled her away from him to hug her best friend. "It makes me so happy to see you wearing this…and living here. Embracing your past lives while creating a new future together."

Tina cast him a loving glance before arching an eyebrow at her friend. "I still can't believe you knew he was going to propose and you didn't tell me. You should've called me the minute you finished clearing this ring."

Allison laughed. "And ruin the surprise? What kind of friend would I be then?"

Tina smiled. "I guess I can forgive you this time."

Gage shook Trent's hand. "Congratulations, you two. Still no signs of any ghosts or demons hanging around?"

"Nah. We replaced the wood floor upstairs, put in wall-to-wall carpeting and surround sound. That old attic makes a fantastic media room. We watch movies up there several times a week. No sign of spirits."

Tina wrapped her arms around Trent's waist. "Trent and I are the only things going bump in the night around here."

Gage laughed. "Lucky you."

"Indeed."

"Awe." Allison picked up Tina's flowers and handed them to her. "You forgot to toss the bouquet. All the single girls have already gone home."

Tina eyed the tulips and grinned. "That's okay. Hey, Gage, catch."

He looked up, and she hurled the bouquet at his chest. His reflexes forced him to catch it, but the look on his face said he regretted it. "Not funny, Tina. Here, take it back." He shoved the flowers toward her.

Tina held up her hands. "Oh, no. The bride tossed the bouquet, and you caught it. Deal with it."

He chuckled and shook his head. "Yeah. Okay."

As the rest of their family said their goodbyes, Logan and Allison were the last to leave. With Tina's arm wrapped around Trent's waist, her thumb fitting snugly into his belt loop, they walked their friends down the driveway to their car.

Allison gave them both a hug and paused as Logan opened her door. "Have fun in Mexico. Drink a margarita for me."

"That's the second thing on my to-do list," Tina said.

"I don't even need to ask what number one is. Be safe, you two. I love you."

"I love you too, Allie."

Logan shook Trent's hand and pulled him into a tight hug. "Welcome to married life, my friend. You're going to love it. I know I do."

"Thanks."

Trent waved goodbye as his friends drove away, and he pulled his wife into his arms and admired their home. Though his uncle's motives for giving it to him weren't in the right place, he'd be forever grateful things turned out the way they did. "This burden turned out to be a blessing, didn't it?"

"A blessing that almost killed you. But, yes, it did. Things have a way of working out, don't they?"

"Our lives have come full circle now—back to the house we were forced to leave all those years ago."

"Mm-hmm." She rested her head on his shoulder and sighed.

"Just promise me you aren't going to summon any more spirits with your newfound ability."

"The next ghost I care to see is my own when I look in the mirror at my funeral. And once I'm sure my hair looks nice, I'm moving on. I know better than to stick around haunting people."

"That's good to know." They strolled to the porch and walked up the steps, stopping in the doorway. He gazed into her emerald eyes and tucked a strand of hair behind her ear.

She batted her lashes and looked at him with a sly smile. "We don't leave for our honeymoon until tomorrow afternoon. What should we do until then?"

"I've never made love to a married woman before. You wouldn't happen to know of one who might want to give me a go, would you? I promise to give her a good ride."

"You promise, do you?" She snaked her arms around his waist. "You are pretty cute. I think I might know of someone who's available."

He cringed at her use of the word *cute*. But if Tina liked to say it, he would have to get used to hearing it. "What exactly is your definition of cute?"

"An incredibly handsome man with smoldering eyes and a charming smile."

He laughed. "Why don't you say that then? It sounds so much better."

She shrugged. "I like cute."

"Well, if cute is what I need to be to get into this sexy, married woman's pants, I'll take it."

"In that case…" She gripped his butt in her hands and pressed her body to his. "I'm your girl."

**Haunted Ever After Series**

Love at First Haunt

Second Chance Spirit

Third Time's a Ghost

**Stand Alone Books**

Flipping the Bird

The Rest of Forever

Soul Catchers

Bewitching the Vampire

# ABOUT THE AUTHOR

Carrie Pulkinen is a paranormal romance author who has always been fascinated with things that go bump in the night. Of course, when you grow up next door to a cemetery, the dead (and the undead) are hard to ignore. Pair that with her passion for writing and her love of a good happily-ever-after, and becoming a paranormal romance author seems like the only logical career choice.

Before she decided to turn her love of the written word into a career, Carrie spent the first part of her professional life as a high school journalism and yearbook teacher. She loves good chocolate and bad puns, and in her free time, she likes to read, drink wine, and travel with her family.

*Connect with Carrie online:*
www.CarriePulkinen.com